ECHOHEAD

T.C. Waas

For my teachers.
Linda, Steve, Kasey, Dan, Sharon, Jo Ellen, Kathy, Ed, Larry, Lamar, Amy, Ryan, Tina Lee, Margaret, Elise, Paul, and Babs.

"Once the soul has been placed in the body, it relishes its own strength. And when the body is put aside, like a cloud that has blown away, the soul becomes completely bright in a state of tranquility without temptation..."

Bishop Evodius of Uzalis in a letter to Augustine, c. 420

"If God give the Devil leave to plague your body, think with yourself, howsoever it be done, that God has so done for your profit and commodity..."

Ludwig Lavater, Of Ghostes and Spirites Walking by Nyght, c. 1569

I felt a Funeral, in my Brain,
And Mourners to and fro
Kept treading - treading - till it seemed
That Sense was breaking through -

...

Emily Dickinson

1

I, Qualiana

And here I thought I was you. Documenting as much of ourself as possible. Editing direct messages. Crafting exchanges in advance, planning ahead—a practice repurposed since we tuned-in our pockets. This is not paranoise but anxio-scrawldom. You send loss, you can do anything. Lie to whomever you want whenever you want. Plan your own demise. Brag about your empathy. Mobile order your next panic attack. Scroll the knife-edge of it all. You can be anyone. Hermit heard instantly, employee abroad. You can be a pin-drop ping, puddle gulp in sea, and I wouldn't fault you, for I'm always me.

Seven when it dawned I was different. My father left behind little more than well-kept appliances and what's more was a six-year-old curlyhair tarantula named Xenu. It didn't start with humans, but with a spider.

In animalia, no part of me knows I'm Ivy. I am the subject. And though I'm well-versed in the perspectives of animals, I find the subjective details difficult to communicate. Early on, I tried to journal the readings, despite the words never mounting sense. I observe and interpret and react, but can only know those are the things I was doing once I'm human again. Perhaps it's a function of neurons. While I'm actually it —being some thumbless, languageless body-mind—I simply am it. Pure instinct. Some unknowable fraction of the animal's identity is lost, untranslatable or incomprehensible. The same is true of every animal I've read, to different degrees. Still I felt every cropped and passing minute.

Hunt—eat—rest—mate—birth—and on. Coming back the first time was a shock of third-eye glory so powerful as to be feared before revered before set as rubric against all my future dreams. Suddenly a thousand times larger I collapsed from what felt like miles above. Burned and smothered, or blank, my very senses a painful rearrangement, extremities somehow reduced, I found the word 'clothes' on me. Awareness clamors without beauty, until its sudden beauty, and this I learned a forgotten soul unspidered on a living room floor, watching myself scurry away under the couch.

If you ever return somewhere and hadn't realized you were gone, do as a reader, as I learned to do that night, and put a thumb to each finger, lengthen and shorten and warm every muscle of your legs, your arms, ankles, wrists. Run your tongue around your teeth, your palms together. Do all of these things many times over and take a week of denial before you learn a bit.

On some late-summer ghost day of a school year the boys discovered an enormous ant pile behind one of the backstops and took to guarding it like the Secret Service. The pile the figurative center of the playground at Sam Houston Elementary School. You were to try to kick it and if you failed to get past Jason or Travis three times you would be banned until the following recess. It seemed an injustice. My sole wholehearted attempt at childhood friendship involved enlisting the other girls in a peaceful capture of the colony—

not 'pile.' Alas, the brutal equalizer war; Kayla fulfilled the charge and signaled our triumph with a dramatic, full-force kick to the system. I fell to my knees and burst into tears. "You weren't supposed to kick it!"

"But we won," she said, confused. "That's the rules."

Thousands at martial speed, burrowing, a frenzy of trauma and repair. The kids laughed, left me alone, and in time I looked up to see a watery Mrs. Warner approaching and thought what use? How could I explain? I couldn't go back to class. I was needed. There was civilization-wide turmoil to be ordered. Then earth gave one ant onto my hand which came to rest on my knuckle and everything around us went silent and I skimmed a finger over the ant's tiny red surface and became my larval form. I remember very little of the rest of my day after returning, but I recall Mrs. Warner's frightening pleasant smile as she said, "My, you've sorted out now, haven't you?"

I read hundreds of animals en route to adulthood. I kept everything a secret, confederate in wordlessness with the immensity of life around me, duly mistaking myself periodically for a God. Fevered, in total worship of possibility, only rarely depressed in the aftermath, I sought animals and nothing else. I sought as though bouldering blind, feeling here and there for a grip to rise the curve of something vertical I knew beyond man's making or measure but host to certain dynamics on those vertices which might prove humans the toughest intelligence to reach. In short order I read spiders, ants, crickets, roaches, ladybugs, centipedes, mice, squirrels, rats, little birds (oh, that good hour spent hand-on-injured-bird, first touch of one, awonder-whether until deep within my hollowing bones decision woke and I read and flew). Then came Madisonville. At a ranch owned by Mom's first post-Dad boyfriend I met a great brown American Quarter Horse named Bulldozer. It was my first experience as a domesticated creature, since one wouldn't call Xenu domesticated in the same respect. Bulldozer's memories and sorrows remain with me now, forever raw. The loss of her mother, separation from a friend. She was no otherworldly blip or simple mind of instinct. With all the grandeur of the term, she was *self-conscious*. The return from Bulldozer revealed to me a profound new scale of time-warp. Xenu had been near my own age when I read her, and I reckoned my collection of garden and schoolground lifespans —fifty days as a cricket here, three years a centipede down there—together amounted to an age far beyond that of my own mother. But there are pretty distinct psychic levels of matriculation in these studies, some more shocking than others. Beware an early lesson from odd-toed ungulata. Having lived a consecutive sixteen years under the mane, within the human markers of time and industry, one is commanded upon return to a state that can only be described as hyper ego-death. Picture a lonely little ten-year-old atop a mare, suddenly herself, perspective freewheeling, splintered, as if she's just come up from a thousand micrograms of L.S.D. For a hairsplice of a moment there she's Buddha in the grove, she's a king in Jerusalem realizing meaningless ecstasy. What kid wouldn't keep going? At the ranch were a thousand heads of cattle, but I was bored by the idea of a life fattened for slaughter. This from a kid with memories of hunt and flight, fangs sunk into small creatures, liquefaction. I read another horse. I read a pig and some wild rabbits. It was the longest spring break of my life and still wasn't enough. Thus from Kayla's Bombay, Bliss, a dozen other house cats. Then any dog I could get my hands on.

Somewhere along the way, even ageless from the cats and dogs and horses, I understood I was not special. Not even with the prophetlike sensation of total cleansing focus that occurred after each reading, and not as that sensation increased with each newly entered clade. Not even because of the power itself was I special. I was just different. I would've been special if I could've maintained true, marrow-deep empathy with anyone. No matter my gift, I couldn't. At the end of the day, quite literally, I was always me. What did I know? I had known not woman or man, nor cactus, vine, or flower. The idea of limits begrudged me a childish anxiety. In animalia, limitation was nary a concern, just an unquestioned reality, but for a little girl privy to unspeakable mystery, limitation was death. I wanted in myself the presence and acceptance I knew to be available to living beings. It's true that, as people, language gets in our way, but the difference is more than that. Forgiveness, peace, unattachment—these are not human mindsets, they are natures. They are valves within the soul, opened only with patience and work.

Nevertheless, I was obsessed. By twelve I spent every free moment in the biology section of the library or prowling fields and parks for life. I had been annelids and arthropods, some gastropods, but my obsession narrowed to chordates, particularly vertebrates with closed cardiovascular systems. There was, understandably, an enchanting familiarity about such a body. In the meantime, teachers admired my interests, admonished my seclusion. My mother for years strove to socialize me before puberty, but at some point resolved herself to my character and my apparent happiness. Through middle school I persisted in methodical collection of specimen experience, pursuing the classification branches toward humanity as much as possible, but just as happily becoming a frog or butterfly. Happiest as a dog or cat.

In reality, I did spend a healthy amount of time with other girls my age, but my friendships were few, and fluid. I was quiet in most conversations. Where others could offer jokes and gossip, I offered eerily accurate mimicry of everybody's family pets. I wanted to talk about reincarnation instead of church, snakeskin instead of boys' hair, but with so much time to kill until adulthood, no money, still little agency, I conformed when I could, tried to blend into the background wearing zebra print and listening to pop. By twelve I was that girl doing yoga in the trees behind the bike racks, the daughter who studied TV coverage of 9/11 to understand how New York's birds had acted and reacted.

Though a teacher proud of her only child's academic pursuits, Mom was relieved when I found myself a secondary passion which might be more social in result than biological fieldwork. It was an interest I discovered gradually. With a cursed gift like mine, one has many kinds of days. Of study, the pre-read days of dreadful excitement and anticipatory malaise. Days of post-read euphoria. But also, necessarily, distracted days of self-reorientation—the yoga, meditation, the stretching, tapping of fingertips, long gazes into an elusive reflection, and the most surprising sound of all registering as the resonance of my *actual* voice in my *actual* skull.

I took to singing.

Impressions of birdsong and cat purrs, not to mention a million foreign memories, had nurtured in me the acute talent to control my own voice. I made up songs in the shower, harmonized to the radio. By ear I could copy the melody and texture of almost any music I heard, with my voice, with the keys of Mom's ancient electric keyboard.

This in turn motivated Mom again to get me socialized in a normal way. She harangued me the summer before eighth grade until I relented and changed my class elective from Art (a path which had produced sketchpads full of animal drawings, but little creativity and less collaboration) to Choir. Indeed, not only did my new interest allow for a diversified social life, it became one of my most trusted tools for maintaining presence in my own body, before or after a reading. I sang because my identity depended on it.

Adolescence rang of Björk and Radiohead, Sam Cooke, Nina Simone, Amy Winehouse. By high school my shallow conformity in taste and appearance had drained some and I found myself with the awkward teenage realization of a personality all my own. Bicycle girl. Park girl. Girl whose mind and very spirit exhibited peculiar complements to those of the old and dying. She doesn't seem bothered by the time or the pressures of a scheduled existence. She doesn't go to church and says she prays to animals. She still goes to petting zoos, for Christ's sake.

I wasn't a complete loner. The Mormon girls liked me because they considered me basically pious. It is difficult to be an outcast amongst theatre kids, too. I earned minor cachet among the skaters, the ravers, the orchestra kids, and some faculty. But there was a facilitating irony there, for to be maturely detached from others at that age with such idiosyncrasy invites the attention of other teenagers, and then prompts their exhaustion, and so engenders a relationship to one's peers rarely deeper than respectable acquaintanceship. As a teen I had a self-assured spiritual arrogance at odds with the southern Christian parents of outer Houston. I had an animalistic bent to all my metaphors and advice occasionally unsettling to classmates, a blunt perspective on life/birth/death more befitting a pessimist philosopher than a biologist, and few pleasant social skills. Of course I couldn't just admit I was a teenager. I blamed it on the roaches. The snakes. Abusive dog owners. I blamed it on my mom in what was to her a predictable hormonal manner. I blamed the nightmares —fleeing a predator, injuring my wings. But I never, not once, considered blaming the power itself. To the contrary, I resolved to revive my use of the power in accordance with the examples set by Xenu and Bulldozer and Bliss. There must be a purpose to the readings, I reminded myself. Purpose in selection, lessons unearthed. After all, who wouldn't fantasize about reading great apes, dolphins, whales? Trees, fungi, mold could be next. Was it only animalia? When could I know another person, really know them?

Ecstatic meaninglessness is as neutral as it sounds. I couldn't bear it to be for nothing. All the secret decades. All the colored pencils used to the stub rendering my goal of the month, the ruby-throated hummingbirds, the Great Danes. I had knelt beside creeks straining eyes against the dusk more evenings than I wanted to count. I lost my virginity as a spider, as a girl on a date with a horse breeder's son. It couldn't be for nothing.

Adulthood implied humans. Other people, no way around it. Them. But if it was to be a conscious choice, what then? Surely I had a choice. I had felt the churn in the stomach, the sickly day-of awareness, the need to defeat the feeling and my ensuing decisions—go for a bike ride, go to the creek— which caused encounters that led to a reading, a surprise Bufo marinus, Aedes sollicitans. But I had chosen them, surely. It was I who leaned down and observed. I who calmed, cajoled. I seduced a hundred beings, three hundred, got near them, in their business, I who sleepily used them for a glimpse of that ecstasy. If this curse were to reach its natural conclusion, I'd damn sure want a say in what kind of human lives I'd live.

I knew I was different, but not for the breath of me could I guess what the inner lives of other people would be like. Yet I knew the point. Empathy. The goal of all good art and science and government. A dictate of worship, empathy. This whole putting yourself in other people's shoes bit, there's a reason we muse on it so much. Still, what horror, what overbearing rapture could one receive upon the return from a separate human mind? What would the other person feel? The dogs, cats, many of my later reads had felt a vague curious surrender in the lead up to my decisive touch. Would these people be submitting, does free will have a role for either them or me? And how might one react in a fresh human body, anyway? I might lose my mind in a food court somewhere, shouting, "You have my face, you have my body!"

First, I considered ages. Child, peer, adult? I'd been a child myself and in each human life would begin as one. That option felt lacking. Besides, would I have the vocabulary of the kid in those first post-read moments, my childlike wonder setting off alarm bells for anyone around? I didn't know any kids apart from the annoying little siblings of some classmates. So then a classmate? But I knew them already and feared every context imagined. It was a big school, I didn't know everybody, but why waste my first (and perhaps, if too psychologically damaging, my last) experience as another person on one as homebound and young as I?

My entire conception of human reality just wasn't cutting it. Call it my first spiritual crisis. I had inherited agnosticism from Mom, found Krishna and Buddha in the book stacks, and grown up square in Jesus country, but I could only venerate the readings, the returns. Moreover, I knew less about those than Christians knew of the Bible or atheists their philosophies. Had no creeds, no codes, no sense of math or history or sociology. Just a sense of wonder. An insight, a collection, yes, but no proofs, no applications. If I wanted to experience another soul's slice of God-given cognition, another person's philosophy of mind, it behooved me to gain confidence in my own, beforehand.

Houston is a religious city. And though as a teen I wasn't always seeking religious advice, in America, such advice presents itself rain, hail, or sunshine. The Bayou City is a place of megachurches, Vietnamese Buddhist temples, a vibrant Mormon stake, Hindu temples, much more. Our religious infrastructure might break down as 60% Protestant megachurches, 15% Catholic churches, 12% small Protestant churches, 7% spaces for literally every other religion and non-affiliation, 3% gas stations, 2% guns, and 1% brisket. Between the other most populous cities in the U.S. it's no contest for Christians until you get to San Antonio. New York, Los Angeles, Chicago—they have their histories, they have New Testament God-fearing folk, but everything's bigger in Texas. During this latter-adolescent spiritual search of mine, Corbin Allen's Riverbed Church bought a basketball stadium near Rice Village and set up the largest congregation in the nation. Where The Who and Cyndi Lauper once preached now came a big Texan grin telling us to believe in ourselves, asking for donations. I visited Riverbed twice, mesmerized but dismayed. It called to mind the one time I followed a friend to a summer Bible camp. I went for the zip-line, but a handsy counselor insisted on having me saved by Jesus. I wept, thinking that's what I was supposed to do. There was no God for me there, except what I felt after reading one of the campground Tabbies. The bad rock music and American flags, the lights, the production of it had sickened me, more offensive to my artistic pride than any latent religious inclination. The same artifice turned me off of Allen, despite his horror-movie handsomeness. He seemed less pastor and person than embodiment of cash-fisted Christian*ish*ness. Similar and smaller churches I biked to on Sundays left me equally unfulfilled. During my senior year of high school, I frequented the Rothko Chapel and Vietnamese monks, spiritual swindlers, palm readers, mediums, and even once visited a Scientology clinic. I spent far too much of my theatre camp counselor wages on this stuff, and in my quest for human enlightenment I went an entire year without reading an animal. Thoreau, Austen, Nietzsche, Marx and Smith, Darwin, Camus, de Beauvoir, Dickens, Arendt, Sontag. The scene kid poetry in English class. The Texan backdrops of *No Country For Old Men* and *There Will Be Blood*. I sought not just guidance but explanation, and I read and watched, but never enough, never everything, permitting canons patriarchal or progressive, never getting the whole story, never knowing what common creed might exist beneath the apocalyptic clash-of-values in the American psychoscape. Then back to the east, to Jaynism and fasting. To the I Ching when in doubt, to the Holy Quran, to Rumi, to the Japanese poets of the eleventh and twelfth centuries. Secluded again. Back to America, to Alice Walker and Langston Hughes.

If I have made excuses for the tendency to seclusion in my early childhood, I submit none for resuming the habit in my final months of high school. I was a recluse when not at school or the local community theatre. My circle of friends included no more than study groups, carpoolers, some of the theatre tech kids during show season. These relationships existed mostly online. The internet in 2008, what a trip. AIM lingering on, Facebook Chat arriving to dominate. The world in our pocket. The perfect tool with which to simultaneously hide from and engage others. I hid, but chatted. I told myself this was part of the process of taming my impulses, those to read, to escape myself. But it was another manifestation of them, because I was still secluding myself for the God of Reading's sake. Instead of knowing people, I was studying them.

But I tried. I was an anxious, self-obsessed wallflower, but I laughed, joked, had crushes. And I would think participation in the theatre and science departments kept me from total existential dread. I wasn't morose, though kids could perceive me that way. I was just intensely preoccupied such that other kids presumed a social condition, and suburban Christian moms presumed me a lesbian. The latter presumption I wouldn't refute. I didn't know. My sexuality was quite diffuse because of the llama sex and whatnot. My sociability however was flourishing precisely because of the readings—my deepest relationships, other species.

We had pets beside Xenu. By the time I was eighteen we were caring for our second cat. Mom had named her at my insistence as I had named the cat who died a few months before, Milk, an A+ black and white cow cat, loving little creature. I loved her and our next gal, Cassandra, loved them like family. So I didn't read either of them. It was for love I didn't ever tell my mom about the readings. Better she be spared further doubts, thoughts of her only child on the cusp of schizophrenia. In the early years I hid it from her with selfish, private awe. In later years with a dollop of mercy. If I were to go crazy after reading my first person, my explanations then would be meaningless, yet were I to tell her everything ahead of time, all at once, in the dusk of my second decade, then she might go crazy, blame herself, and never let me leave.

Eighteen-year-old Ivy Qualiana was not the greatest predictor of human behavior.

Mom would've gladly accepted an empty nest—as a high school English teacher she was around teens all day—but while graduation neared I did absolutely nothing to prepare for my future. That is, my future as other people saw it: college, career, family. I remained preoccupied. Mom and I tacitly agreed I could continue to live with her in my adulthood so long as I kept a job and contributed to the mortgage. She always hid some guilt about never remarrying and raising me alone, unable to afford much, and she probably knew I was unable to focus on providing for myself in the very real life soon approaching. She did urge on me the SAT, the ACT, college brochures, applications. At one juncture she suggested I get work on the cruise ships like many Houston thespians did. Finally over Papa John's one night she practically shouted, "Just become a monk or a nun or something!" I think we both got some clarity as that landed. I was suited for some kind of cloistering, the work of enlightenment in search for the human heart. She could innocently leave me be and start her second life.

As it happened, people came to me, not I to them. There was still an aspect of mutual gravitation, as there forever faintly would be, but with my first, as the current surged between our colliding selves, the power didn't wait for me, didn't consult my agency until it was too late. And I was born again.

Here's how it works. Over a few days I fall gradually exhausted, often sleeping but also often in a trancelike state. If there are people in the course of my days, and there always are, I latch onto them immediately. My brain wiry and seeking relief projects a false deep connection with others for the first moments of interaction, then I feverishly discard interaction and opt for solitude and sleep. Then one of those days, the third fifth seventh (how long can you go without meeting someone?) I meet someone, or hear a voice I know, and enough is enough and there's a touch of vulnerability from both of us and we touch and it's more certain if I want to do it but there's gravitation involved I swear. There's a degree of fate. And I give in anyway. I usually want it. I know it will be relief because I know I'm not myself. So I'm born again. A person's entire life experience, every lost beat and sunk memory, from but the one perspective, unaware of my true identity right up until our moment of contact. The same way it works with animals, except for the extent of my exhaustion in the preceding days, except the preceding days of unease in the lives of the subjects. The scale of this, the age of another soul in another memory? Though I am its witness, even I cannot fathom it. The return is too blinding. Nowadays, I lose a few minutes. That first time, I lost the whole day.

My first was my biology teacher from sophomore year. Under thirty in 2008 and metamorphosed from punk rocker to Biology Club Sponsor, Dolores Dodge was the coolest teacher at my high school. Since I'd left her classroom as a student I'd spent two years returning to it for lunch and after-school Biology Club meetings. She was nearer to our age than most of the faculty, and as such became many a geeky teen's conduit to adulthood, her humor and gossip always reservedly parallel to ours. She liked me. I loved her favorite science and I appeared to speak more with her than anyone else, including the drama teachers and the cast members of each musical. She advised me to pursue laboratory research. She lent me her ragged copy of *Silent Spring*. I didn't think too hard about whether I wanted to read her, but one afternoon toward the end of senior year, after a lunchtime conversation in which she told me she was moving to another state and I told her I wasn't going to college, with tears in her eyes she spread her arms out for a hug.

Imagine you've come to know yourself as Dolores Dodge. Head, shoulders, knees and toes Dolly's. You grow up the eldest of three kids in a comfortable Dallas suburb. You like soccer and gardening and in your early teen years you develop a dependency on punk rock. You start a band decent enough to make it to Warped Tour '99. You oscillate between modes of artistry and economy. You investigate the deepest recesses of your psyche in order to produce a memorable lyric, a radio-caliber hook, even as you pursue an associate's degree, then a bachelor's. Science and music, the science of music, the tones and tremors of art that lurk deep within the scientific method. You fall in love at age seventeen, and roughly out of it only two years later. Your cousin overdoses on his birthday and you read out the lyrics to his favorite Harry Nilsson song at his burial. Your dad suffers through then beats lung cancer. You keep smoking. Lungs, blood, heart. You are Dolores and no one else, but you are many versions of Dolores, the angsty teen, the practical young woman. The punk with close-cropped hair who puts down her axe at twenty-four to become a high school science teacher. You fall into love and out of it again. How many days have there been in your quarter of a life? How many days more? Imagine you're absolutely wrecked by this new version of yourself. Long hours, scant pay, no recognition except from a few enthusiastic students. It's not uncommon for you to wake up in a cold sweat simply because you were dreaming about going to work. Maybe you're just a shitty teacher. Anyway an idea gnaws at your brainstem for a solid two years. The return to your True Self. The songwriter, poet. Enough with the Punnet squares and Latinate turns of phrase. Enough is enough, and despite the gut-emptying nervousness this decision imbues, to change careers yet again, to find some goddamn meaning in your little life, enough is enough and you know it's time and the only person you're actually nervous to tell is this one student, this one girl who seemed to respect your efforts in the classroom. She's just a teen, telling her is nothing special. But you are becoming who you were always meant to be. You are leaving your family in Texas and your teacher friends and whatever career ladder you were on. There is no truth, no purpose, except this idea in your head and your sinking stomach and your tingling arms. No truth except this hug and what a startling truth it is.

And then you're me again. Some twenty-nine years older in the mind, but only milliseconds removed.

Though when I came to, that first return, I was hours removed. I was looking at the front of our condo, Cassandra licking herself in the window. It was almost ten at night. Later I reconstructed the intervening hours and learned that after abruptly leaving Ms. Dodge's room, I wandered the halls of the school with a gloss of rapture on my face. Other kids thought I was rolling. I missed the second half of the day, apparently spending much of my time in the bathroom, staring at my new reflection. Where exactly I went and what exactly I did in the hours before my sudden awareness on our front lawn, I don't know. But I remember a permanent smile. I remember my own wide eyes. Leaves and dreams of the lives of trees. Concrete meeting grass, this I focused on, not the image itself, but the image as it refracted off two old familiar eyes. I remember moving through the world as though floating, two ghosts in one forgotten body.

Once shared a hotel wall with a guy for a week and that was sufficient. Of course neighbors. Coworkers. Dates. A talkative stranger. It's a hug. Sometimes a handshake. Hand on knee. Fingers running through hair, I'm pretty sure I didn't dream that one.

Am I more empathetic because of all this? Yes. Am I any less biased? That's doubtful.

After high school I worked at a pharmacy, at theatre camp some more, and at a movie theater. Time moved very slowly for me between the ages of eighteen and twenty. I wanted to read the population of Houston in its own proportions, an arbitrary endeavor perhaps, but it seemed logical. I wanted to map the religious attitudes of the city, the backwater atheism, and from every angle I desired to participate in our local economy. I objectified demography. All for God. Or the lack of God. And the lack of God it turned out to be, for I lost him somewhere along the way, the population itself fragmented, and I continued to worship only my readings. The people. Houston. One every couple months, then one every month, some bi-weekly binges, breaks for weeks, then relapse and relapse. Building up a tolerance, so to say. I'd return to myself and whichever dead-end job. I'd sing in my car, do sirens and trills, belt, all to denote me to myself. By twenty I'd spent seventy years homeless and twenty-five as a high-end chef, I'd lived in Australia and Boise and along the entire arc of the Gulf of Mexico and a few dozen other places. And yes, quite naturally, the return from a life as a different gender or race was intense. Incomprehensibly unsettling. It always felt like a kind of betrayal. But who was being betrayed and how was beyond us. Seriously, us, which it was for a moment. There was always right at the end some shared moment of awareness—two minds intertwined. That momentary joining and separation somehow made the reversal, the betrayal, easier to stomach. But then I was me again, tunnelvisioned ol' me. Any less bias, any less prejudice? Understanding something or someone tends to reveal more unknowns. So I hoped that the long-term accrual of those brief moments might beget a deeper knowledge outside of them. And I wrote on my palms with chewed up Bic pens: You Are Only One, UR1, UR1, Just A Dream, Ivy Only.

At twenty, desperately needing to feel anything other than self-pity, or perhaps needing the sorrow and self-pity of others, I left Houston for nowhere and lost myself. A vagabond of character, I read person after person in city after city after town. Read them, loved them, left them. I went along every spectrum the American road exposed, was a cowgirl, playboy, operative, cash-fiend, Type A, Type B, Type Without A Cause, proud to know Victims of Circumstance, Workers, Slippers, Risers, Triggers. I was impoverished, lavished, ravaged, homely, comely, lucky, sad, simple. Maybe I was searching for a generalization.

There were no outliers because there was no consistency. I had wanted to be able to say There are five kinds of people in this world, etc. But there are seven billion kinds, there's One kind. Perhaps my story should be one of race or gender or institutions, tensions systemic, but it's a story of God and suicide, the things individual. To wit, the only story I can write with any authority or relevance is what follows, and it's pretty white and male and zealous since that's how it happened to me. At one time I had wanted to find the fundamental, non-stereotypical, articulable difference between the minds of men and the minds of women, but found instead that such a search was beside the point, since true of residents animalia every person navigates existence on the same premise, the id, and the rest is personal. I wanted to confirm that everyone has secret sin, and we do, but secrets cannot define us where actions can. Everybody shares with their fellow humans as many qualities as they possess distinctly, or at least it feels so, and beyond that, if that, generalizations fail. Unfortunately to accept this took me years of body and centuries of mind. My two indulgent months in Las Vegas stretched over eight hundred years.

Morbidly Unhinged Omnisexual Borderline Amnesiac Addict Hypochondriac Marxist Graphic Designer Buddhist Sikh Tattooed Mormon Day-Trader Eagle Scout Marlboro-smoking Anti-smoking Activist Lawyer Thief Priest Dissident you fucking name it. I believed in every god, but didn't. I saw the world, but preferred my own. Me myself at the end of the day, at the end of the day. What day is it? What's my schedule, I've forgotten my real job. I pray to a nameless god in the east. Fast. Sing proud. Repeat your name. My name. I believed in Meyers Briggs and the Enneagram and didn't. I believed in Theories of Self and of Mind and in Groupthink and Love Languages and Types A and B, Cliques and Factions and Seniority, and I didn't. I did believe in things systemic. I also believed everyone's a world, a massive population of versions of themselves, but I didn't know what to do about it. So I grew cynical.

At twenty-five I accidentally read a vicious pedophile and got thoroughly freaked out and stopped for a while, then relapsed on time to flush the memory with an entire biker gang over the course of a month. It was getting ridiculous. It was time to go back home. Home: but a fractal cringe of memories aglow by street and stage lights, Texas sun. I had only regrets to visit beside my mom. I had no money, no job, and as résumé only a list of phone numbers connecting forgetful vouchers of brief gigs past. If anything I was a musician but I don't think I ever answered the question and don't remember who asked. People open up to you if you let them.

I took my time getting back. Meet someone in a library, a restaurant, better a park or theater. Who was I looking for? People with stories. Fun people. Extroverts. Introverts who might be secretly brilliant. People who surely have great sex lives. Those with fascinating or horrendously fascinating families. Those in politics, news, finance. The rich. Then, in turn, out of guilt, those beneath the overpass. Many bartenders, hairdressers, mechanics. I suppose, in the back of my mind, I considered searching for someone who could do what I could. Took my time trying to prove I was the only one who could do this, but with what sample size could one prove that?

Mom put me up for a while. I had a habit of slowly filling and quickly draining reservoirs of cash and credit problematic enough that by the time I tired of the road it was clear for stability's sake and sanity's I needed a steady job or a plot of land to till. Happenstance—a throaty, spendthrift neighbor—made me a vocal coach. Contacts grew, project became hobby became life. Soon I got my own place and something resembling a career. Maybe I didn't materially understand things any better than when I had left Houston, but I was, for lack of a better term, sober. Hadn't read anyone since December 31, 2015.

Then in May I met Corbin Allen.

Corbin Allen

Corbin Peter Allen (b. January 2, 1964) is an American preacher, radio and TV personality, and author. He is the founder and pastor of <u>Riverbed Church</u>, the <u>largest protestant church in the United States</u>, in <u>Houston, Texas</u>. Allen has authored several essays and articles for *Christianity Today, Charisma, The Christian Post* and *The New York Times*. His books, *Let Yourself Live* (2000), *One Life Under God* (2002), *100 Ways to Pray* (2006), *Your God Here* (2009) and *After The Wind* (2014) were each *New York Times* bestsellers, and in total have amounted to 35 million copies sold. His televised sermons are viewed weekly by over 12 million people in 90 countries.

Contents

Religion: Non-denominational Christianity	
Church:	Riverbed Church
Born:	Corbin Peter Allen
	Jan 2, 1964 (age 52)
	Tulsa, Oklahoma
Spouses:	Cynthia Allen (m. 1994-2012)
Child:	Wesley
Parents:	John (father)
	Ada (mother)
<u>Riverbed Church Website</u>	

Early Life

Corbin Allen was born in Tulsa, Oklahoma in early 1964. His father John worked as a mechanic at an aeronautics facility, but quit this line of work when accepted into the newly opened Oral Roberts University, where he worked as a custodian while attending classes. John dropped out of school in 1969, and the family was then supported by Allen's mother Ada, who worked at Macy's. Allen describes his early childhood as marked by intimate religious instruction from his parents and their friends. The family left Tulsa in early 1971, and from ages 7 to 14 Allen was "homeschooled without a home" as they traveled the Bible Belt evangelizing and holding healing seminars. Allen describes his parents' preaching styles as "stern and direct, but ultimately informal." In *Let Yourself Live*, Allen says this period in his life saw him attend "The Church of Motel Bibles." He spent his teen years in Houston before attending The University of Houston.

Career

Allen obtained a degree in Communications from the University of Houston, graduating summa cum laude in 1986. He spent his 20s

working for the non-denominational Faithstone Church, where he
met his future wife Cynthia (Nicolo), who sang with the church band,
and <u>Leland Frank</u>, who would eventually make the initial investment
for Allen's Riverbed Church.

Allen says this time in his life was centered on his own personal
religious growth, as he gradually realized he wanted to follow his
father's lead and become an evangelist, though, Allen writes, "with a
more optimistic, community-oriented outlook."

Leland Frank, an oil magnate, funded the first Riverbed Church in
2000, which seated about 500 people. A second facility seating
1,800 was used until 2006 when it was demolished after a
fundraising campaign and deal with <u>Sirius</u> radio allowed Frank and
Allen to purchase and renovate the Houston Athletics Center, which
seats 16,500.

Allen is the senior pastor at Riverbed, giving syndicated sermons to
millions of listeners and viewers every week.

Let Yourself Live

Allen's motivational book *Let Yourself Live* was published in 2000 by Jedessey Publishers, and was expanded and reissued a year later. The books together spent over 150 weeks on the *New York Times Bestseller List*. Allen also published several other books including the #1 New York Times Bestseller *100 Ways to Pray*. See: bibliography.

Personal Life

Allen's mother died in a car crash in 1990. In 2011, John Allen suffered a severe stroke and entered a coma, from which he has not recovered. He remains in a deep comatose state and is cared for in a private facility in The Woodlands.

Allen and Cynthia Nicolo married in 1994. They had one son, Wesley, born in 2003. Cynthia died of pancreatic cancer in 2012.

Allen has donated to many Houston establishments, including University of Houston, the Houston Zoo, Houston Museum of Natural History, Houston Hunger Fund, and The Gulf Light Theatre.

Political and Religious Views

Allen has noted that he tries to keep Riverbed a "politics-free" environment, but has said in interviews that he does not support the legalization of same-sex marriage.

When asked why he doesn't preach much about hell, Allen stated: "Growing up, I was afraid of hell. Thinking about demons and the devil frightened me. The bad of our lives hardly comes from the devil. We're thinking about misfortune the wrong way. The enemy is sometimes as simple as our own anxiety and worry. Our problem is our misconceptions. I don't want to make the public think about the devil when they should be thinking about God. He's the one with mercy, that's what matters."

When criticized for promulgating prosperity theology, Allen responded, "What is prosperity? Is it just material wealth? Money, is that what you mean? God doesn't care about money. If 'prosperity' means a life full of happiness and contentment, sign me up. If 'prosperity' is just money, then no. Money may be part of it. But 'prosperity' means a flourishing. It means God wants us to succeed. That's not a hoax. That ain't swindling."

Allen has reflected on the Terri Schiavo case in relation to his father's persistent vegetative state, saying, "My father wants to hang on as long as possible. As long as medicine can keep him here, although he never met a doctor he liked. He cared deeply about the Terri Schiavo situation and told me then that he would want to hang on. I'm keeping him to his word, and, besides, it's the proper thing to do."

Allen considers himself a "semi-conservative, politically unaffiliated evangelical Christian," and says he voted for both George W. Bush and Barack Obama.

Hoaxes and Statements

Numerous times, the Riverbed Church website and Allen's personal Twitter feed have displayed unauthorized messages, usually parodic re-wordings of Bible passages or references to historical instances of religious persecution. In response, in early 2016, Riverbed hired a new Media Director.

See Also

Evangelism

Charismatic Christianity

Riverbed Church

Coma

2

Riverbed

You could even call it my second spiritual crisis. Between
some lessons I was slumped on my piano bench staring at the
books cluttering my coffee table—the Bhagavad Gita, the
Bardo Thodol, Confucius, Aurelius, Milton and Kant and
Hegel, *Macbeth* and *Coriolanus*, a pocket Constitution, a Bible,
a biography of Marie Curie, the Tao Te Ching, *Don Quixote*,
Woolf, Morrison, Maya Angelou, Mary Oliver. It was all
piled up. The sacred pages. Returning muted sunlight, still
quavering with the voice of the student just departed. My
phone rang.

"Howdy, is this Ms. Ivy Qualiana?"

"This is very much she."

"My name is Cassandra, I'm callin from Riverbed Church,
on behalf of our pastor, Corbin Allen. Are you familiar with
our church?"

"Yeees," I said, rather drawing out the vowel with
suspicious interest.

"Mr. Allen's son Wesley is lookin for a new vocal coach,
and you come highly recommended. Are you takin new
students?"

I always was. She asked my rate and then said, "Oh, the pastor can pay a little more than that." Her delight when I agreed to take on Wesley as a student came out a tad exasperated, as if I wasn't the first call she'd made that day. "One more thing," she said before we hung up, "Mr. Allen would love to have you into the church soon to meet you in person. How does that sound, are you available this week?"

Bestseller, preacher, megachurch man.

Most visitors poured into Riverbed Church from the Southwest Freeway, onto Buffalo Drive, which ran between the two great rectangles of the complex, and they poured into the back rectangle, the parking garage, in holy waves of SUVs and finery every day of the year. Facing Audley St. was an open-air lot and a ramp with footpath to a modest fountain. But true to its origins as a sports arena near the intersection of two highways, the building's main and most elaborate facade, inaccessible and barely lawned, beamed as advertisement at those in the fastest speed limit. One word: Riverbed. Past American flags I ascended a raindamp tissue of May air, past Tuscan columns clocked the few bodies visible behind the enormous grid of glass. Inside, Riverbed Church immediately introduced the God of Air Conditioning. That south end of the building was loud with kids of the Kid Zone and their parents, the buzz of the fluorescent bookstore. It was a Friday, and the church had this Friday funk the way bored offices do. A staffer helped me to Corbin's office at the northern vertex of that grand oval, up the huge moat of blue-blonde carpet, along the curving wall of solid blonde cement, which was topped by an even larger and blonder saucer of stone, past elevators, up two escalators, by various doors clear or frosted, some plainly administrative, leading out, ushering in. A post-officish inlet marked Offering Dropbox. An office for Minister Services.

Corbin met me at the threshold of his suite and my usher

disappeared. He led me in past his secretary, presumably the woman I'd spoken with on the phone, a small young redhead, who sat there typing with a scowl.

His office had a full wall of glass looking out over River Oaks toward Memorial Park, and with a tall ceiling, fruity incense burning over the trash can, and a plethora of trinkets and photos 'twas a sensory overload of sorts. I narrowed in on him. The tall white preacher. Coal-black hair (dyed?) coiffed so elaborately he'd look like a greaser if not for his suit and tie. Big ears, big forehead, long nose. Narrow eyes, a color somewhere between aquamarine and purple, which anchored his thin brows to the oily tightness of skin around, in service to an image processed but unlike plastic. More like wax. He had a kind of Fred Astaire face with Simon Cowell teeth and overly gelled hair. He reeked of money. And he was smiling.

Almost always. Smiling.

He gestured for me to shut the door and I did and then he said in reference to his assistant, "She doubts me now. She worked from home for four years before I started askin her to come in. Have a seat."

"Why the change?" I asked, sitting, inhaling a big gulp of Strawberry Cream smoke.

"Y'know, it helps, running an organization, to recalibrate things every once in a while." He lowered into and reclined his massive leather chair.

Noticing empty shelves and a train of boxes on the floor along the glass wall, each stuffed with books, I said, "Changing up your space too, I see."

"My mind's already cluttered, why clutter up my surroundings? The only book I need is right here," he said, patting a worn leather Bible on the desk. "Are you a religious woman?"

I must have scoffed because he said, "I don't mean to pry,

just curious. You came recommended but you're somethin of an enigma online accordin to Cassandra out there."

"I have had a lot of religious phases in my life."

"Who you fightin for now?"

Sobriety, I thought. But I said, "My students."

"Great answer. Now let's blow past the business, alright? How long you been teachin, Ms. Qualiana? And my goodness what a name that is."

"It's Hungarian. Or so I was told."

"Hungary. Budapest is marvelous, have you seen it?"

"Yeah, a long time ago," I said, which in this body wasn't technically true, but I did remember a life there. "I've been teaching for about a year now, but I've been a singer and pianist my whole life. Music is what I live for. Teaching it is the best career possible for me."

"That's great to hear. Wesley's friends with one of your students, that's how he heard about you. Taylor Camp."

"Taylor's a sweetheart. Good student. I hope she sticks with it."

"See, here's the thing," he said leaning forward and lacing his fingers, gravity on his face for the first time. "Wes has been takin lessons with our music director here at the church, Jordan Barshius. He's a good teacher but frankly Wes is tired of him. Jordan is a bit dogmatic about what songs he wants Wes to practice. He's known him for a few years now but Wes has always been frustrated with... I suppose the best way to put it is that there's a lack of freedom in the instruction. And more than the songs it's how they fit together, now, apparently. He doesn't feel like he's growin anymore."

"What kind of songs has he been singing?"

"Lots of Christian songs. Jordan keeps things modern, y'know." He said 'modern' with a hint of distaste. "But he sticks to our brand, that's for sure. Wes is thirteen now. He's kind of in a rebellious phase, if you will. I shopped around for vocal coaches, no offense, even some pretty rough-lookin guitarists all tattooed-up whose musical preferences I certainly wouldn't agree with. But Wes hasn't taken to any. He trusts Taylor and Taylor likes you."

"What do you think he's looking for from me? I doubt it would just be what songs to sing. Like you said, those other instructors could have—"

"To be honest, I think he wants a woman as a teacher. His mother was a singer. Think of him like a bird tryin to figure out his mating call and he needs to bounce its development off a wiser, older... bird. Or at least I thought that's what it was. I tried to get him to meet with some women teachers but he's not havin it anymore. He doesn't trust me or Cassandra to figure it out. He wants to make this decision for himself and he trusts Taylor when she says you are fantastic."

I filed away the weird bird comment for later assessment, and tried to stay on subject. "Well, if he's trying to figure out what his voice is capable of beyond...?"

"Hymns and Christian rock."

"Hymns and Christian rock, exactly, I can help with that. I teach everyone from adults learning how to sing opera to kids who want an R&B hit."

He leaned back and seemed to get more comfortable. But *comfort*, to him, it soon became clear, meant adopting a half-playful antagonism and dominating the space.

"You don't have a specialty focus?"

"I grew up doing musical theater. You have to be adaptable."

"Who are some of your favorite singers?"

"I'm a sucker for the popular greats. The people who reach a lot of people."

"Aretha, Sinatra?"

"Both. Nina Simone. Diana Ross. Freddie Mercury. Sam

Cooke."

"Few of them got some Christian tunes. Do you ever listen to Christian music?"

"I live in Texas," I said with a smile, and I realized it was the first smile I'd shown him. It occurred to me that he was famous and I was nervous. He grinned wider in response.

"Who do you like?" he asked quickly. It was a quiz.

"Amy Grant has a nice voice."

He only nodded.

"What about you?" I asked, trying to keep a friendly demeanor going despite a nebulous accumulation of worry somewhere in my mind. "Who's the best voice on your car radio?"

"No." He looked down. "I've spent too many years workin in radio to listen to it anymore. I've found myself lately listenin to the music of my youth." He paused for a long time and seemed to be carefully choosing his words. "My father only liked hymns."

"Mr. Allen," I started, but he promptly asked me to call him Corbin. "Corbin, what do you want out of my sessions with Wesley? The songs, and the direction he should go in, like what he should practice to reach wherever his goals are, that's all stuff I can work out with him. And we will work it out. You don't need to concern yourself with that. Something tells me I won't have him practicing his death metal screamo voice at home anytime soon. But this is your money, so what kind of a musical education do *you* want for him? I have to ask."

"You don't have to ask that, actually."

I shrugged.

"Obviously, I want him to be happy. I think he's a good singer and he really cares about it. He could have a future in it. I just want to make sure it's a safe kind of future. Music is Godly but the music industry not so much."

"I'm not a career coach, I'm a vocal coach."

"I know, I know. I suppose the better thing to say is I want him to learn discipline. He's a teen, it's a critical point in his life. Jordan's come close to zappin the passion out of him, but Wes is lookin for a vocal *mentor* as much as a vocal coach. He needs a good, *disciplining* influence. Do you get what I'm drivin at?"

I couldn't help but sigh. Parents. "I don't let my students slack off. They have to do the work. We figure out the path together. I am a demanding teacher, but to keep the passion alive, like everyone wants, of course, a teacher has to read the room. I have all sorts of tricks for getting kids to practice. Gamify it, get them to sneak it into their days. Being demanding and strict and dogmatic is not the same as instilling discipline. Or inspiring discipline."

"I am glad you feel that way." He dropped a fist on his desk as though to say: *Topic resolved! I decree this subject dealt with.* "Now tell me about your religious phases."

I laughed. "Right now I might consider myself a disaffected Buddhist."

"Aren't Buddhists supposed to be disaffected?"

"That's true. And disillusioned. But maybe not in this way. I have been a Christian, a Muslim, you name it."

This was when his expression turned somewhat negative, near a sneer. "Name it?"

I nodded.

"You've practiced how many religions? And to what extent are we talkin here?"

"You name it, I've been it."

His brilliant white teeth returned. "You're quite young, that's a whole lotta change."

"Exploration," I said.

I was wondering why he was wearing his suit jacket on a warm afternoon, why he had packed all his books up. Such a manicured image, the perfect blue suit and unblemished TV face. I thought I knew that kind of life, up at five for morning devotionals and a shave and a workout, crisp outfits in the office and the car, catered lunch. I had read some minorly famous people in my life, but Corbin Allen was in a different league. That's not to say I wanted to read him that day in his office. I didn't, then. But addict that I am, the prospect came to mind.

"What led you away from Christ?" he asked. It's an uncomfortable question.

"Oh, nothing personal."

He didn't know what to make of that answer, so I followed up with, "Nothing led me away from it—"

"From Him," Corbin said.

"Yes, him. It's still a part of me but so are all the beliefs I've held. There's only one thing which I forget what it's like to believe in and that's Santa Claus."

"How do you discriminate?" he asked.

"I don't."

"Between ideas. It's hard enough with the one book." He gestured to his Bible.

"I don't. They're all in me."

"But now you're a disaffected Buddhist." His voice was getting louder. It was still friendly but his eyes, his azurite and drilling gaze, didn't seem to match his voice or his smile.

"That's the sum of things to this point. It's all a cycle, I hope. Maybe there's a religion I haven't found yet."

"There's always Christ."

"How would you define your faith? You have the biggest church in the country. And it's non-denominational, right? I'm sorry I'm not familiar. I came twice a long time ago."

"Did you? That's wonderful. And that's right, we are just 'Riverbed.'"

The rest of the meeting he was quite still behind his desk,

rarely shifting or repositioning his arms. I mirrored him. He thought for a long time before speaking again, and then rapid-fire he said, "Let's see I come from a line of Tornado Alley Pentecostals and separatist Baptists and I think an evangelical Presbyterian or two slipped in somewhere down the line. But my daddy didn't like labels and neither do I. Houston has a lot of love for Jesus, and Jesus is the only thing that matters, not ecclesiastical minutiae. We all agree on Jesus, but all the other questions... It's a preacher's job to make the case for his view of Jesus, but everyone's got their own path to Him. And the looser the label, the further the message goes."

"Well I'm happy to report," I said, "that you've definitely gotten the message out."

"Does seem that way, doesn't it?"

3

Gods Worshipped, 1990-2016

The God of Parents

Born in Santa Fe, New Mexico (1960) and San Antonio, Texas (1962) and took the forms of Misi Qualiana and Renée Taylor, respectively. Misi, now deceased, stood six foot even with thin limbs and early-grayed hair the density and look of a brillo pad. He worked as an electrician and handyman and had few friends, despite his ability to connect with people instantaneously. He was found dead of alcohol poisoning in his car in a mall parking lot in late 1996. His high school sweetheart and co-God Renée outlived him, in all senses of the word. She was the adventurer, she the hunter and he the gatherer until she took both roles. She was born in the exact image she would impart on her only child, and she worked as a decreasingly chipper but increasingly wise schoolteacher whose only commandments for pupils and daughter were Question, Engage, and Give.

The God of Play

Arose from and vanquished the primordial chaos. Ruled forgotten years before constraints of the new order displaced her. She is something of a recluse.

The God of Animalia

The god with countless prophets. Revealed in every life. Every little being. Every ant and cricket. Revealed in stunning fashion the moments after a read. Her oracles enthralled me every day, and called to me with placid eyes, and they preached a steady god, one bending benevolent, but whose mercy could not outlast the present.

I too became her prophet, and life and lives and time immemorial spoke through me. My only regret is not sooner learning that the exponential gain of time and perspective demands an equal loss of… shall we say grounding?

The God of Daydreams

I was to be a famous piano player. I was to be a singer. My father was to rise from the dead. My mother was to vanquish gravity. I was to read plants one day.

The God of Loneliness

An angry god. A demon in action. Jealous. Has never acknowledged a fellow deity.

The God of the New Testament

The most famous god there is. I met him in suburban Texas. My mother considered herself agnostic but deferred to Christian tradition in spirit and decoration. Rarely did we attend church and if we did we did at the behest of a boyfriend of hers. I had my phase. Was saved, then prayed, then let modernity roll Christ off me.

The God of Theatre

Dionysus, that is. Rehearsal and performance offered a chance to use my own body, to feel entirely within it as it developed. So I sang, acted. I pounded my heart with art to resurrect my broken, tumorous humanity.

The God of Puberty
    Who only reveals divine agency in her aftermath.

The God of Dating
    The godchild of gods Puberty and Loneliness.

The Gods of Sex
    Need I say more?

But life happens between people, and there are a lot more people than gods.

4

Barshius

Wesley would start the following week. Corbin paid for four lessons up front (!) and told me Cassandra would handle any coordination needed on a regular basis. Someone named Lorena was to drop Wesley off at my house after school. He told me to stop by the church anytime. I gave Cassandra a list of three music books she should order for Wes and she said, "He probably already has these."

"Could you check?"

I walked out into the massive oval hall trying to recall items in Corbin's office. Several calendars on the wall, a Newton's cradle. An empty chessboard. There seemed nothing to do with the nervous worry that had accumulated during our conversation, so I obsessively replayed the meeting in my head. After those two visits as a teen, and some visits through a few people I'd read in Houston before hitting the road, Corbin Allen existed only in the background of my life, in cable commercials and sunbaked displays at Barnes & Noble. Before meeting in person I'd Googled and found him getting roasted on Twitter for some clips that were resurfacing of his interactions with Donald Trump. A few years prior Trump had called into Allen's first episode for the newly branded SiriusXM and blustered and Allen had been sycophantic and of course the only thing they really had in common was money. This reappearing, mind you, shortly after the springtime surrender of the Republican party to the inevitability of Donald Trump. Just weeks before, Ted Cruz and Mike Pence and Carly Fiorina had tried to pull off something that most megachurch preachers would have respected. But they didn't. In May of 2016 the evangelical leadership of the American South was reckoning with what their congregants already understood, that Trump would pull things off for them, at least on the only issue that united evangelicals anymore, the Supreme Court. No one knew quite where Allen stood. He considered himself an evangelist but he was essentially a motivational speaker. He didn't tend to see the issues of the world through a political lens. And yet there were clips of him chatting with Trump, calling Trump a good guy, using him as a reference of success in the world. The man who had been publicly if sarcastically flirting with runs at the presidency for much of his adult life and was now in the final stretch of a campaign entirely too controversial for Allen to endorse, or even parse aloud. It was the question being posed to every evangelical leader, but especially those who knew the man: What about Trump? I could've asked him. I should've asked him.

Then again, why think too hard about how Corbin Allen felt? It's a slippery slope for me from curiosity to relapse. *Fame is toxic*, I told myself.

I was repeating this in my head and only dimly aware that I was still inside the church, milling around somewhere on the second floor. I descended an escalator and checked out the bookstore by the main entrance. There was a wide selection of Christian texts, and of course three shelf units full of Corbin's books, various iterations of his blank-joy face on every cover. I bought a paperback copy of his first book, *Let Yourself Live*, and tempting myself even more I decided to find a spot inside the church to read.

About halfway up the curving hall I found a sort of museum-lounge. Four leather rocking seats sat regarding one another, and encircling them was a wall show of photos, captions, and cartoons, with a long calligraphic quotation: *I believe in Christianity as I believe that the sun has risen; not only because I see it, but because by it I see everything else. - C.S. Lewis.* Photos and illustrations of Billy Graham, Martin Luther King, Jr., Jimmy Carter and Ronald Reagan, Corbin and Wesley Allen, Corbin with his deceased wife Cynthia, Corbin with Presidents Bush and Clinton and Bush. Cartoons meant to encapsulate the historical significance of Roger Williams, Patrick Henry, John Adams, Sam Houston. A rack of pamphlets and maps. A sandwich board stowed away there, not part of museum or lounge, which read in bold, wearable letters: FAITH IS A RIVER. In fact there was even a rich and glittering river winding through the faces and the script on the wall. Whether the room was meant for regulars or drop-ins, I couldn't tell, but by the time I had absorbed enough to take a pause in one of the leather rockers, I wasn't alone. I was met by a young white guy in bright green chinos and an unseasonably thick pullover. He exited one of the frosted doors across the moat and scanned his surroundings before walking my direction, while pretending he hadn't noticed me. Then he pretended to notice.

"Hello there," he said.

"Hi."

"I take it you're on Team Comfortable."

"What's that?"

"The rocking chairs. Do you think they're comfortable?"

"I could fall asleep on gravel," I said. "I'm probably not a good authority here."

"Jordan," he said, stepping into the alcove and extending his hand. I stood to meet him and we shook.

"Jordan something with a B, is it?"

"That's right. Have we met?"

"I'm afraid I just stole one of your students."

He smiled. "You must be Ivy." I nodded. "Rivalry aside, nice to meet you."

I gave a chuckle and sat back down. He took the seat diagonal from mine. He was about my height with a diver's build, somewhere near thirty, sporting a shaved head and short beard, with the rounded edge of a neck tattoo protruding from his collar. Not the image of piety, but not exactly anything else. Though I knew I was apt to be imprecise in gauging possible zealots.

"Who are you reading?" he asked.

I showed him the cover of Corbin's book.

"Indoctrinating yourself, eh?"

"Let's call it research."

"This is some coincidence. I promise I didn't know who you were."

"I wasn't sure you knew he was changing teachers."

"Wes is a good kid. Known him for a while. No wonder he got sick of me as a teacher. I haven't taken it personally. Corbin asked me if I knew you."

Not knowing where to take the conversation, I asked, "What are *you* reading these days?"

He considered for a while and said, "The news."

"It's a comedy now, right?"

"Indeed," he said, and stood up. "Would you like a tour of the place? The arena's empty."

It was then I realized he was determined to flirt.

"Only if you share some inside information."

"What do you want to know?" He leaned on one of the rockers.

"How is Wesley coming along as a student? Mr. Allen seemed to imply... well, he said, there was some tension between you and Wesley. But I'll trust teachers for a more accurate take on a student than the parent."

Jordan shrugged. "I have a certain way of doing things. Wes just got sick of it, that's all. I wanted him to stick with the junior choir here. He doesn't want to. Corbin can't wrap his head around the fact that Wes is, to put it simply, losing his religion. Though Corbin can't wrap his head around much these days."

"What do you mean?"

He was on the verge of answering, but then he frowned and scanned the surroundings again, as if the preacher would be eavesdropping nearby. "Come check out the place."

Jordan first led me to the choir room, which was beyond the door from which he had emerged and down a long cluttered hallway adorned with posters of church events past. Referring to one of the posters he said, "Have you seen any of our Christmas pageants before? I imagine Wesley's extrication from all things Riverbed meant finding a teacher who has never even stepped inside this place."

"Is that what he's doing, extricating himself from all things Riverbed?"

"He's a teenager now." Jordan flicked his finger onto a photo beside the choir room entrance and held it there. "Time to piss off Dad." He opened the door and passed through, as a small fog dissipated from the glass and his fingerprint settled onto Corbin's face.

"The Christmas pageants are our real show of force," Jordan continued, crossing the chamber to a fold-out table on the other side, "but we're at every Sunday service. The band leader rehearses all the musicians, of course. The songs, the programming, and the choir are all on my shoulders. The magic happens here. This room is my home."

I looked around and took in the rows of bleachers, the scattered songbooks, the foam sound-guards biting from the walls. The chamber had a fresh glow to it and soon my eyes landed on the source, a large skylight.

"It's no corner office window, but it's natural light," Jordan said. "Makes the trek from the parking lot worth it, almost."

I opened up one of the songbooks. Contemporary Christian. "What did you mean earlier? About Mr. Allen?"

"He's been a bit distracted lately. When he's distracted, he changes things up. He gets his team to change things up. Schedules, room reservations. I heard he's gonna repaint his office walls and put new furniture throughout the lobby. He didn't come to the Cinco de Mayo party the staff had. He's in a mood this month."

"Is that part of what's turning Wesley off of the church?"

He shrugged again and began to mark packets of sheet music. "It's just the two of them, isn't it?" I asked.

"And Corbin's dad, of course, who's in a coma. The father, son, and the holy ghost."

I didn't react.

"Sorry," he said. "Bad joke. He's upset that I wasn't able to keep his son involved. But that's not on me, it can't be. The kid's thirteen. Did you want to go to church at thirteen?"

I was a bit surprised at his cavalier attitude with a secular stranger like me. Something fake about him, but I followed him assuming there would be a better punchline sometime soon. Jordan lured me into other rooms, another hour. He met my every subtle indication of departure with a tease of some other Riverbed peculiarity, some destination that would keep my interest in both the church and him. Before long, I resigned to his direction and his effort. He chatted me up, and I played along. Eventually he returned to the curious subject of Corbin's mood.

"His latest swing has had an effect on Wes. He's getting

really… dogmatic."

"Funny. That's what he said about you."

"I've always been this way. He hasn't. Somethin's up."

"Rearranging furniture seems pretty mild."

Jordan softened his voice. "I'm not the only one who's noticed it this time. His sermon writers—" and here Jordan cautioned me like I was a journalist "—off the record, by the way, that he has writers. But one of them came to me the other day and said he hasn't used their work in six weeks. *That* is new. I mean, he got his start as a sermon writer for someone else, it's not that crazy, but I don't know. Somethin weird is going on. He's going up there every week with unapproved text. I think the congregation is starting to notice. He was always pretty light on theology before. Metaphysics. Come on, follow me."

He brought me through a series of cramped, windowless hallways, until we found ourselves in the wings of the main stage. He led me out onto the polished boards, and though the stage lights were off, the entrance still felt unavoidably theatrical. Images of my own teenage self flashed before me— thin little thing, consumed by her mysterious power, a lonely kid passing time in the ensembles of *Peter Pan* and *Grease*. With a sweeping motion Jordan said "Voilà" and presented the sea of seats before us. The view was absolutely monstrous. Rows and rows, aisles, levels. A pulpit for a whole population. I sidled up beside him.

"The acoustics could be better, but it's quite a space," he said.

"You're pretty young to be the musical director for this big a congregation, no?"

"I'm very proud to be. I have given a lot of my time and energy to this place. I was the assistant to the last director for several years. They say a church's voice is a harmony in two parts, pastor and music. Happy to do my part."

"Shouldn't God's voice be the voice of a church?"

"God?" Jordan asked with comic confusion. "He can't afford this place."

I genuinely laughed. Then I disingenuously made a move to physicalize the laughter, and placed a bracing hand on Jordan's arm. "Don't be sacrilegious."

For a moment I thought I had somehow offended him, so quickly did his demeanor sour. His arm flexed under my touch and he looked down to where we connected. I withdrew my hand with instinctive speed and silence, like I had accidentally woken a beast, or marked the young of some over-protective species. Cast down, Jordan's eyes lingered there for a moment, nearly closing, before he looked up.

"Sorry," I said, though I didn't know why I apologized. Hadn't he also just been evaluating our momentum? Hadn't some connection been his play? To be honest, I wasn't sure if I was tempted to read him or fuck him. Neither seemed like a good idea.

But as quickly as the strangeness flamed up, it died out. Jordan's smile returned to his face, and he swallowed a lump in his throat. I didn't know what to do with my hands, so I crossed them behind my back.

"I wanted to show you this. These are the acoustics I've been training Wes for. But you know how kids are. He wants to sing into a laptop microphone and compress his voice onto YouTube. This is where he started. This is the space he's trained for."

"And that harmony?" I asked. "Pastor and choir. Are you two dissonant now?"

He nodded gravely. "The pastor has gone," he took a deep breath and sang loud with a slow vibrato, "SOLOOOOO." He turned and then smiled again, proud of his space and voice. I couldn't help but roll my eyes. The auditorium echoed back to us: OoOooOooo

5

The Allen Boys

Wesley Allen was a very bright kid. A better pianist than singer, perhaps, but he understood the mechanics of vocalization in discretely physical ways rare among his peers, crackling pubescent execution be damned. A rather obvious aspect of his voice, that it was dropping when not squeaking, had been completely ignored in my conversations with his father and former teacher, and when I addressed it with him in our first lesson he literally breathed a sigh of relief.

"Mr. Barshius wanted me to keep singing tenor."

"What we've got to do is flush, and hone, and tune every part of your range. If you don't want to sing in a choir anymore, don't worry about those labels."

He may have even teared up a little. He was a sensitive kid. At first he would arrive in his school uniform, but when summer came his dress got darker in hue. He'd wear graphic tees of album covers, New Order and Nirvana. His hair was straighter than his father's, swooping across his pimpled forehead, almost covering his ears. He was very quiet. If I didn't see Lorena's car pull up, his knock at the door always surprised me. When they showed up early, he'd wait in my tiny kitchen with his earbuds in and his eyes closed.

But in every lesson, even in that first lesson, and increasingly, I thought more about his dad than him. I couldn't shake Corbin Allen. You know those people, something in the eyes. You look into them and onto some future calamity, windows giving view not to a soul but to a slivered reflection of terrorized thought. The eyes of violence or psychosis, characteristics admittedly easy to project onto the religiously at-peace, but still. Wesley did not have this glint in his eye, not as his most bitter teenage self nor even when his eyes lit up with passion.

I became obsessed with this preacher. I started reading his articles, watching interviews, watching his sermons on YouTube.

Corbin Allen lived dressed to his best among crowds dressing the like, a bestower of custom Bibles, flanked by slick logos, washed Sunday in the blue and silver light of a place where basketball and hockey were once played but neither drew such a crowd as him, way down there below that mezzanine and the next, the humbly suited chalkslab of a man of God. Corbin started every televised sermon with an audience say-along prayer like:

Jesus is my God

I can be what He needs me to be

I can do what He needs me to do

I let Him into my heart

Forever

In Jesus name, amen

And there he was and there my obsession fixed. It was June 2016 when I admitted to myself that I wanted to read Corbin Allen primarily because I was afraid of what I might learn. Let me be honest, it was mostly his eyes. Though six months sober, many lessons of my many souls had never left me, for how could they? His class of glint-in-the-eye I had met before, and chased, and read. Cold-hearts and brutes, all of them. I thought I'd learned my lesson with that breed. Maybe I was wrong or maybe I had been desensitized beyond caring. I had centuries of relative normalcy, of course, normal beauty and normal pain, but as months can mar a decade so can lives a population. What was I but a collection of minds aware some sick few can really spoil the bunch? Why should I entertain the ideas of a possibly twisted preacher? Why because of the eternal fault, temptation.

See, each time I had chased that glint, I knew not whether I sought innocence or guilt. Did I want to empathize with those people as I did the others? Or was I wanting vicarious evil? Whatever the answers, I had searched for nearly every kind of mind, pedophiles and killers aside. Exhaustion with that search is part of what brought me back home, but new interests, new suspicions can always arise. Something about Corbin seemed different. And that suspicion I deemed warrant enough for another pursuit. Sue me.

His assist to my fixation was his fame. He was all over Houston, all over the internet. He was quoted, memed, called a pillar of the community, called a scourge to true faith. Need I know how he began his sermons with a joke I simply checked YouTube.

"I want to share a story a jovial friendamine told me this week. He said 'My wife and I, we were driving north and seeing signs for Nacogdoches and got into arguing over how it was pronounced. I felt like the G was there for a reason and she didn't, and favored the *ch* sound. We fought and fought and decided the only way to settle it was to wait until we got there and ask a local. We drove in hot silence for the next thirty minutes. When we finally reached the town, we stopped for gas and went into the convenience store there. Ma'am, we pleaded to the lady at the counter, we have been arguing for an hour about this. Could you *please* help us out and very slowly pronounce the name of this place? The woman leaned close and very clearly said SE-ven e-LE-ven.'"

And he pronounced the Gs of his gerunds and present participles when onstage, when recorded, as he hadn't when I met him in his office. The shine in his long I sound, that twang of his, restrained by the enunciation of his performance.

Need I know the lines of thought he cast into his congregation I simply skipped the video forward.

"Life is full of contradictions and confusion. It has been ever since He created us. So what's at the end of a complaint? You have the only end you need within yourself, and it's the grace of God. Faults, troubles, pains, horrors—these are not indications that God does not care about you, they are reminders of His mystery. They are signs that He believes you are strong, you can overcome. If you're waiting for God to change something in your life, lack of change is not an accident. Don't fall into bitterness. Bitterness corrodes. When God's path for you takes you by pain and terror, tap into His grace. You will soar. The only solution is God's grace. Every message from every corner of life, every story ever whispered to you by devil or angel, every preface and every punchline is faith. Prove to the Lord above that you can give without receiving. That's what life is. Every strand of circumstance is a reminder to believe."

Need I know my subject I simply watched hours and hours of his sermons, got to understand his rhythm, his preferred allusions, his favorite passages. Corbin Allen was a man of staples, Proverbs and Job and Mark, *The Brothers Karamazov* and Billy Graham.

Need I know the surface of his character I simply examined his attire—at the pulpit, loose blue suits with pastel shirts and fat-knot ties kaleidoscopic in pattern; in press, fitted plaid matters with notch lapels and pocket squares of thick accent; as casual as he came, solid polos or muted fleeces or anything trim, anything slick, as long as it had a collar. Need I know his tastes I directed our scarce banter foodward (twice he called to check in on Wesley's lessons) or in my shameless moments I just asked Wesley outright, "Did you and your Dad have any nice dinners over the weekend?" Weak. Need I measure the projections of his libido I regarded his Tesla and the palatial nature of his home (as seen on Google Image searches), his swagger, his diction. Need I know his X or Y, there's an article in the *Chronicle*, or *Texas Monthly*, or where have you. Need I learn his Z, peruse his rumored faults, oh message board, oh op-ed! Christ, I needed it all, I needed him entire.

But if there was one moment that really did it, really crystallized my intent to read him, it was that time at Mom's house, after she had gone to sleep, when I was flipping through the three hundred channels on her TV and found a repeat of his latest sermon. Jordan was right. What I had scoured online was Corbin Allen from 2000-2015. What I heard and saw that night confused me. It was the same man, in yet another blue suit. Same hair, same crazy eyes. But the words were new. The tone. The spirit behind his God that night. New.

Corbin Allen was now preaching with someone else's voice.

6

A God-Given Lot

Wesley slouched by the door, clutching his folder like a lifebuoy. "I'm supposed to invite you to this thing," he said.

"What thing?"

He opened the folder, rifled past the sheet music, and produced a small envelope embossed with the Riverbed insignia. "It's an Independence Day party. Cookout, I mean. My dad wanted me to say 'cookout' so you know it's personal."

"Okay, then." I said, and laughed a little. "That sounds fun." He handed over the envelope. "Why are you upset? Do you not want me to go?"

"It's not that."

"I would understand if that's it. Sort of like seeing your geometry teacher out of school."

"I just hate the party is all. We do it every year. We always did." In that second 'we' a note of sadness sounded.

"Hey, you want some tea?"

"I've never had tea."

"You've never had tea?"

He shook his head. We went into the kitchen and I put

water on to boil. Wesley's experience sometimes baffled me. He had told me about a musical setup in his room that probably cost north of five thousand dollars, he had been to New York three times, yet he had never had tea.

When I placed a mug in front of him he stared at it, then said, "Lorena makes me tea when I'm sick."

"So you have had it. This is black tea. Your dad doesn't mind you having a little caffeine does he?"

"That's Mormons," he said.

"I know."

"It's hot, why are you having a hot drink?"

We were seated at my little wall-side table. I shrugged and my shoulder clicked the lightswitch off. "Makes you sweat. Then it's not as bad."

Wesley was silent. I turned the light back on.

"Y'know I met your old teacher a few weeks ago. Mr. Barshius. He said he'd pretty much been your teacher forever."

"He's weird."

"Well, regardless, he said you've been trying to keep your worlds separate, kinda. You can always be honest with me. If you don't want me to come to the party, I won't be offended."

"You can come, you can come. Jesus."

"Hey," I almost snapped. Wesley whipped a look at me. We both knew I had almost snapped at the name Jesus but I didn't know why.

"What?" he said, and with one word it was the sharpest I had ever heard him speak.

Some shame and nerves charged up within me. Maybe I was a better instructor to adults.

"Nothing. It sounds like a fun party. Cookout, excuse me. And I want to see your house!"

When Wesley had first been inside my place, he had

looked around and asked if that was the whole house. I could tell he was embarrassed having said that. Guess I couldn't help myself. I felt like a teen weaseling my way into that invite. If Wesley cooled to me, so would Corbin. I needed every ounce of trust I could get. "We do it every year," he had said sadly, "We always did." If I was to earn trust as an authority figure in the life of Corbin's son, I needed to be ever conscious of the ways in which Wesley loathed and needed authority. His dead mother would again miss the Independence Day party. His fucking comatose grandfather might not make it either. But I could. In this I found some blushing relief.

"Everyone's always boring."

"You know, it took me a long time to understand, but I think everyone's really interesting."

"Everyone?"

And for a moment I was him again, driving with his terrified little cousin in the backseat, taking her to an isolated spot.

"Most of them. Let's get started."

He practically leapt from the chair. As the lesson wore on, we drank our English Breakfast, and before he left for the day, I questioned him. "What did you mean earlier, when you said Mr. Barshius was weird?"

"He's such a— He thinks he knows everything."

"A lot of grownups think that." I felt I should have used the word 'adults.' "Men especially. That doesn't make him all that weird."

"Sometimes it felt like he knew more about me than my dad did. That's weird, right?"

I knew something was wrong when I slept through my alarms and missed Taylor Camp's lesson. Her mother called me and I missed that too. I woke up around noon after having gone to sleep early, and still after stretching I felt tired. I took a shower hot then gradually colder and washed my hair and slapped my face a little to get some color into it and I put eyedrops in and still after breakfast and tea I fell asleep on the futon. Unmistakable, like the pre-cold tickle at the back of the throat. But instead of a tickle I have a little luminescent octahedron rotating in my middle vision, pulsing gridlines changing color on my periphery. I sleep too much, dream other people's dreams, and I have thoughts of being trapped within a decaying body or leaving one in slow bright death. That's it, it's like being entranced and raptured on a deathbed. Obsessed with no object and all objects. All planes of sight and all references of distance. Any idea brilliant or awful. There is no centralizing of the mind, only entropic decay. Not depression, seclusion—not a borderline, a revolution. Knowing my tendency to latch onto others while in this state, or either reject them unceremoniously, I canceled lessons for a couple days. I knew I needed the money but it would have to wait. I didn't want to risk too much interaction with any of my students or their parents, scornful of the gravitational aspect of the readings and thinking cloudily like an addict that maybe I could avoid it this time. But then again I wanted Corbin (even watching his sermons in bed) and I slept and groggily fixated, unfixed, until the Fourth of July. Pride may be a sin of mine, but my mortal sin is gluttony.

That holiday Monday, I sat sweating in my parked car for a long time, watching outside the Allen house as flocks of finely dressed people arrived at the mansion. The cul-de-sac had curb space for at least three mansions, but there were only two, across from each other, and one was but a wood frame. The Allen house was a broad brick affair, a rind of maroon and copper with white-blinded windows, with a wraparound porch and thick white wooden pillars supporting a balcony. The neighborhood itself was low, shaded by the reaches of an ancient network of oaks, but the tract there at the cul-de-sac was clear and high, sloping behind, treeless, windblown, so of its sky. All the visitors stopped to examine something behind one of the pillars, where they then climbed a ladder and returned with upturned hands.

As I approached the porch, a tribute station revealed itself. Two small circular tables presented a collection of framed black and white photos of the Allen family. Visitors creaked about the patio, waiting their turn to ascend the step ladder, and admiring the main attraction, a painting. The backboards of the porch's overhang, visible only when looking out from the house, were streaked with the beginnings of an abstract geometric mural. Tins of paint—green, blue, white—had been placed on the deck wood beside the bottom of the ladder. One at a time, people dipped their hands in the paint of their choice, climbed the ladder, and stamped the image of their palm onto a mottle of handprints bursting sideways from the mural. A large woman barely contained within her dress struggled onto the second step of the ladder as a young man braced its frame with his knees. The woman agonized over where to leave her mark. Her husband, de-painting his hands at a courtesy plastic wash basin by the front door, told her, "It doesn't matter where." She glanced to me for opinion, and I shrugged with a smile.

Nailed to one of the pillars, a plaque explained.

Cynthia wanted this part of the house to be an artful welcome. We humbly ask all visitors to get your hands dirty and help us finish her dream.

I chose green.

Inside, people milled, ate, gabbed. We clogged narrow passageways en route to cavernous rooms where we boomed and echoed. We gratefully filled our plastic plates with cheese cubes, salami, crackers, grapes, apple slices, all fresh and filling. We washed ourselves out with Merlot or local beer. Communion jokes were made as we went for seconds. We were the congregation of Texas's largest church, diverse, diversely devout. We were families and branches and our children's friends. We introduced one another. We commented on the spaciousness of this room, the luxuriousness of that kitchen, the prints of Reformation era art so carefully decorating the study, the nostalgic scent and firmness of that bar soap in the bathroom. Which bathroom? Did you know there's one with a urinal? And the view out the rear of the house, oh my. The beautiful spiral staircase in the foyer. "God save the man," we said. "A single father." "And yet this place has got a woman's touch." "But he can pay for that." "Don't say that, Keith."

In a pristinely arranged music room near the back door people gathered around a piano, and there I glimpsed my first Allen of the day—Wesley, at the piano bench, distinctly having fun as he swore he couldn't, waving people more compactly into the room. "If anyone knows guitar, hop on," he said. "Country blues coming." He trinked some high-octave keys, hummed. He saw me and nodded hello. I smiled back. It struck me that the other kids at the party were elsewhere, not listening to the music. Then Wesley's tenor sounded, his being dilated, and the room brightened as he took it to a genre surely none of us had heard him voice.

He sang "Dear Doctor" by The Rolling Stones. He was leaning heavy on the diphthongs, for effect I understood, but try as I could to think like coach or audience I was distracted by something, someone, outside myself... The day of the plunge.

A guitarist had joined, and for the second verse nearly strummed along in key, and several feet in the room were tapping between the *woo*s and claps, but then with one fluid rest father and son connected eye-lines, one set passing behind me, one all daggers at the other, and Corbin's voice dopplering through the hall cut into the music with paternal disregard—"It's a God-fearin crowd, Wes, don't get too blue."—and Wesley kept playing.

With a suddenly rapid pulse I pivoted and stepped into the hall Corbin was then exiting through the back door. Two golfish men followed him, day drunk men, and following them was a cigar-mouthed Jordan Barshius, who in passing pointed ahead and joked sideways at me like a '20s gangster, "Lookin for him, creep-o?"

The backyard rolled out from a square patio of planate stone. A dozen people strolled about the lawn and its symbol sculptures—a small cross, mini-Mary of Nazareth. Couples drifted to the edges of the yard, which was double fenced and ivied over. How much money could a preacher make? They call it *prosperity gospel*. I saw the bayou and the skyline, but wasn't the city supposed to be flat?

Some paces away, Corbin showed off a table's load of fireworks to the two men. Jordan paused between us, lighting then puffing his cigar to life.

"What's creep supposed to mean?" I stepped into his smoke.

"You've got a line before you can greet the host," Jordan said, nodding at the men. "I'm just teasing. Feel free to make fun of my flip-flops."

"You are indeed wearing flip-flops." He was also wearing shorts, revealing a tattooed series of interlocked impossible triangles spiraling down one of his legs.

"I've heard it all by now. Damn me if I'm not comfortable."

"Don't you get all bitten up out here?"

"Good for the circulation."

"Is it?"

Corbin led the men to the other side of the table. "Enough of the kid stuff. Here's the Black Cats for whoever wants to ruin the party."

Jordan puffed away through quieting words. "I get it, I do. Millionaire widower, sexy."

I rolled my eyes, crossed my arms.

"You ever been to a psychic?" he asked.

"Why?"

"I went to one this week. Second time I've been to one."

"Did the second say the same as the first?"

"I don't remember. I'm still trying to discern if what she said to me could have been said to anyone else."

"Sure it could," I said, "but it could still apply."

"You ever been to one?"

"Yes. She wasn't psychic. But I believe some people are."

"Really? But not her?"

I barely remembered it. It was before Vegas. "Nothing she told me came true."

He regarded the burning end of his cigar and said, "Maybe you changed your fate."

"If there's fate, you probably can't change it, right?"

"If there's fate, there's probably much more, too. Who knows what you could do?"

My eyes glanced reflexively to Corbin, opening a box of bang snaps, and Jordan noticed. "Or who you could do." he said.

I smacked his shoulder. "You heard the host, don't go blue."

"I think he meant the music, not the jokes."

"It's not any of your business, but I have no interest in seducing a man twice my age."

"Good, because I'm pretty sure there's a line for that, too."

"Are you in it?"

"Not my type. And before you ask, yes."

"Yes what?"

"Yes, you're my type."

"Jesus…" I said, starting to move around him. He stopped me with his cigar hand, with force and urgency.

"Ivy," he said, practically glowering, and before I could pry his hand off, he let go. Like *he* was recoiling. And then he winked. "Almost got me," he said.

His words hung dead in the air but I was whooshed off by Corbin, speak of the devil.

"Ms. Qualiana, hello but there's no time for manners, he's singing for real now." Corbin with all his rush, and his huge hand to my elbow, bid me turn and go with him, which I did. These fucking guys. Always another line or destination, or just plain overreach.

Jordan's words had caught in me, but distancing from him my familiar tingle flared and spread over me a warm exhaustion. A part of Not Me ached with my movement, and I saw Jordan left behind smoking in the warp as in a Hitchcock zoom, Corbin all the while launching from word to word for what instantly I knew and cared not, self so muffled and shaken. The joining. One filter I knew so well, tearing against another. I was going to read. Today. That much was apparent. I was beyond my exhaustion and felt less like someone who had been hibernating than one who'd stayed awake for days on end. Time cracks up in these moments, how it would under sleep deprivation. Here again was Wesley, playing, singing. The crowd in the music room had thinned and grown serious. Beside me Corbin watched with pride. Wesley, on point, caroled with the relaxed and flowing vibrato he reached around the 59th minute of our lessons.

"T'was grace that taught my heart to fear
and grace, my fears relieved.
How precious did that grace appear
the hour I first believed.

Through many dangers, toils, and snares
we have already come.
T'was grace that brought us safe thus far
 and grace will lead us home."

The room crooned along, I assume. I heard only a voiceless impression of the words, between heartbeats, twice my own, sinking within. Everything in measure.

Corbin showed me to the good beer. Time cracked and I awoke behind him, outside, at the door to a detached yard house. I scanned the backyard for Jordan to no avail. Corbin *ahem*ed.

"I.P.A. or pilsner?"

"I.P.A."

He entered the shed and called out to me while maneuvering bottles.

"I dare say I already hear improvement. You have got him to practice more than Barshius ever did, I think, y'know, at least it seems that way. I hear him all the time now."

"The voice is an instrument, you can't let it stagnate."

"D'you teach him that 'Doctor, doctor' one he inflicted on us?"

"No, I believe you can blame that on The Rolling Stones."

"Shows how much I know."

He emerged from the shed—which at a glance inside betrayed its cost, more amenity than utility—and he handed me a beer.

"Thank you. Hey, what kind of name is Barshius anyhow?"

"I think it's Czech," Corbin said, shutting the shed door.

"Is that Wes's game room?"

"No, this is my sanctuary outside the summer months. Wesley's in his room or at the piano all day long. But seriously, thank you for your work so far. He likes you. Sometimes it's a racket, gettin your kids to pursue somethin, to really care and work toward somethin."

"Wesley has a serious interest in music, Mr. Allen. And he's very talented."

"He won't take piano lessons anymore, or guitar. He's insistent on teachin himself. But voice? Maybe Barshius beat it into him that, for that, you need another ear. A second opinion of the ear."

"It's a blessing that you can provide him with lessons," I said.

"Amen, but you're the one teachin."

"Are you musically inclined at all?" We ambled toward the table of fireworks.

"God's gift to me was speech. The devil's probably responsible for my singing voice."

I laughed.

"Hope you've gotten to mingle some," he said before a swig of beer.

"Sure, a little. Thank you for hosting. Wesley says you do this every year."

Corbin's clean-shaven rock of a jaw split with some burgeoning response, but time slipped and I missed it. In some whorls I'm a little self-conscious slab of a person— that's what I judged myself in the moment. No musician, no boy of God, naught but another unremarkable little dude...

"Ivy?"

Corbin was reaching toward me, his hand turning under to a point, and he placed the tip of his index finger under the bottle I was holding, or rather letting slip.

"You good?" he asked. He had this look of trivial but sudden doubt. A look I've seen many times, the look that says *Oh she's just crazy.*

I set us in silence. Corbin's hands were back folded over his beer before him.

"Would you like some water?" he asked.

I was numb. All I could think to do was go find Jordan and make him vulnerable and read him. Corbin, my jewel, my question mark, right there in front of me. But I knew that day would not be his. This was merely social discomfort written on him. Plus I felt younger than Corbin. Now wearier every second, now wired past delusion, now tired again.

"I'm fine, thank you," I said. "I'm sorry, I just suddenly got very tired."

"Am I that boring?"

"I promise you're not. I'm also nervous. I'm a big fan of yours."

"Are you now? I thought you said you weren't a believer? Or goin to services."

"It's true, it's true. But I've watched several of your sermons now."

"Have you? And what'd ya think?"

"You're a very compelling orator."

"Why thank you."

"And you put on quite a show."

"Well, we hope it makes you pray. Do you pray?"

"I meditate."

"And do you reach that flow state?"

"A state of stillness maybe."

His face changed after I said that, it brightened or relaxed. He took a moment before responding. "The avenues to God are many and exist in all religions. Meditation is communion with the breath and the mind. Prayer is communion with the idea of a dialogue with God."

"The idea of it. But isn't it a dialogue with God?"

"I'm putting it in secular terms. I do view it as a dialogue with God. I think God is in our subjective faculties of language and reason and our inner monologue. Rabbis pore over text, and contemplate text, and tap into it. Christians pray, Buddhists meditate. Many people meditate."

"God's always there?"

"God's always there."

"Well, Mr. Allen, your sermons do make me meditate."

At that comment he narrowed his eyes, but not his smile.

"I was curious, though," I started to say. What was I doing? Wired and unraveling I was still carrying on. Talking. Autopilot. "Your recent sermons, it seems like you're taking a different tack. I haven't heard you talk like that on stage recently."

Then his face soured. It was always impressionable when Corbin Allen's demeanor soured. So sudden. He frowned, then nodded almost furiously. "I have been strippin things bare of late. You're perceptive. It's a fundamental summer for me."

"You were talking about organization the other day."

"That's right."

"Felt a little… I don't know. Isolationist, don't you think?"

"Pro-family but individualistic. That's what I was goin for."

"I get it, I get it."

"I know how it seems," he said. "Leader of an organization bein skeptical of organizations." He clicked his tongue against his cheek. He always had that sheen to his face, the perfect broadcast look. Hairlines finely edged, posture strict, imposing. "But what if I told you the good of organization comes from the good of individuals. Same as the bad. Cooperation ain't bad, group purpose ain't bad. Groupthink, that's a corruption. No matter what." He could tell I wasn't satisfied with his answer. "What?"

Time was cracking but I was there, thinking of a childhood, but there, refocusing on conversation at a party. I was blathering, "You seemed to base that sermon on the premise that all organization was inevitably bad, though. Or inevitably *tending* toward groupthink. But how could that be?

Churches, charities. How could that kind of groupthink be that bad? It literally produces good."

"You're not the only one who took issue with it. But you know what, sometimes I gotta hold Corbin the TV preacher accountable. I gotta remind myself every day just as I gotta remind the congregation. Fundamentals: perseverance, trust in the word of God, trust of His word in my own ear. He made us individuals for a reason. We're not supposed to know it all, but we can hear it. We can taste it. But we hear and taste and smell on our own, don't we? And all of us together, well what could that accomplish? Life lies between you and God, not you and I."

"It's a little pessimistic, don't you think?" I asked, instead of what I wanted to ask which was how often he referred to himself in the third person.

"What's pessimistic about humbling yourself to God?"

"It's skeptical, at least."

"It is skeptical," he said, and there was that broad smile again. "We'll have you at Riverbed any time, ma'am. Mingle some more!" And with that he walked away. So disjointed was I I hadn't realized I was already back in the house, at the threshold of Corbin's study. Why was I alone there? I almost threw up. Braced myself across a cabinet bench. Voices drifted around me and the swallows started deep within. Wait, sorry, that was later. First I was standing with a group in Corbin's study, with the preacher, the choir director, and two socialites straight outta *Gatsby*. Jordan kept eyeing me and I kept looking out of someone else's eyes. I was on autopilot still, time acrack, and one of the socialites was teasing Corbin about his onstage tics, and then Corbin said, "She watches a lot. Hey, Ivy, any criticism from the outside?" And I was agreeing, "You do blink a lot." And there was laughter. Then I was still speaking, dimming the tone in the room, apparently, saying "You do do this one thing also, where there's a thesis to your sermon. It's the name of the YouTube videos too. But it's like plugged into a format when you say it. So even if it's not grammatically correct you'll say 'Today I want to talk to you about Leave Doubt Behind,' or 'Today I want to talk to you about Remember A Proverb.' At least that's what I hear. It's kinda funny."

No one laughed. Corbin tensed up and Jordan... And there was Wesley still on the piano, now there I was talking to Shannan from Dallas about British comedy. At one point I noticed it was dark outside. Then I went to the bathroom, *then* I was back in the study, alone somehow. I chided myself for allowing it to get to that, and all in public. Jordan would be twenty something years and then I'd wake up wine-tipsy in someone else's house and have to deal with the shock. Fuck Dad. I meant 'fuck me' and thought so. I was in the fetal position and thought I should probably sit up and at least pretend to be okay. So I got my bearings. I wasn't in the study. I was at the end of a hall, first floor, next to the study, on the cabinet bench piled with pillows.

And with the speed of rock, the now! Wesley appeared at the end of the hall. I smiled what I could of me. He walked the length of the hall and stopped an arm's length away from the bench. Like rock, like Xenu, there I was!

It wasn't Jordan or Corbin, it was Wesley. I was going to read Wes.

At least it would be quick. He was young.

"Umm," he began, though I swear I heard *ohm*, "Ms. Ivy, I need to tell you something."

He sat next to me and I knew it was only half to hide his tears, for now his voice cracked and hands fluttered up and any pretense was futile. A weeping student. What one can muster, in a moment like this, tapping the system of all teachers lived and gone! But alas I already knew what Wesley was going to say.

"I have to quit lessons," he said. "I'm sorry, Ms. Ivy, I just want to learn other things."

We lost to the wobble. Wesley convulsed once, a flapping stick in cargo shorts, and he gulped it all, consciously embarrassed, and he turned to me. "Oh, dude…" I said, scooting over, taking in a hug, folding into ourselves, on the verge of some truth, before time disappeared.

Wesley

Hollowed out and brightened, you're undone and tightened. Sickened, tricked, or tripping, you learn with repetition. The dirt is not for licking always. Your teeth have hardly bitten, but your ears now make some sense. Led by Mom and Dad, with friends. Linear responsibility, parabolic sin. You hide things now and again. You count on toes and fingers just how long until you're ten. Wes, yes, that's you alright. Wesley James Allen.

Now rare frost, icicles crowning the garage—Christmas. Tucking your knees in backswing. Now Mom and Dad crying with laughter after you taste a jalapeño. Your trucks printing tracks in the carpet. The bulldozer and Godzilla fighting. Now your being showing in the face in the mirror, now you. The deep green at the far reaches of a mirror tunnel. How the right of someone facing you is your left. How you've been given a body and bounds. Mirages on the highway. Grandpa, ever grouchy. The way Mom and Dad kiss in front of others. The way your voice reverberates in the atrium at the mall even among so many people. Now pray.

Sundays, remember the stories, engage with the morals. You got lucky with Dad as a dad because he knows this stuff better than anyone. Not *anyone*, he says. But everyone listens to him. The people who come to your church are welcoming, waggish sinners. They all love Daddy's books. You love those days Mom lets you help sort the collections and place the money in the electric bill counter. Now apply hand sanitizer. Sit on the pastel concrete stairs of the parking garage and eat a granny smith apple. Throw a tennis ball against the ridged wall, chase. Smell your sweat. Try to think of something the church doesn't already have—but it has candy, books, puzzles, games, instruments, everything. It has maps, people, machines, screens, music, Bibles, paintings, closets, dressing rooms, dining rooms, meeting rooms, mailboxes. It has walls entirely of glass and entirely of marble. There's hundreds of those long tube lights and hundreds of normal lightbulbs. There's TVs and even some video games. The only thing the church doesn't have is next week's sermon. Listen closely as Dad 'spitballs' and Mom 'brainstorms' next week's, next's. Wash your hands. Take the jagged ride home. See the sunset through the car window. See those cloudbursts, Wes? See the fading at the edges of that rainbow? See the traffic here and these mudcaked tires and the smiles people trade after a storm? That's God, Dad says.

Mechanosensation—hearing and balance, touch and pain. This is the world. Exchanges are vibrations. It all goes: World to auricle to canal to eardrum, tym tym tympani. It counts when the world plays on your brainstem. But you and Beyond You work inversely, too. Brain to lungs to windpipe to voice box to throat to tongue to lips to world. You and Beyond You form an echo chamber, within which some thought rings ever grander. You try to explain this to Dad and he says, "Like a game of Pong."

Speak the truth in love, and know you'll grow in every respect to become the mature body of the head—Christ. Note: you have fluid, cartilage, joint capsules, spinal discs. You have blood that could spill. On the pinnacle of the temple, Satan twisted scripture in an attempt to convince Jesus to jump. But Jesus wasn't hung up on pointless magic tricks. Remember that.

Mom's favorite part of the Bible is when Jesus rises. Dad says he doesn't choose favorites. Sometimes, the way he talks makes you feel like a stranger to his God, while Mom, at her best, makes you feel like everyone shares the same purpose. She understands that Christian kindness is more useful than Christian preaching. All around, all the time, she's a smoother soul than Dad. She knows when to get mad at you, when not to. Plus she's smart about things other than the Bible. She can explain how satellites work. She can sing harmonies to a song she's never heard. She was born in Manhattan in New York City, lived in London for two years. Worldly, as it were. Every day, she's more Godly, and proud of it. She and Dad must really love each other, because they work together, and they love their work.

Mom is pretty, too. People often tell her this. After services, on the street, anywhere. Dad likes to say she's radiant. He whispers more than that in her ear. One day, he leans over to you, points to her, and says, "That's how you take a compliment, bud."

Both of her parents have gone to be with the Lord, but Mom's sister, Aunt Zelda, claims you are just like their dad— righteous, diligent, with a full-lunged laugh. You can't ever know for sure if that's true. Dead is dead. But you can trust Mom when she agrees.

Really, you must be more like her than anyone. You may have Dad's teeth and frame, but everything else about you comes from her. Your cheeks, your eyes. She teaches you how to use the voice she gave you, how to trill it, how to warm it up. The two of you sing along to the radio and she teaches you how to harmonize. When you dial onto a song she calls screamo, and shy away, she teases you, says, "There's some things in this world to be scared of, Wes, but music isn't one of them." And she's right. This song playing right now, this is her favorite. Follow her lead: *Thunder only happens…*

And playing, playing is all you do, such the kid. On your seventh birthday, in the stolid mustard air of Grandpa's apartment, where there sound but clock chimes and game shows, your father's father leaves a thought slamming in your ears. "You're the age of reason, Wesley. That means no excuses." And him a preacher just like his son.

"Grandpa doesn't preach anymore."

"What does he do?"

"He watches TV and plays with numbers like he's some kind of medieval wizard out of ideas. And he eats frozen meals and he yells at telemarketers."

"Corbin," says Mom, mad.

"Numbers like math?" you ask.

"No, not like math. Wes, if anybody ever tells you when the rapture's comin, don't believe em. No one knows."

Mom says quietly, "I didn't know he was apocalyptic."

"Didn't used to watch TV either. Age maybe?"

"Your grandpa's just a stern man, hon."

Behold—School! For a year now, no, more now, you've worn a uniform, carried a packed lunch. It's a fishbowl, the people say, you're all fish. Madison, Matthew, Tyler C., Tyler G., Victoria, Hopper, Angela, Alejandro, Garrett, Elijah, Dominic, Rebecca, Gavin, Lily, Gabriella, Hunter, Isaiah, Ryan P., Ryan Q., Jordan, Aidan, Gannon, Ashland, Sydney, Jenna, Taylor, and you. And Mrs. Slazak, whose glasses are so thin you can barely see them, whose voice is like wet concrete at a rolling boil. And how come the teachers don't have to wear uniforms? Why does Taylor say this school is going to heaven and the other ones aren't? If Noah only took two of every animal, how did the second generations reproduce? What's it like to be a sibling? A parent? A teacher? A fifth grader? The only thing you know is what it's like to be you—what a trap.

Of the kids in your class, you are neither the most annoying complainer nor the most ardent student. You are curious, though less vocal about your curiosity in school than around your friends. Of you and the Tylers you are the tallest, the second fastest, the third strongest. The Tylers tease you for liking books, for singing to yourself so often, for so often being friendly with Taylor. Too frequently, you let them infuriate you, but don't show it. Dish it right back. You have chums.

You have a big arrow on your being, an attribution everyone sees, which points up at Dad. The world has defined you as your father's son, and this you understand because people pretty much emphasize it. He is famous in the truest sense of the word, famous like a celebrity. He has books and a TV show, that's what he's done and doing every day, broadcasting God across the globe. A preacher, but still famous. Sending himself gleefully into other people's lives.

There is time enough in this life for you, Wes. Time to gamble what cents you got. Time enough to be wrong, some time therein to be reassuringly correct. There is an hour after dark but before midnight when suburban sprawl lulls itself into a repose blissful enough to conceal the mischief of kids. Time to perfect the pranks of that forgotten hour, when you can lay strips of duct tape sticky-side-up across both lanes of a street such that the neighborhood thinks guns are firing every time a car blasts over them. Even at moderate speeds, tape getting tangled in a car's wheels produces that fulfilling boom. Time to run. Time to get caught TPing a house. Time in an autumn to listen to Mom's half-drawled reading of *The Chronicles of Narnia*, time for a winter move within the same zipcode, into a house—don't kid yourself—a *mansion* in a gated community, with a cul-de-sac all to itself, with a pool. Remember the punch-code: six, eight, one, six. Remember where the hide-a-key is. Don't swim alone.

Once Mom buys a piano and fashions a music room, the possibilities of your time retract as if on the surface of a deflating balloon, and the days and hours move ever nearer the same outlet—music. Mom teaches you. Pitch is only the perceived positions of a scale. Consonance, a construct. Dissonance, a default. Melody is the weaving of roots. Rhythm and timbre, mindsets. Progression is chemistry, but each measure is a different art. Listen to composition. Time signatures, tempos, bass, rests. To master the art of music, you must internalize its conventions. You must be counterpoint to yourself, even if slurred, or too often refrained. To master anything, you must practice, practice, practice.

The house fills up with friends, mostly Mom's and Dad's but also yours, convening for America's sake in the mug of summer. You watch from the safety of Mom's lap as Dad and Mr. Frank set off fireworks in the cul-de-sac, launching a hundred laughs and tearing the sky apart with color. You survey the destruction in the morning with the Tylers. At some point you say, "We're older than the age of reason."

"What's that?" asks Tyler C.

"Means we're not stupid," says G.

Pet Sounds and that yearning deep within it. How a major key can still bring sorrow. How wordless music can still have a narrative. You listen to Mom's favorite Fleetwood Mac album many times to study what she calls its "perfection of pop." Spend hours online and marvel at how Mom and Dad don't think twice about the amount of time you spend on the desktop computer. Tupac, Nirvana, Pixies, Radiohead, Gorillaz, Björk, David Bowie, Tom Waits, Kate Bush, Taylor Swift, OutKast, Katy Perry, Maroon 5, Kanye West, Lady Gaga, there's a lesson in every sound and every dollar. Mom and Dad hardly notice when you go to sleep anymore. In this life there is time for secrets hidden from everyone but God. God alone knows, and that's okay.

Dad reads to you one night and enforces the Book of Job, barreling on with the same drama Mom uses for *Lord of the Flies*. "Then Job replied to the Lord: 'I know that you can do all things; no plan of yours can be thwarted. You asked, 'Who is this that obscures my counsel without knowledge?' Surely I spoke of things I did not understand, things too wonderful for me to know. You said, 'Listen now, and I will speak; I will question you and you shall answer me.' My ears had heard of you but now my eyes have seen you. Therefore I despise myself and repent in dust and ashes.'"

"That's sad," you say.

"It's a lot of things. Sad, true, but also it can be an uplifting sort of reminder. There's things beyond us we don't understand."

"So God is supposed to question *us*?"

Dad absorbs that with warmth. He smiles and reaches out, puts the back of his hand to your forehead, then runs his hand down your face and directs you jaw, chin, and nose toward heaven, like he's regarding his bust of Plato. "You amaze me sometimes," he says, then he reads the epilogue. "Son, some people in this world are going to tell you that this doesn't mean anything. They don't believe in the same God we do, or they don't believe in God at all, so they don't believe any of these words. They don't think they have meaning. But I promise you, no matter what the Bible means for you, every word here matters. Every word is true."

Yet there are other religions, other nations, seven billion other people. Seven billion.

And you are rich. Dad is on TV every day, dude. Your friends and the other kids at school ("a priiivate school," some kid at the ballpark once sneered) may be rich, but their dads don't have a private driver, haven't been on TV, haven't met President Bush. He is famous for believing, can you imagine that? No, he no longer expects you at every service, but he still expects Christ to be the centerpiece of your days. You wonder if he's so distracted that he's decided to leave your religious instruction to school, or to his public preaching. Didn't he used to read you Bible stories every night?

Sets and contrasts, sounds and forces. You are what you consume on the internet. You are hours of fail compilations, evidence of the scale of human stupidity—hopping onto the back windshields of cars in jest only to shatter them, snowboarding with such energy that a safe landing is impossible, blundering with a quarter-ton ATV. Why do we put frozen lakes to the test? Ice always proves it can break. Why shouldn't we watch? So watch: the buckling of uneven half-pipes, the faltering of headstands and kegstands, the collapse of weak roofs, overpowering gun kickbacks, falls into cacti, waves dispensing of surfers, wheelies gone awry, elephants charging tourists, the remnants of race cars pluming into oblivion, so many people failing to land back flips, the odd car crashing into a home, manatees snubbing, parasails tangling, dogs bellyflopping, weightlifters crushing themselves, mountain bikers meeting trees, bridges breaking, trains derailing, runway models tripping, broncos bucking, bonfires exploding, cops noticing, toes betraying, gate arms closing too fast, and, generally, faces planting.

Mom has book club the night of a concert you've discovered, so you beg Dad to take a night off and take you there, which he then does with stilted pomp. Alas, the Midtown Civic Center, a squat teal bucket with a shingle roof, just folding chairs and a step-stage, the scene of your most childish crime, a night thankfully already receding from your Now but stuck forever where it was. Curse the hour Dad asked if you needed the bathroom before the show and you said no. Two classical guitarists proceeded, the room alive with their fretwork, their rhythm measuring the time it took a hot bowl in your stomach to fill and capsize. This shame preserved in amber: You sat numb and afraid of every choice, afraid of interrupting the show, afraid of any willful action's impact on one normal night with Dad. So you sat and sat and distraction prevailed over confrontation. All your self-direction to notice that slight syncopation or that funky chord or that bass-line smoothing out a key change, all to no avail, the bowl spilling onto your lap, wetting everything like you were a stupid little kid, until your last distributary drained itself into the puddle beneath your chair and still you sat. Dad never noticed. Not there, not on the ride home. How could he not have noticed? How could he have ever noticed?

From Merriam-Webster, definition of *stroke*. *(tv)* 1. to rub gently in one direction, to caress 2. to flatter or pay attention to in a manner designed to reassure or persuade *(n)* 1. the act of striking 2. a single unbroken movement 3. a controlled swing intended to hit a ball 4. a sudden action or process producing an impact 5. a sudden diminution or loss of consciousness, sensation, and voluntary motion caused by rupture or obstruction (as by a clot) of a blood vessel of the brain

From Merriam-Webster, definition of *coma*. *(n)* 1. a state of profound unconsciousness caused by disease, injury, or poison

Disease, injury, or poison. Grandpa has a stroke playing chess with Dad, and becomes comatose, and things move quickly at first, then glacially. After a month, your visits to his hospital room grow infrequent, but they always terrify you.

2-A. With his monitors, his drips and tubes. The venetian

blinds, the daylight cast through them and onto his stillness. The metal bars siding his bed, the weight of his body on the mattress, his adjustable angle. His breathing. You're here with this giant void of family connection. This time, it's just you and Dad. You pray together before sitting.

"What did Grandpa talk about when he was alive?"

"He's alive, Wesley."

"I mean awake."

"You talked to him," says Dad. Then he reconsiders. "I know he wasn't much of a talker. When he was younger, he... he talked like a man who always thought he was right. Usually he was. I always thought his voice sounded like a cheese-grater. One of them big ones."

"Grandpa's... not gonna wake up, is he? You don't think he will."

Dad inhales, holds the breath, and keeps holding it as his expression evolves from one of disinterest to one of alarm to one of sullen duty. He exhales, and speech races over his breath, as if the words were just now unstuck from some crevice within him by the force of air. "That's why we pray for him to wake up, we want him to wake up, but no we can't expect him to. We need to hope, but can't expect. Part of me is sure he'll wake up when the time comes, but if it ever comes the time's from God, so I don't know. I don't know."

"Do you think he's dreaming?"

"I hope. If he is, I bet he's convinced he's wide awake."

That slow, inward rasp, and slow, outward hiss. Radagraaasp, hnnnnnsss. Your grandfather is the living dead. The veins in his hands, the creases on his face, the stubble that someone who works here must regularly shave. This is maybe the dozenth time you've looked at him asleep like this, but the first time you've seen him for the lack he really is. He can't see, can't hear, can't feed himself. God only knows what he can sense. In that room, be conscious of your eyes and breath, if not for yourself, then for him. After all, you'll never know him.

You turn fuckin nine, yo, and still you are what you do. Some play soccer, some play football, you play piano. Some are restless gamers, but mostly what you do is scroll and scroll and scroll. Click click click. Newscasters accidentally curse. Meteorologists euphemize. Greatest broadcast bombs of all time, here they are. Vlogged routines of amputees. Narcoleptics' inaction. All hail the Russian dashcam. The sex jokes hidden in children's content. The comments sections of footage of your Dad preaching. These centuries old photos recolored, this gruesome war footage remastered, this hilarious embarrassment replayed, replayed. Chauvet cave. The Falling Man. Haiti. The B.P. oil spill, right nearby. Tahrir Square. Occupy. A baby biting into a lemon.

If you are the people around you, you're best around Taylor. She's special. She laughs at your good jokes and rebuts your bad ones. She makes you think more than any boy, and not just about her. You have fun together simply with silly faces and sillier voices. She's really good at drawing. She's not alien, not removed, as are other girls at school. And look at that face. Look at the daylight on the edges of her hair as she sits fake meditating on that stump in the clearing by the bathrooms in the park. Ask her again to do that impression of your dad.

On the day before Halloween, she's all giddy and giggly. You chase her to keep up as she leads you to an especially autumnal-feeling spot way at the south end of the neighborhood clubhouse grounds. She twirls in the leaves and whistles. From somewhere beyond a fence drift the voices of teenagers. From behind you come the blaps and grunts of a casual match on the clubhouse tennis courts.

Between you two there sounds a subtle, arousing static. You ask, "Can you whistle? I don't know how."

"How could that be? You play piano and sing, you should know how to whistle."

"I can't really sing."

"Yes you can," she says. "I've heard you. Want to dance?"

"Dance?"

"I love this time of year. It makes me want to dance." On cue, a long-chilled gust of wind circles you and shuffles the leaves and pine needles around Taylor's feet. All the trees—some golden and orange, some dumped bare—shake with approval. You expect Taylor to say something like, "See, the trees are dancing," but she just whistles.

"Can you teach me how to whistle?"

"I can try. Purse your lips. Like this, yes. Now blow air out."

"Pwoo."

"Not all at once. Like you're singing, but don't sing like with your voice. Just air."

"I can't do it."

"Hey, you asked."

"Yeah, well..."

"You give up easily," she says.

"I just can't do it."

"Don't get mad. That's a fact. You give up easily."

"That's not true! I didn't give up on piano."

"But that's because you're already good at piano. Like naturally. You think you can't whistle, so you give up."

"Well you're a twat."

"You're a twat. Did I make you sad? I mean, you're really good at music."

"So what? No one can do everything."

"You could try harder at some things. Like how you talk to me at school."

"What about it?"

"You *never* talk to me at school."

"Yeah I do."

"No, you don't. But it's okay. Hunter doesn't like me, so when you're with him, you pretend like you don't like me either."

"It's school, though."

"But you want to."

"Want to what?"

"Talk to me in front of other people. You sometimes do in front of Tyler and Tyler."

"Sure."

"But you want to do it more."

"I don't know." You shrug. Taylor sits on the ground and starts untying her shoes. There's a big splashing sound from the backyard with the teenagers, and ooing and screaming.

"I love pushing people into pools," she says.

"We're not school friends," you say. "You know how you've got school friends and church friends and other friends? We're the other kind."

"Gee, thanks."

"Why are you taking your shoes off?"

"You know that's a pretty dumb way to have friends. So you wouldn't talk to Hunter if you saw him at church?"

"I guess I would."

"It's normal, Wesley. It's okay. My mom says it's normal for boys to be like you. Online says so, too."

"Be like how?"

"The way you like me."

"I don't like you."

"You don't like me?"

"I mean, I like you."

"Yeah. You think I'm pretty."

"Shut up."

Taylor stands and runs and cartwheels and falls, stands, cartwheels again, again. She laughs to herself as if you aren't here, like it's just her and the wind and the sounds of the neighborhood. She crunches some leaves between her toes. She says, "Watch this." She tries to kick leaves along the arc of her feet as she cartwheels more, but she keeps getting a face full of pine needles and dirt.

"Have you ever had a boyfriend?"

"I knew him at camp. His name was Roger. He kissed me."

"No way."

"It was on the cheek, but he kissed me. We held hands. The counselor told my mom and my mom told my dad and he grounded me when I got back home."

"I don't know what my dad would do if I kissed you and he knew it."

"You said he liked that we played together. "

"Well, sure, but just like friends. Do you want me to be your boyfriend?"

"I don't know. I want you to talk to me in school."

"Okay."

"Yeah?"

"Yeah, okay."

"You promise?" she asks, lighting up.

"Do I have to kiss you in front of people?"

"Nope. Just talk to me in front of Hunter."

"I will."

"And come dance with me right now."

"You're not dancing, you're flopping around."

"Come flop around with me."

So you do. After a while, she says, breathlessly, "Truth or dare."

"Truth."

"You're a wimp," she says. "Pick dare."

"You gave me the choice."

"You better do what I tell you, poop scooper."

"Fine. Dare."

You expect her to dare you to kiss her. For a brief moment, you expect and wish this more than you've ever wished for anything. You know she must be thinking the same thing. But she says, "Go jump in that pool."

"The clubhouse?"

"The one behind the fence, where those boys are."

"What? That's someone's house."

"It's a dare."

"Climb the fence and just jump in someone else's pool? Just like that."

"Uh-huh. Come on, I want to see the looks on their faces."

"You know, I think you and Hunter would get along if y'all tried."

"Do it."

"I'll get all wet."

"You can come dry off here in the dirt."

"If I do it, will you teach me again how to whistle? I won't give up this time."

"Deal. But that's not how truth or dare works."

You shake hands. You hold each other for a moment more than necessary. She curtsies and releases. You bow, turn. She watches as you climb over the fence and run toward the pool, with singular focus, but silent, without a battle cry. The kids shriek as you plunge into the water. You come up for air, then sopping wet you run back across the yard and narrowly escape a boy's grasp as you roll over the top of the fence. You and Taylor flee the scene, laughing. It's worth it.

And then death.

In better days, Dad said The Lord Giveth, and the Lord Taketh Away, and this you must mull over and over, every disappearing sun. You can't stop crying when Mom tells you what kind of death God is giving her. What's happening happens too fast and now it's gone. Mom is gone. Dead. And you're still crying.

What did happen? She died the same day a man murdered twenty children in Connecticut. Pancreatic cancer. The hospital swallowed her up like it swallowed Grandpa, but he remains trapped, and Mom is gone, so it is said, forever. Hours of silence, or tears, or awkward preparation. The last time you saw her, it looked like she was sinking into her bed, her face gray, her teeth with a weird sheen you're certain you didn't imagine. That last day, you and her were each aware of every brutal detail, at once horrified and fascinated. Dad sat in the corner in the same clothes he had worn for three days, not so subtly pushing the conversation this way and that, trying to keep you engaged with some moral. You tuned out so many of his words. He tried to twist it into a lesson, a sermon, didn't he? Sort of. And what moral could there have been? What lesson could be worth those hours? None. It was a meaningless and Godless death, hers. Mom shriveled and passed, simple as that. Along the way, you and Dad exchanged maybe a dozen honest sentences. He got hung up on stupid bits of scripture like they were gonna help any of y'all. Song of Songs 6:7. Psalms 48:10. You thought: What is this shit? You prayed with them, but, duh, had never so viscerally hated the act of prayer. Once it's past, you keep praying, but you angrily entreat God on her behalf, for her to be alive again, for even her dying days to be the present. But it's past. Never forget what she said to you then, the way she hugged you and whispered, softer than Dad could hear, "Life is really big. We gotta share it with everyone. We can't all have it at once. We gotta share it, I guess." She guessed.

You could still be guessing on your deathbed.

At the memorial service, Aunt Zelda holds an ironclad grip around you, and tells you three times it's okay to cry. Not that it matters, you're crying anyway. At the burial, Taylor holds your hand. It's all the world just to focus on her hands. The contours of her knuckles, the texture of the dried polish on her nails. Think: This is the first time you've seen Taylor with nail polish. Think this as they lower Mom's casket into the ground. Mom's casket? No, it's not hers. It's the other way around. Mom is the casket's.

If you're being honest with yourself, you've long suspected that God doesn't exist. Now there's proof. In the weeks after Mom's death, your belief bloats, then one day completely evaporates. It pops, disperses, gas from the balloon. If authority can disappear, if commanding love and the literal source of your life can all disappear, then authority and commands and sources are meaningless. Right? People die, yes, but *meanings* can too? You spend hours madly playing the piano, singing along to Pandora. You listen to the old radio—it's so rare, to plug in that thing—and you tinkle over the songs and commercial jingles with the upper range of keys. Then out comes the burrowing bass line and stretched-out, rained-on jaunt of Fleetwood Mac's "Dreams" and Mom dies all over again. You know you cannot add harmony to it, but still find yourself singing along. So here you go again. If there is a God, he's a cruel God. He's a sick fuck to think it's okay to leave you with just a glitzy-pious Dad, to have taken away half of a Godly pair, someone so fundamental and pervasive that her absence reveals the truth that she was half the world. And your head and heart drop with the cymbal crash of the chorus, and you burst into a messy cry, and thunder only happens when, when, when...

You cannot determine whether your relationship with Dad has drastically changed or merely revealed its true form. No longer vigilant about your part in the cleanliness and order of the house, he lets the maid do everything. He doesn't care if you fall asleep on the living room couch. He doesn't care what time you go to sleep. Where he used to scold, he now explains, sans enthusiasm. Where he lamely quipped he now dryly remarks. Where he proselytized he now states. You are what you say. You are how you say it. A place—a gesture, an articulator, a passivity. A manner—your intra-action. Phonation. Your resonance and consonance and consonants and vowels. You are belting with free and careless vibrato. You are what you sing. You are whispering to yourself, "We gotta share it, I guess." You guess you are what you mourn.

Meanwhile, you wish people would stop prompting you to talk about her. Wish you didn't think about it all day, every day. If only Dad stopped mentioning her in his sermons. If only he would quit preaching altogether. He has enough money, he's said enough peace. If only he were a closer father, and if he could just stay away.

"I want to take voice lessons," you say, a week before your tenth birthday.

Dad shakes off that signature dumb, blank gaze of his. "You mean speech lessons?"

"Singing. Vocal lessons."

"Oh. Okay."

"And—umm. Music. You know? Dad, soon I think I'm gonna need a computer."

"We have a computer."

"I mean one of my own. In my room. Good speakers."

"There's a lot of bad crap on the internet, Wes."

"I've seen more of it than you."

"If you get a laptop, you'll never leave this house."

"Aren't laptops so you can leave the house with them? I don't want a laptop, I want a desktop of my own. It's what I want to be."

"What is?"

"A musician. I need a computer."

"We have a piano. Shouldn't you need more instruments?"

"I need a computer."

"Is that right?"

"Uh-huh. Come on, it's not much. My friends have iPhones, I'm not asking for that."

"A computer's more expensive than an iPhone. You're just going to play games. I see you with the Xbox."

"I won't just play games. I'll make stuff. Music. For church, even."

Dad buys you an iPhone and wireless speakers, tells you just to use the computer in the study when you need a computer. It's as though he's pretending to be an overly cautious helicopter parent but also half-assing it. The internet says Dad's net worth is thirty million dollars. He says, "Don't believe it, trust me." In what may be a bid to keep you in his purview, he gets you private voice lessons from someone who works with the church choir, whom you must call Mr. Barshius even though he's barely more than a teenager. But Mr. Barshius's lessons are both fun and challenging, and he makes church music exciting, so the bluntness of instruction washes out the dullness of venue, and by thrilling inches you learn yourself closer to the mastery of two instruments, the piano and the voice. You join the kid choir and find two new crushes.

Life in double digits, life in the year since Mom died. Dad has the gall to insist on throwing another 4th of July party, never seriously considering your protest. "Mom would want us to keep having fun," he says. You and Tyler C. spend the party listening to music in your room, but except that hint of fun, the day dredges up memories of Mom, the time she explained how every other continent's history became American history, and how Dad didn't like her candor, or how she would cover her ears when Dad lit an artillery shell even if it wasn't going to be loud. She didn't mind the screamo music but covered her ears for fireworks. Later in the year even the anniversary of her death passes with little ceremony from Dad. Fuck it, you're all YouTube and Wikipedia and Instagram anyway. You read all of the best and worst things about Dad you can find. What is faith in the face of clarity? If there's a God, he'll forgive you for not believing in him right now. For as long as you can remember, you have been told to pray. Did you ever know what to say? How dare you ask, how dare you broach any subject? God only answers with profound silence and unrelenting circumstance.

You stop behind the Berrys' mailbox and watch Taylor as she kisses her mom goodbye and nearly skips off toward the street. She stops to pull earbuds from her backpack. She plugs in and her skip becomes a dance. You run to catch up to her, tap her shoulder.

She squeals. "Why'd you scare me like that?"

"Did I scare you? I'm sorry."

"You're... hi. How was Christmas?"

"It was weird," you say. "Sad."

"Oh. That sucks."

"I mean, I got some good presents. You?"

"Sure. My dad made such a good turkey."

"I miss you, Taylor."

"Yeah, I miss you, too."

"Sorry, I just really do."

"I missed looking at your stupid face."

"Nuh-uh."

"Uh-huh."

"My face isn't stupider than yours."

"How can a face be stupid, Wesley? Don't be silly."

"You said it first!"

She punches you. You punch her in return. Y'all scramble, and she gets you in a headlock, but you get out of it and tackle her. Kiss her. Kiss!

She slaps you. "What are you doing?"

"I'm sorry. I wanted to kiss you."

"Do it again," she says.

You kiss her again, on the lips, and you join there, in the hard press of stupid faces, for a still and breathless beat. She gets up, wipes dirt off her pants. "How do you know how to kiss?" she asks.

"I don't know."

"You can't do it unless I say it's okay."

"When is it okay?"

"Not on our way to school."

"Then when, after school?"

She doesn't say yes, but nods.

Smell the library—Dewey. Read aloud in class—an intimacy unwound, judged. Write enough to cover both sides of a sheet of paper. Understand that Houston is a tad boring, ecologically speaking, but the rest of Texas ain't boring, and the rest of the world ain't, neither. God damn, look at this natural world you got. Spit. Ride your bicycle all the way to the bayou. Here's your environment for ya: a great spread of bottomland hardwoods, pine forests, wetlands, grasslands. Here's a bit of truth for ya: your dad's money has bought him the ability to ignore you. Your most immediate environment is your room in his mansion and it's a place too big even for Mom's ghost to haunt. The irony is that you curse God in a house built by praise of Him. You have your music, Dad has his work, Grandpa has his hospital bed and darkness. In one another, the three of you have some semblance of family. Supposedly.

You thought the world was made of sound and sight, but that can't be it.

Now behold—a full family. All you really know about the Camp family beyond Taylor's traits and anecdotes is that the

Mr. and Mrs. adore your own father. They're one of the big donor families listed in the lobby of the church, and they give every year, though they don't attend service very often and as you know Taylor takes Sunday school elsewhere. They explain this with their arms around each other. As you watch snotnosed little Peter yawn in front of *Family Feud*, you realize you haven't been inside the Camp home after sundown. Behold—this lovely night. Taylor is so cute here in her own environment. She talks a mile a minute about the house and school and "stupid" Peter, and she grabs you by the hand with every exit. You cannot name all the ingredients of her energy. Is she nervous? She transparently enjoys any awkward silence between you and Peter, or you and her parents, yet does everything in her power to avoid a beat of silence between you and her. Like she's hiding a worry. Like you are her experiment, her long-studied discovery now thrust into some testing moment of truth.

At dinner, arms unfold, hands upturn, and Arnold Camp with his huge forearms asks if you would please like to say grace. Taylor grabs your hand, but any electricity there fizzles as Arnold takes hold of the other. Peter has already taken a bite, but his mashed potatoes suspend in pre-swallow. The refrigerator's motor starts up. Mrs. Camp's smile relaxes as it becomes obvious you are deliberately not responding to Arnold's question. Taylor squeezes your hand.

Mrs. Camp says, "Wes, would you like to?"

Your esophagus lets out that odd high groan you sometimes get when thirsty. You clear your throat. Taylor squeezes your hand again, but softer.

"No, thanks."

Peter swallows his mouthful. Your palms sweat. You notice Arnold's grip hasn't changed at all. He looks right at you as he clarifies. "No?"

Taylor says, "I always just say one I memorized. You know

some, right?"

Through a second ungracious bite, Peter says, "Of course he knows some. His Dad's—"

"Stop chewing," says Mrs. Camp.

"Why don't you want to say grace?" Arnold asks. "Don't be shy."

"It's not that," you say. "I don't know. My dad says grace for us. When we eat together."

"What does he usually say?" Taylor asks. Her voice has gummed up, her nerves overpowering any appreciation of the awkwardness. She turns to her mom. "Can I?"

"Sure," Mrs. Camp nods.

But then Arnold Thick Neck over here pipes up. "Come on, Wes."

"He's not used to it," his wife offers.

"He's the guest," says Arnold.

"I'd like to hear Taylor's," you say.

The fridge motor gurgles. Somewhere inside the freezer, ice falls. Arnold holds the silence for two long, dreadful beats, until finally he breaks from the circle of hands and shrugs and says, "Okay. Taylor. Say it."

"Our Father, thank you for this food, and thank you for all our nice neighbors, and for the weekends, and also thanks, Mom and Dad, for the food, too, you know. And um. God, please help another family tonight, one that doesn't have food yet. Thanks. Amen."

You take a huge bite of mashed potatoes. Its stone bolus of heat pounds down through your chest, throbs. Your tongue sizzles. You spend the rest of the meal sweating and wondering how Peter kept those samplings in his mouth for such a long moment without reaction. Some weeks, you see Lorena more than you see her boss, your father. Some months, even, what with him in South Carolina or Florida or New York. How many dinner graces does he really lead?

One day, for no particular reason, you review Dad's browsing history. The websites for Bank of America, Chase, and Riverbed auto-sign you into his accounts. You stare at the balance of his checking account until your heart rate increases, and when Lorena sounds at the top of the stairs you exit the page and room.

You quit the junior church choir, so here you go, have time enough for every pointless thing. Mondays for the envious scrolling of Instagram, Tuesdays for vocal lessons while all your peers play pee-wee football, Wednesdays for piano lessons, until you ask to stop them. Halloween falls on a Friday this year, and costumes are for kids. Aren't your ears just sharper every day? Aren't these growing pains, as they say? On a Sunday morning, deep within a jazz scale, you can feel flow, just as Daddy Corbin says a Sunday sermon flows through him like a river. But he has less time and will die one day, like Mom. He has no time to date, he has a publisher's deadline, he has to go plug and defend himself on CNN. He has sermons to edit, hardly has the time to write his own anymore. He takes you to New York again, but again you spend most of the trip in the hotel room. You sign into his email and marvel at the volume—he certainly has time to write to donors.

But enough about Dad. There's a farce going on all over the world. The earth is suffocating and everyone is about to burn and we're ignoring it. Mr. Barshius with his references and accents, Mrs. Gilbert the Social Studies teacher the object of every boy's jokes, Hunter Pastel with his memeified ribbing, Mr. Todd the obviously closeted orchestra teacher, Simone who numbs your mind when she tells you what she and Brad did in a closet together, Arnold Camp, even taller than your dad, the ghosts of great musicians, the ghost of Mom, the placid, studied suspension of Grandpa Allen. He's been asleep for over three years, lucky bastard. "Black lives matter," says Dad, "and all lives matter. Why do you think we pay to keep Grandpa alive?" And it's the first time he's phrased it that way—honestly, but strangely and like a cruel joke. If you didn't have the money, Grandpa would've been six feet under long ago. And Dad didn't answer your question about the protests.

Then one day at the end of a lesson Mr. Barshius gets very serious and asks you to sit down for a minute. He scratches his dumb beard throughout and dandruff sprinkles onto his pants. "Wes, I want to tell you a story and I want you to really pay attention."

"Okay."

"Do you know who Aaron Swartz was?"

"Kinda"

"Who was he?"

"The Reddit guy? Who's dead?"

"Yes. He was a really smart kid. Knew a lot about technology and science, became a programmer and more. Bit of a hacker, bit of an activist. Good guy, he fought for an open internet, he fought for freedom of expression. High achiever. He starts working for big universities. And if you ever go to college you'll meet this thing called JSTOR, which is a huge database of academic articles and books, history, science. It's a vault of knowledge available only to people in school or working for a school, really. I mean you need cash for it. All owned by these private companies so it costs a fortune to get. So Aaron, who's working for Harvard, goes over to MIT, puts a computer in a closet and starts downloading from JSTOR. Might as well go for some ethically justified digital piracy. But the law catches him, and comes down hard. The system. The government. This is one guy up against many systems, he was staring down a trial that could end with him in prison for decades. And before it started he was found dead hanging in his home."

"Why are you telling me this?" you ask, ears hot with the thinned pounding of blood.

"Because I think you especially might want to consider how tricky this digital world is. Your dad's famous, but you're a little rebel. If that story is how noble intentions can end, what do you think it's like for all the people who hack and pirate and snoop *without* good reason?"

"I don't know."

He stops scratching his beard finally. He dusts his pants off. "I'm just saying, for every action there is a reaction, and when you look at something, you change it."

"I'm not a pirate." You can barely get the words out of your mouth.

"Oh, who knows what you kids do on those things." He winks. "Have a good weekend."

You can give only an *okay* and a hasty exit. For hours you torture yourself with his warning. Could he know about you looking at Dad's accounts? Have you ever done that at Riverbed, on any computer there, or in theoretical view of Mr. Barshius? With a slip of the tongue have you ever betrayed some suspicious awareness? No. No, there's no way for him to have known. It could only be coincidence. Unless Dad himself knows...? But Dad never says anything about it. Dad's behavior but a natural bitter decay.

Twenty-seven million people in this state and you're stuck hearing the same ones. Your parents set you on a track long ago. Not everybody goes to the same school their whole life. At this rate, you'll share high school graduation with the same kids you shared naptime. Taylor says eighth grade will be her last year at Westland Grace, because her mom wants her in a public high school. Does Dad even know the names of your teachers?

Ugh, just shut up and be a kid. Or grow up. There's

nothing in between that isn't awful. Play hours upon hours of *Destiny* and *GTA* and *Borderlands* with Austin Wallace. *Call of Duty* with Hunter those few times. Be a kid and be snarky with Hunter if he's snarky with you. Be a student and pick up the slack you've let out in math. Dad doesn't know when progress reports come, but Lorena does. Always an A+ in Orchestra. You are one of Mr. Todd's favorites, but make sure not to relish that. Be an all-around student. Give your solemn opinion on *Night* by Elie Wiesel. Wonder how you'll feel about frog dissection day when it finally comes. Be astute, be pious. Really work hard on your essay about the golden calf —the religious instruction here is finally gaining some complexity, nuance. So, Wes, what or who do you think your generation falsely worships? You know without a doubt. You know every one of these kids should say the internet. So be more specific, kid. We worship WiFi. And be you, you. Act your age. It was always there, so you start playing with it, and one night stuff comes out. When you absolutely must walk around, use a textbook to cover your erection. Just standing? Just lean. Sitting? Spread, get the right angle. Consult Hunter about porn. What were those sites he showed you long ago? (You were a kid once, right? There were times you and Dad played catch with a muddy Nerf football. Surely it mattered those times on a road trip where backseat imagination reigned more immediately than the world.) Be quiet when you masturbate. Experiment with technique. There's sensation, oh yes. There's janky rhythm and with rising nights a jerked climax. Then something comes out. Alright then. Wonder when Dad's gonna give you the sex talk. He must realize you've searched, you've clicked. Still be careful where you click. Imagination is limitless. One picture and you're good for the night. One mental picture—probably of Rachel Ozro or Brittany Joyce, guiltily Taylor—and you're good for the week. So that's what this is. This is what you do.

Slowly all the boys start to talk about it, share pointers, spread urban legend. Wonder what role evolution plays in the way you swap stories with the boys. Wonder if Dad believes evolution plays any role in anything. If Dad was anti-masturbation, he surely would have made that known to you by now. Wonder if Kyle R. really was able to jerk off six times in one sitting, like he claims. Now wonder about something else.

"Dad, do you believe in evolution?"

After a dubious beat, he says, "I believe in science, son, yes."

"Like Darwin. Do you believe that?"

"Do you mean natural selection?"

"Yes."

Dad spins his fork slowly, like it's a rotisserie spit. "Yeah, I do. Science is real, Wes. God created evolution like He created everything else."

"Why don't you ever talk about it in your sermons?"

"People don't want or need to hear about that from me. People want practical lessons, drawn from scripture, that remind them how to behave in the world, and view it. I don't need to get political."

"It's not political."

"Well, to some people it is."

He doesn't really give you a 'talk.' He gives you a book and tells you to let him know if you have any questions. There is such a frozen sense of him that overwhelms you sometimes. Whether his hands-off approach to parenting is due more to his insensitivity or his aloofness, his fears of confrontation or his respect of privacy, these questions knot inside you frequently, but you can only answer with gray assumptions. So fuck that warning Mr. Barshius randomly gave you that one time, fuck privacy. You've got plenty of mischief-makers in your tool box. Rig every poll Riverbed's media team attempts. Make it so Dad's cheapo hack of a webmaster can't ever find your entrance, now violate that site. Spam them all. Ensure the Riverbed Board of Directors receives a weekly update from the Texas ACLU. Stay quiet, look innocent, and don't laugh as Dad grumbles about these things at the dinner table. By summer you've finally got the decked-out room you need, and Dad can't even figure out what you're doing in there. He's not even trying to.

Houston rainwashes itself to ruin, politics arise everywhere, the summer of 2015 is just another season, just prelude to autumn to winter and on and on. You can hardly mark the endless scroll of time as your digits facilitate it of their own volition—how automatic it is to keep things moving, open, refreshed, refresh. Snapchat, the social badge ephemeral and immutable. The streaks of airless moments accumulating into these most basic of stories, the stories, the updates, TL;DR people suck. A hackneyed truth: it's all feed for the never-full, easy to rue, easier to use.

How much would a swimming pool fill if you filled it with all the soda you've ever had? All the mashed potatoes or carrots, which is more?

Arnold Camp is sawing meat and splashing sauce all over the table while Taylor says over and over Jesus is my God, I can be what He needs me to be, I can do what He needs me to do, and Mr. Barshius is there, arms crossed, like waiting for you to prove you practiced, and Arnold is talking over his daughter's prayer asking you why you didn't bring your guitar, and you wake up on the couch sweaty and sticky against the leather and it's daytime outside.

Why is no one in your life normal? Ms. Doerre breaks down and cries every time your class gets rowdy and yet she's been a teacher for twenty-five years, what gives? Tyler and Blake smoke weed with Blake's older brother every weekend now and Tyler's getting all proud about it. Meanwhile Hunter's sense of humor has gotten so twisted that when Blake passes out in the auditorium during the church lock-in Hunter uses a Magnum Sharpie to stain a swastika onto his forehead. Rachel Ozro kisses you like she means it, and in some backward way your union and reunions heighten your social standing while diminishing hers. But she doesn't even seem to care. And Taylor isn't jealous anymore, she actually approves, like believably approves, of you and Rachel. Yet you keep having dreams about Taylor, not Rachel.

Then there's Mr. Barshius, forever sneaky about something. When the U.S. Office of Personnel Management gets hacked, when Ashley Madison gets hacked, Barshius brings up the news click-clacking with his tongue like you had something to do with these things. "For every action, reaction," he says. There's a moment once, as you're checking Dad's latest bank statement or reviewing the details of a nameless event on his Google Calendar, and you wonder what exactly Mr. Barshius is driving at and whether he could possibly be unaware of the synchronicity of his warnings and your temptations, the outside world and your father's.

The outside world and your father's. Alternate realities, or parallel. There is this distinction. A split. Good God-fearing Christians are the evangelizing protestant Jesus-trusters of the Bread Basket and Tornado Alley and the wooded south but forget geography because it's really just them and you, the good God-fearing folk and everyone else. The outside world. It's that dogmatic dichotomy of spirit and purpose spat in form from lip to spittoon to porch to weedy yard on down through the generations and your dad is just as siloed as any of them.

Throughout 2015, Dad's decay—in morality, self-assurance, sanity, what have you—that slow corruption you thought you sniffed at the edges of his being turns out actually to have been a rot from within, and even though it belongs to the most famous preacher in the country, your father's very being, his soul perhaps or something otherwise *of* him, presents a final burst and putrefaction. This eaten state of his becomes the norm, but at first the merest changes in him unsettle you. You get unsettled enough to start praying again. Jesus is your God, you can be what He needs you to be, you can do what He needs you to do.

It begins with small turns of phrase, an anachronistic word every now and then, copacetic, halfway to Sunday. But words are actions, don't let anyone tell you differently. Dad starts asking if you should be playing football. He's busy, always busy, often traveling, but there was a time, wasn't there, when you two maintained a ritual of scanning the channels together once a week. You usually landed on John Oliver or Stephen Colbert, but now he just loathes those guys. Watches TV during the day now. When Mom was around and he was fun he wouldn't necessarily encourage risqué humor but he didn't totally freak out about it either. There's no blushing no more, no respites allowed. No suppressed smiles nor flushes of discomfort. He is anger incarnate if not fervor. He has no sliders, no levels, no operation but an ancient series of rudimentary switches flipping him yes-no at every stimulus like he's some mute image coded on a loom. You don't have to wonder about him anymore, you can just ask. So ask about evolution again.

"Darwin wasn't smarter than anybody else."

"That's not what you said last time."

"Last time what?"

"You said natural selection was real."

"It's incompatible, son. The only things naturally selected are those ordained by God."

Those ordained by God. Please. Give it a rest.

"So you don't believe in it? What about like fossils and stuff?"

"Fossils are fossils. Fossils are fuel. We've gotta remember to look around and see what God is doin right now. Right now, we're here, and fossils are in the ground. So? We're here for the mystery, son, not the answers. We already know the answers." And he points guess where.

He pays for your school but insults it. "Waste of money," then, "waste of Bibles, tell you what." He pours out all of the liquor from the cabinet above the microwave, pours it down the sink with some old pickle brine, and he starts having Lorena stock the fridges with beer. He spends the cooler nights out in the yard shed, reading, writing, attacking whatever publisher's deadline he's on in hunch and candlelit yes candlelit out there still up at two in the morning every morning for weeks. Other times were different. There were other flurries of his, forty pages and six coffees in a day, piles of earmarked theology, piles of notecards. But this time it's just a notebook and his Bible. This time for better or worse he keeps rubbing his eyes and leaning over and squinting along the same lines, that same text, that same leather copy, that same old story of stories, over and over like a madman.

In a folder marked 'misc' you discover a file named *birthday letter*, and it takes all of ten minutes to decide whether or not to open it, which you do. There in single-spaced Garamond is a screed meant for your comatose grandfather, whose now inescapable brand of stone-still hopelessness descends on you like hail, the damage of the storm more apparent with each word.

31 December 2015

Today would've been 75.

I mean it is, a coma doesn't equal death I know. Technically somewhere life is going on. There's a beating heart in there. Not that I can feel it over there. That body is gone. A body that can't feed itself. Stuck away. Some of the doctors look at us almost as if to say isn't 75 enough years? But that's not your decision anymore. For once, I'm in charge. So for all those bloody fantasies I know you've had in which I die or fade away, what do you have to show? What do you have to say? I'm waiting.

You sit there dumbfounded for a long moment, then read the whole letter again, and again. On the verge of some hypothesis, you realize the document continues. You read on.

December 31, 2014

My handwriting is getting older. Type slow. Even my voice sounds older in here. Joints creaking non-stop. This is what aging is —moving as much as you can and then right off feeling stiff again. I'm not sure what birthdays mean anymore. I hope they mean something. I found this file every year for the past couple. Why not. I know we're losing it here, everyone's getting older and no one's getting smarter. Maybe I should make a record, I thought. What if I can watch myself unravel for you year by year. I won't know if this is a good idea or not.

December 31, 2013

Happy Birthday, Dad. Today I took Wes to visit you and he asked if you had ever done anything bad. I mean he really just asked it. I asked if he meant did you ever go to jail and he said sure and I said no and he seemed kind of disappointed. Maybe it's the way I talk about you that made him think it up. Can you believe it? Imagine that. You in a prison that you didn't build for yourself.

December 31, 2012

You outlived her.

A few minutes can change every subsequent hour, no doubt about it. With one stroke, you discovered about your father something hidden which by being hidden legitimized itself as worthy of uncovering. Was it his deepest hatred, his most obvious hypocrisy? Which characterization of these entries would help you make sense of him? Or do you need to make sense of him? To hell with the preacher who hoards his riches. Who cares that a supposed moral authority like him remains tight-lipped about Trump? Dad's true sin is so much simpler, so close to home. Those last three words—first three, actually. He assigns different values to different lives. He is a son who scorns his father, a hypocrite of Biblical proportions. Honor thy father and mother, does he just not care? Do the words not mean anything to him either? Confusion fades, but the world and all its systems are real despite confusion and they continue devolving, prey to entropy, spiraling out. Some days, you feel unwound, you've run aground, you know not who you are or've been, and you hope and fear that as you age entropy won't win, and fear and fear and fear yet hope that as you age you'll spiral in.

Your school bleeds photos for weeks. If you've got beef with someone, submit a candid, embarrassing photo of them in class to the finsta Kelsey and Morgan run. Full-body cringe as they go after Ariel so hard one day she cries at lunch, stands up, starts taking off her clothes, wailing and stripping, until she's covered and rushed off and never returns to school.

Meme in the flesh, Trump says he could stand in the middle of the street and shoot somebody and he wouldn't lose voters, and he's right. This comment, of all the shit this guy says, inspires Dad to bring him up during a car ride.

"Why don't you denounce him at church?" you ask.

"I could only denounce the things he does, not him. I can't tell people how they should vote. God will pass judgment on Trump. Besides, son, religion and politics are connected. I used to hate it, but that's how it is."

"I guess I don't see what's so Christian about Trump."

"You know the expression 'the ends justify the means.'"

"Yeah."

"Yeah, well, that. For a lot of people, all politicians are bad, and they're all the same. Donald Trump is not a politician, and he's definitely different."

"Who do you want to win?"

"I'm supposed to say Jeb."

The winter is a cold blue and one day the sleet becomes almost snow. Then the winter gets washed away, and you keep scrolling. Dad hires someone to figure out what's with all the Twitter and email hacks, so you cool it. On occasion, you reflect on his letters to Grandpa, and try to reach conclusions—like *he is lonely* and *he is a hypocrite, this is why he doesn't even have friends*—but you too are lonely, your friendships play out primarily behind a screen, so how are you any different? You're just younger than Dad, your beliefs are thinner, but you've got the same pettiness he does. Like, if you took every text, every message you ever sent Austin or Blake, and all the words you've exchanged over Xbox Live, and you stacked them next to all the words you and Austin and Blake have exchanged face-to-face, it's a blowout. Why is that, Wes? Is that the times? Is that your environment, or is it a thousand little choices of yours? Dad has stepped on five of the seven continents, he has heard many more voices and his own voice is louder and more widely heard than 99% of people. You have never even left America, and you type into a void.

Dad asks you to come to church again, then again, then he's back in the habit. He's pestering you, really. He spends more evening hours hanging around in the kitchen or living room, trying to be around you as you scroll on your phone or practice fingerpicking. But he's just there to read scripture aloud, from his phone if he has to. And he looks so old now, juxtaposed against any technology. So set in his ways. Is this just your revelation dawning or is this a new reality emerging? His silent tussles with the word, his private scoffs exploding off the end of verses as if bested by a friend in debate. His eyes shifty.

'Apocalyptic' was the word Mom once used. Is he there yet?

You start praying again. You pray to Mom. You try to spend less time scrolling and more time listening to music. You practice scales and songs. Dad asks if you want to start going to teen Bible study. Remember how much you liked the junior choir? Do you want to join the real one? You say no, and further daring Dad to disapprove, you ask to stop taking lessons from Mr. Barshius and get a different vocal coach. "I need someone who can teach me how to sing like a real singer, you know, not like a choir boy." Enter Ms. Ivy, flint-eyed and scary pretty. You like her lessons and think about her for several jerk sessions in a row. You only sometimes feel guilty after jerking off nowadays. There's enough guilt to go around. Puberty is new hair, growing pains, NRBs, and the constant projection of your worst impulses onto the girls closest to you, and still it's better than what the girls are dealing with, and all of this moves by the great invisible hands of shame and curiosity. That hand, God's or a ghost's, worthy of curses, worthy of praise, unsparing. For some reason you get stuck on one definition of the present. The Now. It's that moment in a song where you can hear fingers changing chords on an acoustic guitar—the changed use of a tool, the breathy, tinny scrape of action against time. Everyone always says, "I can't believe it's summer already," but what else would it be? Everything alive keeps living and moving, of course time will pass. Not a week after 49 people die clubbing in Orlando, Calvin Harris and Rihanna drop the video for the song of the summer. Life keeps going. If you live long enough, you'll get to write a few songs of your own. And look at that, you've lived long enough to do it! You've written two whole songs.

And now you've got today, tonight. At Bridget Boroughs's

birthday party, at her rich-ass dad's house, dance with all the hormones of your class, really dance, for the first time, and when Bridget grinds on you, nearly cum it's so awkwardly right. Go into Dad's study with the intention of snooping, then swear off snooping and pranking forever. Not for morals, but for fashion. You're cooler than that. Wake up at 3 A.M. and realize it was just a nightmare. Wake up on a summer schedule. Play Fleetwood Mac on the piano. Pray for Grandpa, try and remember the sound of his voice. Realize all you need to do is keep your voice warm. God and Dad have blessed you with a music room, that's all you need. Decide to tell Ms. Ivy you're through with voice lessons, you know how you need to work and you can work on your own. You have the fundamentals but now you need to hone the craft. The creative craft, of course. Tell her this on a holiday, under the cover of American independence. Pass the party entertaining in the music room, look at the clock and wonder where an hour's gone, then, loopy and splitting, find Ms. Ivy on the bench outside Dad's study and ignore your tears and nerves and tell her this.

7

Nel Mezzo

The night above rent by the whining flare of an artillery shell, an eruption of green and yellow, a quick shower of light, "ooh" from the kids. My body on the move and a figure several feet in front of me not slowing as I was now, my nascent reality unnerved by some tired adolescent thrill as if I was sneaking out of the house, but I was just sneaking out of someone else's party and that was Mr. Barshius ten paces ahead. This is how I came to and again it was like some ecstasy wearing off.

We had gone beyond the crowd gathered in the cul-de-sac and were walking up the street. Jordan must have sensed I stopped for he turned back to me and himself paused mid-stride. "Wait," a voice said, and I suppose it was mine.

"What's up? Forget where you are?"

I didn't answer.

"How much did you drink?" he asked, stepping closer.

I looked back toward the crowd as another series of artillery shells began to rip. Turning to Jordan I saw his pale dry dome of a head display the alternating hues of the fireworks in all their shimmer, America-colored, incandescent.

"What are we doing?" I asked.

He smiled, mildly confused. "A minute ago you were very insistent."

Again I couldn't answer.

"You wanted a ride, right?" he said, gesturing behind him up the caravan of parked cars on either side of the street.

"There's still Uber, but it's probably extra right now."

"I asked you for a ride?"

He was still confused, but no longer smiling.

"You said you wanted to ask me something."

But what could I want to ask Mr. Barshius? I had been avoiding him all day. I had been playing and singing and jinxing that he'd reserve judgement from another room. He was creepy Mr. Barshius and he was just Jordan and these two conceptions of him arose and collided and arose and combined in some M.C. Escher loop of definition in my head and I couldn't straighten it out even as I stared into his eyes.

"You okay, Ivy?"

Ivy, there she was.

I decided to trust myself. It's a coming-to, followed by a rather exhaustive mental process. It's a complete decoupling of mental signs, a deconstruction or breakdown of all suppositions by will or circumstance which allows for the arrangement of some newer, realer perspective. It is a coming-to, but also a coming-out, as I come out of that brief overload of truth and back into my one biased self and then one brain is left sorting through two. If in my rapture I thought it prudent to ask Jordan for a ride home, I would go along for now. Hell, I couldn't remember which car was mine. I knew the look, glancing it in Ivy's muddy driveway at each lesson, but I couldn't tell you the license plate or where I parked.

So Jordan led me to his truck and I climbed inside. I pulled down the visor and looked at my reflection in the small mirror there and was shocked to see who I knew to expect. I turned to Jordan. He gave a small nod of sympathy.

"There's some aspirin in the glove compartment," he said, turning the ignition.

We didn't speak much on the ride to my place. I stared straight ahead and focused on breath, focused on the rubble in my mind and some important search through it which I knew to be necessary. At a stoplight Jordan asked, "Do you remember what you wanted to talk about? It seemed important."

Was it about the spying? Was it about Dad?

"I'll remember," I said. "Later."

We rolled to a stop in front of the little peach clapboard structure I had said was my home and I stared at it for a long beat. In retrospect, Jordan's patience throughout this evening and his lack of real questions probing my odd behavior should have been some kind of hint. But I couldn't think straight. Was busy disassembling memories, identities. I had been watching fireworks flare up and die across the city and had been calculating my age. There were centuries behind me, but more important there had been that clarifying span of time, core happenings of perception, fixed in spot a few minutes prior, after the return but before the coming-to, and these moments of clarity were receding with every mile and minute and my memory as it were became gradually revisionist until what I knew was profound and true seemed little more than a dream. I did indeed remember asking Jordan for a ride. I remembered wanting to confront him, to question him. I didn't remember why.

"This is it, right?" he asked.

I nodded, still looking at the tiny house. I knew how to walk up and knock and go to the side room where the piano was, but what else? And yet this was my house.

"Thanks for the ride," I said. "Sorry. I don't remember what it was…"

He shrugged. "It's okay. Can I give you my number in case you remember?" He kind of shrugged his eyebrows, too, as if to say he knew the timing was weird but can he hit on me later. While he typed into my phone I searched my bag and came up with keys. He handed back my phone. "Gimme a holler," he said. "Whenever."

A home comforting, but unclear. First things first, the mirror, my image. There came such foundational denial from that image. Denial became anger. I tried too hard to reconcile myself with Wesley. My potential had been abandoned, my soul had been restored. So I fled the mirror to investigate my home. I marveled at how distant and obscure the fridge felt, and the stove, and like this I marveled at my sink and futon and table and mail, and throughout the night every object, every tool of mine hailed me through my fog with a jest, like an old friend, surprise surprise. This was Ivy. Her stuff and mine, then mine alone. I dwelled in a rented one-bedroom tinderbox on a plot of dead grass about where the north loop hits I-45, my own private swampshack with a mud path and a private road onto the property of a restaurant supply company. I had only boxfans and a window unit to survive the summer, and there were often ants, but the place suited me just fine. Cheap, central. Quiet at night save the cars.

I awoke on the futon after four hours of sleep and spent some time stretching, tapping thumbs to fingers in 3/4 and humming one of Wesley's refrains. I surveyed my body and in shock after some time I laughed like a maniac.

Refamiliarizing, I showered and brushed my teeth, stretched more, made a slow circuit of each room and tried to think of my own life. Losing a student was no bueno. I was down to nine, and with no other gigs my income stream was quite low. Savings would last only two more months. Before the summer was out I would need a few more weekly hours booked or would have to raise my rate. I figured I should promote myself somehow, maybe try to find my way back into community theatre where vocal director jobs could mean work for a solid season. Schools needed music teachers. So did churches...

On Wednesday, after lessons, it occurred to me that I still hadn't picked up my car. So I ordered a Lyft, input the Allens' address, and on the drive there I finally allowed thoughts of Wesley to break their dam and empty into me. I had read him because I wanted to know his dad, but Wesley hardly knew his dad. Corbin Allen was obviously not the most present father. He was a provider, an instructor, and at times a voice of reason, but it's not as if he liked to share much, or even very much liked bonding with his only child. Wesley seemed to think this absence was due to his father's workaholism, or greed. He imagined his dad as someone who got lucky in life, who was able to write and say things within a certain modern Christian framework that rewards success with abundant cash, who was able to succeed within that framework because he was something of a selfish attention hog. After his mother died, Wesley resented going to church, but Corbin didn't make him go very often. To my eye, Corbin was actually quite respectful of Wesley's space in most scenarios, and the main motivation for Corbin to get his son back at Riverbed was simply to be near him, not to indoctrinate him. But these two were afflicted with different strains of loneliness, and thus there was always a barrier between their quarantines.

The real question was: what had I learned either to allay or energize that vague suspicion, my fascination with Corbin? Did I still fear evil in him? Wesley never thought his dad was evil, just negligent. But Corbin was hiding something. He had gotten starker. Firmer these past two years. And as I considered the letters he had typed, those never-sent screeds to his bedridden father, it became clearer that those letters were the funnel into which all my weird fascination should pour. What was the exact phrasing? *All those bloody fantasies you've had where I die or fade away.* Corbin had journaled as though keeping his father on life support was a conscious decision to torture the man. Like him wishing life upon his father was retribution for his father wishing death upon him. Or is that just how Wesley read it? I pictured the document and felt Wesley's sweat, the guilty choke of a swelling Adam's apple. Little snoop. Then the Lyft pulled up beside my car, which greeted me with that foggy friendliness, and I returned to my mind. The matter at hand, so to say. I was gazing dumbly down the street at the facade of the Allen house as it struck me. How natural. I wasn't alone. I wasn't the only one who knew about Wesley's snooping. And there were at least two people in this story hiding something.

8

Whataburger

I knew whatever might be said could fall on deaf ears, so before I went in, I started recording audio and hid my phone in a clutch. Jordan had arrived first. He waved from the corner booth and came to meet me at the door. It was that late lull hour between dinner and the early morning honey-butter chicken biscuit rush. I was confused and fuming and didn't know how to start, so I just nodded along to Jordan's natural manner for a minute. He ordered a veggie burger and onion rings, I some fries. We got a corner booth and sat down to eat, Jordan beginning promptly. I watched him chew for a long moment.

"You're a vegetarian?" I asked.

"Vegan when I can," he said. "It's not vegan batter on the onion rings here, but you pick your battles."

"Do you know why I asked you here?"

"Because you owed me."

"I think you're the one that owes me," I said. I was deliberately whittling my tone to a sharp point. Jordan remained casually disengaged.

"D'ye figure it out so quickly?" he asked.

"Almost got me."

"How do you mean?"

"That's what you said. In the backyard at Allen's party. Why did you say that?"

I expected him to feign having forgotten the moment, small as it was, but real flat he said, "You know why, Ivy."

I waited for him to speak again.

"I was toyin with ya, a little bit, I admit."

"What do you know?"

"Listen, it's staring you right in the face. I know what you want me to tell you. But you know it already. Say it."

I said nothing.

"At least eat your fries," Jordan said, taking another mouthful.

"You know what I can do," I said.

"I know what you can do."

"How?"

"Well," he started, over-enunciating like what was to follow was common sense, "I can do it too." He looked me right in the eye and took another bite of his burger.

"You can read people," I said.

"Yes."

"Like I can? Exactly like I can?"

"Exactly."

"You read me."

"I did."

"You fucking read me."

"You call yourself a reader. I like that."

"What do you call it?"

"Having the keys."

"Having the keys? So what, you keyed me?"

"Took you for a spin."

"What the fuck is wrong with you? When did you do that?"

"When do you think?"

"At Riverbed," I answered straight away. "Standing on the stage."

"No, but good guess. Right then, you touched me. But I could tell."

"You could tell from when I touched you?"

"Yeah, there's... let me see. I gotta watch my phrasing in this conversation. We're gonna be dealing with a lot of information, okay? Yes, when you touched me, I sort of sensed you were like me."

I noticed how heavy and monstrously fast my heart was beating.

"But when did you read me? That's the only time we touched."

"No, it's not."

"I guess we shook hands when we met."

"That was before the stage."

"When, Jordan?"

"Right after you left Wesley. You asked him to come get me, you were—" here he huffed and nearly choked on his onion ring, "—pretty whacked out, but Wesley seemed worried in the moment, honestly, so I was bracing you..." he gestured toward me, then retracted, "Unfortunately... shoot, you get it. One of those 'Whoops, adios thirty years' detours. I didn't mean to."

"But it wasn't thirty years," I said.

"You're twenty-six."

"If you really read me then you've read everyone I've read."

"Oh yeah, and that."

"And that?"

He nodded.

"And that's it?" I asked. "I'm a few thousand years lost and it's nothing to you?"

"It's not nothing. But basically it's a cakewalk, yeah."

I didn't know what to say so we sat in munching quiet for a moment. The whoosh of a soda fountain, passing headlights like more fireworks through the windows. Jordan would have been removed from himself by a factor of one of my eternities. He kept eating.

"You read me when I was..." I couldn't think of the word. "When I was blacked out on a mind high. I was incapacitated."

"I mean, you were capacitated. Listen, I know nobody's ever done this to you before, so it probably feels like a violation. But before you get too worked up, let's just remember exactly who you are and how many people you've spun without their permission."

On the recording, my voice sounds like that of a person in shock. But if I was in shock I couldn't have known it then. I felt nauseous. "You were everybody I was."

"I lived every little minute of your life and all the minutes of every other life you've lived and do you know what that time meant to me? It was a little jarring, but really it was just some holiday Monday. I drove you home right after that, and yet you were so exhausted just from Wesley Allen? No, you have no idea. As far as I can tell, you know nothing but your own conceptions of this power and you're in for some earthquakes."

"Okay. Tell me everything you know."

Jordan laughed and finally stopped eating.

"Philosophy is odious and obscure, both law and physic are for petty wits, divinity the basest of the three. 'Tis magic, magic, that hath ravished me."

"Are you gonna quote at me all night or answer my question?"

"What question?"

"What do you know about this power?"

"You wanna know what I know?" he asked, and he wiped his hands with a napkin and presented one to me for a shake. "Take me for a spin."

I didn't move. "How long would that be?"

Jordan withdrew his hand, smiling. "Now you're getting it."

"Will you answer me honestly?"

"I'll do my best."

"Why did you read me?"

"I could tell you were a *reader*, if you insist, and wanted to know what you knew."

"Why didn't you just ask?"

"It was an accident. But. One thing I have learned is to be cautious of other people like me. Consider it a background check. Accidental, but not unforeseen."

"How many others are there? People like you and I."

"I don't know."

"How many do you know of?"

"Eleven now, including you and me. Only eleven for certain. There are others."

"Why can we all do it? What's the connection between us?"

"There's no connection, they're just people."

"You and I... we're both musicians."

"So? That has nothing to do with it. One's a salesman. One's in prison for wire fraud."

"Tell me about them. Can I meet them?"

"We're not a community, Ivy. What would you guess it's like? Things are complicated between people like us. Vacuums open up. No one knows everything, though some people pretend to. There's not much trust. There's a fair amount of bad blood. Some actual blood. I don't keep in touch with anyone. Two I met were nutso. Count yourself lucky. You're probably depressed, but you never thought you were crazy. And you weren't. But you could've gone."

"Please don't psychoanalyze me."

"I'm here to help."

"Okay. Fine." My voice rang with disdain. "What am I doing wrong?"

"You're not doing anything wrong. It's actually quite admirable. You know what you could've done with the information you've learned. You could be a millionaire, you could've gotten away with anything."

"You mean been a criminal. Steal from people."

"And you didn't. You just keep meeting new people. More and more people."

"What else would I do?"

He grinned and seemed to think about it.

"You don't even try to retain the languages other people know."

"They slip away. When I'm me again."

"Do they?" he challenged me. "You know Spanish. You live in Houston, it's around you."

"You don't think I do very much with my life."

"It's not like that. It's a matter of exposure. You've taken things at a nice pace. You're aged and disgruntled but, comparatively, I'd say you're a sophomore."

"What about you?"

"I got my PhD, baby."

"There's that much more to this?"

"Yeah," he scoffed. "There's more to it."

I thought for a minute on what to ask, then said. "Don't beat around the bush. Tell me."

"I'm being generous here, okay? I know how this is playing to you right now. I know your blind spots."

"But you're you again, and I'm me. You don't know what I'm thinking in this moment."

"True. That's why I want you to ask me. And, answering,

I'll measure the doses as appropriate. You do have sort of a romantic view of this thing. It may not be healthy."

"What do you mean?"

Jordan ate another onion ring. "Do you remember when you were, like, sixteen or something, and you wanted to get close to death? You wanted to read something right before it died, right as it was dying. Remember exactly how you were gonna do that?"

"Yes," I said. "If I grabbed a bee. In my fist. If I let it sting me, and held it there, maybe I could read it right before it died."

"But you didn't ever do that. Why not?"

"I just... lost interest. I didn't want to get that close to death."

"It was more like you didn't want to get stung, I think."

"Alright. So I was selfish. I was a kid, I thought I was a God or something."

"You were gonna kill a bee just to see how it made you feel."

"Is this your pitch for veganism?"

"Partly, sure."

"You say there's more to this. So, what? Can you read the dead?"

"Is that what you want to do? Read the dead? Where are you gonna find a corpse?"

"I don't know the limits we're dealing with."

"Jesus. You're an addict, right? You're addicted to this. Don't be shy."

"Okay."

"So imagine you're an alcoholic but all you've ever had was white wine, and that's your poison. I come along and tell you there's an entire goddamn distillery in your attic you've never noticed. There's a vineyard in your backyard and a brewery in the basement. Are you gonna be happy I told you?"

"Will it kill me? If I'm an addict and this is poison, will this thing kill me?"

"It's killed before. But let's mix metaphors. It's not poison. It's a tool."

"A tool."

"Yes."

"So how do you use it?"

"You know how to use it."

"You can use a hammer to build a house or take it apart. I mean you. How do you use it? Just go around mind-raping people at every party?"

"I spin on occasion just out of pure curiosity, much like you. But you find your animals. I like dogs, of course. But I really like the ancients. Iguanas, birds. If I'm gonna take a person for a spin? I might really go after someone who I think is a bad person."

"Why?"

Jordan thought for a deep beat before he said, "I promise you'll find out someday."

"But you read Wesley. You knew he had been spying on his dad."

"I do read students sometimes, if I'm worried about them. Wes is a rich and lonely kid. You never know these days. Something was off. If it wasn't abuse or something... he could've been a school shooter."

"You really think so?" I doubted that.

"It was just grief," he said. "So anyway I put it to use. Scared him from his sin."

"Is it a God thing for you? The readings. Your life is in church."

"I get to play and teach music for a living, I get to go on missions for the church almost every year. The pay is good. And I believe. But the difference, Ivy, between you and me, is that I know when and how to let this thing rule my life."

"Because you understand it better now."

"What were you gonna do for Wes? After you read him."

I didn't have an answer. "Alright," I said, "clearly you have some judgments about me. If there's only one way to give it to me straight, do it. You can give me a PhD right here, right now. Let's do it. Let me take you for a spin." I showed him my palm on the table. "If it's not gonna kill me. Show me how it's done."

Jordan's natural smirk faded. "You're trying to lose your wits in a Whataburger?"

I flexed my hand further open. "I want to do it."

"You would regret it," he said.

"Do you regret that much of what you've done?"

"It's not what I've done, it's what's possible. It's a lot."

"Are you the better for it?"

"Not all of it, no. There are better ways to learn. You don't have to be tricked into an eternity, like I was. Besides, Ivy, the deepest purpose of life is to be your own person, no?"

"You know me," I offered. "Addiction, blindspots, all of me. You don't think I could handle your life?"

His smile returned, he reached over, placed his hand on mine, and pushed me away.

"So you get to decline. I didn't get the chance to."

"I'm sorry about that."

"You won't tell me, you won't show me."

"Do yourself a favor. Don't read Corbin Allen, either."

"Why not? What will I find?"

"I've never been him. But I've got a bad feeling about him."

"What's that?"

"I know him. I've worked with him. I sense nothing fun in his life. It's that. He seems like he's a mess on the inside."

"You thought he was abusing Wes, but he's not."

"Somethin's been going on with him lately. I told you all about it. It's more sinister than mental illness. Or radicalism. It's some… new form, some new regression of his. When someone's a real haunted mess on the inside, it doesn't end well for people like us if we're too curious."

"You really like to warn people about how things end."

"I've seen a lot of things end."

"So you're immortal."

"No." Something came over him then. Pity, or a memory. "But doesn't it feel like it sometimes?"

"So what, then. Some spins aren't worth taking?"

"He's haunted. He's a haunted person. You don't really know what they can do to you."

"I don't see how that's an issue. No one ever knows we're in their head."

"Mmm," Jordan murmured. "You found a clue." Then he began gathering trash on his tray and shifted to the edge of the booth as if to leave.

"Being coy or mysterious isn't charming, you know," I said. "You know me, so you must know I won't just let you leave like this without saying more."

"I bet you're pretty mad it's me," he said.

It was true. I realized then how angry I was, how angry I'd been the entire conversation and how fast my heart was still beating. Him pointing out my anger only enraged me further. Of all the people with whom I could have shared this, it was this skeevy Christian choir director. There he was teasing some grand scheme of things, proud of his calculated restraint, proud to withhold. Hey, someone says, I read your diary. I read every diary you've kept since you were a little girl.

"Why shouldn't I be mad? This place is twenty-four hours, we've got all night. I need answers. You think I'll be able to sleep after this?"

"There's stuff you should figure out on your own. There's stuff you'll want to figure out on your own. There's stuff you don't need to hear yet."

"You love this." I sneered. "You love lording information over people, that's it."

"I like that we could be friends, okay?" he said, snapping at my sneer. "I like that there's actually a chance we could both benefit from knowing someone like us. It's a first, alright. But that's not gonna happen, you're not gonna be satisfied and I'm not gonna learn from you, either, if I let you take me for a spin or if I just babble at you for ten hours. You thought you were alone. I owed you this much."

"Just tell me what I am."

He sighed. He scooted back to the center of his side and faced me, the wrapper of his burger expanding, mewling on his tray where he had crumpled and left it. There was that pity again as he looked me over.

"What are you?" he clarified.

"Who I am. How I fit in here. You know everything I want to ask."

"You're a collector, Ivy. That's you specifically. You collect them. You traveled around the country, tallying up perspective, seeking experience, dabbling in class and race. Always yourself again and always pissed about it." He lowered his voice, though since there was no one near to listen he must have done so for effect. "So many people. Haven't you known enough? But you keep collecting. Then you stop cold turkey. You have an unhealthy relationship with your abilities. All or nothing. Distraction, depression, distraction, depression."

"That's me specifically." My voice on the recording raw now. Fury in a fog with no idea where to aim. "What am I, generally speaking? What is a reader?"

"A reader. Someone with the keys. An archivist, a collector, a psychic, an anthropologist. A psychologist. Thieves. This is what we are. Not literally, not necessarily. But deep down. We're voyeurs."

"Is that the full definition?"

"No."

I gave him a sour look. "What then is a healthy relationship with it?"

"That's a matter of debate."

"What do you think?"

"I like iguanas. I only spin people if I know it won't fuck with me too much, or for security purposes."

"You learned about this. The power. You learned somehow and now you say I shouldn't learn the same way. So what do I do? How can I educate myself if I don't know where to start?"

"Hand to God," he said with his hand over his heart, "my advice is that you start writing it all down. From the beginning. As much as you can remember. And see what you've missed."

9

Indigestion

He would tell me nothing more that night, so we parted, and as he backed his truck up he rolled down his window and said, "Sleep on it, we'll talk again soon." He drove away and left me there in the hazy summer dark. I leaned against my trunk for a long while, watching the line for the drive-thru populate, change. After some time I found my phone, still recording, and stopped it. I listened to the entire conversation again and then just kept leaning against the trunk. A voyeur. My mind simultaneously high-speed and suspended in stillness, I could think of nothing to do. Finally figuring I should do something, anything, I crossed the parking lot to a 7-Eleven and bought a pack of Camels, returned to my car, sat on the trunk, listened to the conversation again, and chain-smoked until I felt sick. The Whataburger crowd was getting drunker, so I drove home in a daze and sat on my futon. Sleep would not take me, nor did I want it to. I passed the night watching the spare moonlight rappel down my bathroom door. At 6:00 A.M. I consulted my calendar for the day. No lessons to teach until the afternoon, and nothing else to do. Thrice I checked the mirror to insure, nay, enforce myself, and I went for a walk. The sun rose as I left across the field behind the supply warehouse, over four hundred mostly flat feet of dried grass, between shrubs, tufts of little bluestem, through a shallow ditch, up to cross Grady Street where it met with the narrow cemetery by the highway. I continued under the concrete, avoiding eye contact with pedestrians and drivers. Following any zig-zag jaunt of green, I came into another undeveloped field and walked toward its surviving pack of bald cypresses, then onward along the fence of a city water pumping station, about the waking neighborhoods, recalling by sight and smell the history warred between the land and its people.

Was I really to have figured it all out on my own? Of course not. Jordan said he was tricked into an eternity and I believed him. I conceded that would not be the best way to learn. But if there was more to learn, did I need to know? Could I handle much else? To walk in someone else's shoes at the speeds of light and sound and touch, that alone had rocked me. Should I be a colony of bees? How I'd imagined. To be spaces throughout a family, or the dual secrets of a marriage. How I'd imagined life beyond animalia. An existence just of germination, breath, and water. To be rooted life. To know no phenomenons or metaphors. If I could, would I read a row of switchgrass? Should I become the thoughtless stillness of a tree? I had thought I should if it were possible. I always wanted what was possible. And, to loiter in metaphor, I had sought the poetry of life and found prose, but wasn't I reading things wrong?

On the phone, she could tell I was upset and summoned me for dinner at her house. I drove the forty minutes north to Lethland and listened to a news report and roundtable discussion about events in Minnesota the night before. Driving with his girlfriend and her daughter in the car a man named Philando Castile was pulled over by police, shot within moments, and dead within the hour. From the passenger seat, his girlfriend livestreamed the immediate aftermath of the act, the slaughter. By the time I pulled into my mom's driveway the broadcast was investigating the release of Pokémon Go.

I knocked on the door and heard my mom call from inside, "It's open!" Shutting the door behind me, I saw her standing at the TV, barefoot in a long checkered dress, watching PBS NewsHour. I slipped my shoes off, shuffled over, and hugged her with all my weight.

"Oh, honey," she said, and she patted my head. She turned off the TV. I fell backward onto the couch and let out a great sigh. "Long week?" she asked.

"They really do get shorter, right?"

"Well, years get shorter. Come help."

It's true I didn't visit her as often as I should have. But in all fairness, she had been independent of me once I became an adult, and in a self-assured, infectious way. Throughout my life, there was only the one thing I ever kept from her— my keys, as Jordan would say. She never knew what I could do, though she was always aware that some distinct part of life consumed my habits. Still, it wouldn't have changed her mothering one iota if she had known. She would've said what Jordan said, it's more important to be your own person. And she should know. That's who she always truly was, Renée. She was consistent, no-nonsense support after my father died. She let me wallow in her home for a few years to play piano instead of going to college. And she always trusted me, warned me away from cynicism, her heart all the while golden with care.

Head in the fridge, she asked, "Why the pall?"

"The what?"

"You're morose. What's wrong? This is your crisis visit, I

know it." She placed a bag of spinach on the kitchen island and with an armful of vegetables kicked the fridge shut. It was very subtle, but in those days I thought I could see her body getting stiffer, older. When I think of my mom now I think of the light in her eyes, her glasses, her voice. She always had that glow like a natural star on a movie screen, but with age expression centralizes in the face, and in those days her cinematic presence suffered a slowing frame rate.

"No crisis" I said, fetching the cutting board and knives. "Why do you think that?"

"You're always in crisis when you visit," she said. That comment deflated me. "I don't mean it in a bad way, honey. I'm glad that you can count on me. Grab some bowls."

"I don't only visit when I need something, do I?"

"Well, you wouldn't have to if you dropped in more often," she said, but she winked, just teasing, and it made me feel better. "But listen, I will need something from you. I'll trick you into coming back more often. I'm gonna get a dog."

"Shut up."

"Yes…" she began, and there was the slightest hesitation in her voice, "I saw so many dogs in Berlin I just couldn't resist the idea."

"Oh my God," I said, "I forgot to ask." A wave of guilt crashed over me. Early in every summer, between her years of teaching, my mom went on a trip she had saved for. That year was international, a treat, and though I had seen her before she left and called her when she returned, I had called when she was jet lagged en route to bed, so we hardly spoke. I had let nearly three weeks slip by without really talking to her. "I've been so distracted…" I said, but what kind of a distraction was it? "Oh Mom…" I moaned, and I walked around the kitchen island and hugged her and started bawling.

After a minute of this she told me to snap out of it, no big deal. She had really been enjoying her summer. She made me wipe my eyes. I made a spinach salad with red onions and peppers and artichokes and feta and she tended then let sit a chicken from the oven. We set the table and poured wine while she told me all about her nine days in Berlin. Hours she spent in the Tiergarten reading, people-watching. She told me about her favorite cafe and bookshop, and about the drizzly solemn silence she spent in the memorial to the murdered Jews of Europe, stones falling and rising deathproof. She had spent upwards of three hours at Charlottenburg Palace in love with symmetry and swans. She talked about meeting a retiree from Florida, a pirate Jimmy Buffett type with whom she shared a late night doner kebab. On her last night she almost splurged on a restaurant where you eat in the dark, but then went to the movies instead and watched *Captain America: Civil War* auf Deutsch and got confused for a second when there was an intermission halfway into the flick. While she spoke I watched her reflection in the night-blinded window and felt a surge of love like a rip tide.

After dinner, we curled up on the couch and watched some TV, first *Property Brothers* then *Seinfeld*. It was the episode with the close-talker, and Elaine was prodding him about his day at the museum with Jerry's parents when my mom turned to me and said, "Alright, then. Spill it. What's wrong?"

"Just this student," I said, and after a very long beat, continued. "He lost his mom."

"Oh, awful. How?"

"The thing is he lost her before I knew him. But I just... see it on him. I see his hurt, there, and it's sort of contagious. He dropped lessons. But now I'm worried. I feel like I didn't do enough for him."

"How long were you instructing him?"

"Just a few months, this year."

"If he quit, though…" she said.

"I know. He's just talented and young and sad…" I trailed off.

Mom put her hand on my ankle and squeezed. "Remind you of someone?" I shook my head. She got up to change the AC and draw the curtains.

"Mom, do you think I'm cold?"

"Cold how?"

"Like unemotional," I said as she sat again beside me. She put her feet up on the coffee table and the bottom of her dress draped limply over the leather of the couch like a tired dog's tongue. "Sometimes I feel like I'm cold to people. Desensitized or something."

"Are you spending too much time on the internet?"

"I'm being serious, Mom."

"Hey, me too. You're not cold. You've always been an introvert."

"I've always been aloof."

"Aloof, sure, but you're warm with me. You were always warm with friends. Animals. No one who loved animals as much as you could be cold. You were obsessive in interest."

"Been thinking a lot about that," I said. "Growing up. I was so lucky you were there for me. This boy, he lost his mom, and now all he has is, yeah, the internet. I feel so bad for kids these days. For him, losing all that warmth of a good mom." I was picking at my fingernails. "Sometimes I think if Dad had been the one to raise me, I would be a sociopath or something."

"Don't say that. Your father was not a sociopath. He was an addict."

"That wouldn't have worked out so great, either."

"No. And it didn't. But so when are you not feeling cold? You're not cold to everyone."

I thought about it for a moment. "I think I have to be really, really invested in someone to open up with them. Y'know I let other people open up to me just like that, because everyone wants to be allowed to be themselves. But for it to go the other way? Me to open up?"

"You have to trust them," she said.

"I'm not sure that's it. I wish that was it. I was a sad kid. Now I'm an addict. I'm addicted to other people's sadness, like I have to be really fascinated by their troubles in order to not tune them out."

She digested that for a minute, patting my knee, then said, "You're an artist, too. Maybe you can't control why or how you like someone, but there's no need to be a sadist. Is there someone you're not telling me about?"

"Sure," I said. "There's seven billion people, but no matter who I meet, I'm still me. And if I know that, other fish in the sea, other students, all that, then how come I can't just flip it off? The interest, I mean. Like a light switch. If I know there's somebody who I want to know just because I want to know their troubles and their secrets, that's not me really respecting them, is it? It's me using them."

"Using them for what?" she asked.

"I don't know. To fix myself?"

She laughed, really loud. "What, by comparison? Don't be ridiculous. No one can fix someone but themself. Or medication. Have you tried talking to a therapist?"

"No."

"Let me guess, you wouldn't open up to a therapist unless they were more fucked up than you? Is that what you're thinking?"

"You do know me," I said, smiling. She laughed again.

"You've come to me like I was a therapist before."

"You're my mom, seeing you is therapy."

"Well, as your doctor, I'd recommend following the feeling."

"Which feeling?"

"Any feeling. If you're desensitized, or cold, as you put it, or uninterested in people, and you feel something from someone, sure, follow it."

"But that's what I'm asking. Short of them being a danger to me and me being a sadist, aren't I kinda using them by doing that?"

"Without the sadism, what you're describing is friendship. Dear. You're not a sociopath. Maybe you're depressed."

"My happiness isn't someone else's responsibility, though."

"Who said anything about that? Friendship should be mutual. You're numb, someone comes along who makes you feel not as numb, great, embrace em. Your main responsibility is to pay them back. If they can make you feel a certain way, or teach you something, or do something meaningful for you, good. You won't be using them if you pay them back. Help them in return. I feel like I'm talking in platitudes, but so are you."

By this time, Jerry was bluffing his way through the plot of *Schindler's List*. Mom kept her hand on my knee and watched the TV while I thought about Wesley. Another line of Corbin's letter floated back into my head— There's a beating heart in there. Not that I can feel it. A commercial break came and the local news plugged upcoming coverage of the election.

"Maybe it's a small comfort," Mom said, "but it's not just you. The world is actually going crazy these days. I thought we all knew each other but maybe that's the problem."

On Mom's couch that night I had a nightmare. I was some combination of myself and Wesley, sitting in Grandpa Allen's nursing room, listening to the slow, medically induced breathing. I wouldn't look at the figure on the bed, and could only hear that weakly drawn breath, in and out. I became aware of someone next to me and turned and there was

Grandpa, John Allen, wide awake, red in the face and puffy with health like he was before the coma. With his sandpapery voice, he said, "I'm sorry, kid." I turned back at the bed and realized it wasn't Grandpa Allen in the coma, it was Dad. I got up and approached the bed, but moved as if in a long hallway, stepping up real slow, my nerves blazing, and behind me John kept saying, "I'm sorry kid, I'm sorry kid," until I got to the bed. I watched Dad's face and listened to that breathing, that rasp somewhere between life and death, and horror overtook me. "It's not your fault," John said. "Some men have demons in them." Then I looked down and saw Dad's wrists were bandaged, and in a most pressing panic I started unwrapping them, unwrapping, but there was so much gauze getting stickier and stickier and I started crying because my hands were now stained with blood. And I woke up in a sweat, and my heart kept racing for so many long minutes that I had to force a calm upon me by listening very closely to the quiet noises of the suburban night—katydids and cars, the hum of sleeping appliances, a raccoon, an airplane overhead.

For the next couple weeks I tried not to think about Corbin or Wesley. I meditated every morning, went jogging, and began reading at night instead of surfing the web or watching Netflix. I got through *The Brothers Karamazov* and started *Middlemarch*, neither of which had I read with my own eyes. Between lessons I focused on improving the goals and song selections for my students, and would tinker on my piano with a renewed purpose for hours at a time. Twice in these weeks did Jordan call me, and neither call did I answer. I figured if he really believed me equal to himself in ability, if not experience, he might exhaust of pretension before I did. Maybe if I sweated him out, he would tell me more. Essentially he promised to tell me what I needed to know if I asked for it at the right time. But I wasn't ready anyway. As much as I thought I was enlightened before Jordan came into my life, I hadn't really examined my past, my pasts, as much as my self-assuredness suggested. So one muggy afternoon, I sat down with a notebook and a pen and tried to name every person I had ever read. Nearing two hundred names, a great shame seized me, and I could list no more. Two hundred names and barely a selfless act to show for them. I had been collecting lives like they were fucking stamps. What did I do for them, the ones I loved? The ones I admired? The ones like Corbin, in whom I feared uniquely troubled minds? I could have been a detective. I could have been a private investigator, or a therapist, or a journalist. I could have used my power for some objective good. But I had never wanted to admit there was such a thing as objectivity. Everybody is the center of their own universe. They truly are. And everyone a filter, forever refining their bias of the world beyond their skull. My mother was right. I didn't know anyone, because simple empathy was never enough. Empathy is not action. It is a condition, a subjective condition, necessary in order for action to have objective good.

The nightmares lingered that summer. Jordan a frequent guest in them. He guided me through a theater. It wasn't the Riverbed auditorium, but a dustbombed vaudeville venue beset with litter and architectural flourishes which morphed when I looked at them. Jordan kept telling me to keep my eyes on the road but we weren't on a road we were walking through a theater, a place I knew was hell, starting out from the bowels of a green room Jordan called devoid of blame and praise. The lightbulbs bordering the mirrors aflicker. Scrawled on the wall, in Sharpie or eyeliner, Don't Abandon Anything. Sounds everywhere, horrible sounds of anguish and a confusion of tongues somewhere in the theater, whose dreaded sources these dreams never quite disclosed. Jordan led me from the green room through passageways of stone, up and up, out in widening circles, up and up, by a scene shop full of guillotines and guns, through repositories of costumes, rack upon trip-hazard rack of disguise, me parting and suffocating on the centuries, him always ten paces ahead and chattering in verse like some self-appointed Virgil. He kept saying, "I know readers who were gluttons, it's fine. I know hoarders and the treacherous. All of us diviners, all of us diviners." The house seats you could punch a hundred times and dust would still come out. Every theater is haunted, I think. "Hell is the conscience, worse than the worm," says Jordan. The sound booth the site of a crime, the spotlight with a mind of its own. And I kept trying to think of something to ask Jordan but couldn't until one night I dreamt that on the ladder to the catwalk I asked him "Why are we going up?" and he said that in hell everything is upside down so in reality we're going deeper. I asked him what hell would be like for someone like me and he said there's an answer written down somewhere and then he checked his pockets.

Let me put this into words, please. The tricky thing about trying to dethrone a vice is that in doing so you must confront a sin, and when one of your sins is threatened all others rise like generals in a coup. I was a glutton before I returned to Houston and began my fast. Which sins had reigned supreme since then? Wrath and envy, no doubt. Hierarchical sin, this is what sobriety reveals.

I had relapsed by becoming Wes. Maybe I was just some benign collector after all, a harmless version of what I could've been, but there was merit to Jordan's question— Haven't I known enough people? I'd been an addict before, I'd known true physical dependency and the shock of its interruption, manic wanderings, reeling analysis, the give-in. And the shame after a relapse. This was it. Was it not a sign to stop?

Jordan told me to write everything down but I didn't yet. Played piano instead. I resolved to avoid Corbin Allen for good. I took my copy of his book to a Starbucks and placed it innocently on a table for someone else to have, but I placed it front-cover-up as is not my custom and the cover arched open and revealed a folded note. I recognized it instantly as my list of names. A list of my names. I took the people, left the book.

In my idling car, under penalty of summer heat and the broadcast of the Democratic National Convention, I wallowed in those two hundred souls. Was that a good enough sample size yet? Where do numbers and people meet? One death one tragedy, a thousand an event; one life a miracle, billions too many. I bore my gaze into the blue strokes of ink which made a letter, a word, a person. I read that one name over and over until it summoned a meaning. A meaning not for me but as me. I had been her. She had been everything. You don't notice it until you open your eyes and you're not there anymore. The dream, the euphoria, or the delusion. It's there and you're in it and you're it until you come back to reality, as it were, which means as you were. As you know by now this is the issue of my being. Jordan's too and everyone's. It is an old question, born in caves. Thus the potency of opening. I didn't notice that I wasn't her until I opened my eyes, saw the ink, heard the crowd, and smelled the traffic. But for a moment—imagining—I wasn't anything, didn't have the capacity to notice. I was detached imagination itself. A borrowed memory. The unborn. There was a life in that moment, yes—there was a girl with a name thrust Californian into something called a first generation, a girl with a limp second tongue whose ideal days panned out on screens, who changed her hair every other year yet felt ever more anonymous, who broken by invisibility glimmered off the eye of a charlatan, a psychic, and found herself subsidizing fortune on a weekly basis, who in commerce leased a friendship with this liar and after about a thousand dollars heard the real truth, the truth that rattles between the lines of someone's story as they tell it, as the psychic told it to her, over coffee a secondhand tale about her own brother and his verbal outbreak in a CVS, his interpersonal demise, alienation, isolation, obsession with temptation, a girl who heard her psychic tell this in one long archaic monologue until she understood that no matter how widely someone can perceive a view is a view and inherently limited—but I opened my eyes and she was only ink on a page, at most a memory, and I was myself again, yet again.

They say in times of panic you should center yourself, meditate and focus, remind yourself of the good things. They say you should turn to your god or your ancestors or history. You should write down your thoughts and burn them. You should call a friend.

10

The Chapel

"I was hoping you'd call," he said.

"I want to ask you more."

"What's on your mind, Ivy?"

"At some point... you must have been as lonely as I've been?"

There was a long pause. "Was that a question?"

"Yes."

"Sure. Lonelier than most."

"It makes me want to have pity for you."

"You can if you want, but I don't need it. It's just a matter of coming to terms with yourself. Ain't it?"

"If you have so much context for yourself... and you do, you said as much, you have more context for yourself than I do. For this thing. So what do you think of the world? I mean people. You know what I think. What I've thought and what I wanna ask."

"You're anxious," he said, and I could hear he said it with a smile.

"Everything is lonely. Not just people. Horses are lonely. Spiders. Is life really just you versus the world? It's that way for everyone."

Another long pause. "Life is more than lives. Single lives."

"But you said yourself I've read enough people."

"Quantity versus quality," he said.

"You mean what? Define quality of life."

"Not the quality of someone's life, no, of course not. The quality of your engagement with them. Quantity is irrelevant if we're all one, and we are all one, and I know you believe that sometimes."

"Why do you believe in a god?"

"Well… there could have been something or there could have been nothing. And here we are. There is an initial condition here. A premise."

"A premise set by a god."

"I think so. And life is the reaction to that premise. Like a series of logical statements. Like math. No mind exists except in relation to what it encounters. No animal or person. Every idea of ours rests on some previous conception all the way back to our first interpretations of reality. At the individual level, and at the societal. Humanity figured everything out long ago. I mean happiness. Peace. Even your prayers were formed sometime before you. But it's piled up, all these misinterpretations or knee-jerk reactions to creation, all these ideas good and bad, illusions too. We know peace is in the surrender to underlying reality. There's peace in losing yourself in something. In no action, in automatic action. Or if conceived of desire, an act conducted in flow. Because you're a part of that greater… movement. But still closer to the earth. And nowadays, shit, there's so much to surrender, so much in the way, religion's the only thing that'll get me there. That or art. Sex. Death. God is that which persists unchanging through innovation and through the centuries. It is what slips through the middle every time. God persists in the hypermodern age because creation was the premise and our most exalting reactions to that premise have always by their very conception been designed for eternity. We're our most distinct selves when we are creating, so we know instinctively, individually, to trust creation. We identify any creation as personally relevant the moment we sense it. We are overstimulated, but the ultimate creation is anywhere we look. So we trust the reality even as we question its meaning and question our sense of the real, and we must use belief to reject belief. Where did belief start? In thought. Where did thought start? Somewhere on the tree of life. Life springs from the earth, the earth from the cosmos, the cosmos' creation the premise. God means the first conception, who came bearing sex and death. Puns intended, I guess."

"But why the Christian god? Why America's Evangelical god?"

"That's simple," he said. "I was born somewhere, as someone, inheriting temperament and tradition, and I became me. A surrender to the biographical flow, in a way."

"You have no free will?"

"I like the Christ story."

"What about free will?"

"What about it?"

"Does it exist?"

"Some readers would tell you no. How should I know? I'm here same as you, aren't I? But it's the right question to ask."

"Have you done everything with it? The power. Have you done all you can do?"

"No, but no one can do everything." he said.

"Does that leave you empty?"

He sighed. "You've been collecting, remember? Filling yourself up. There's a good kind of emptiness. To live overflowing is to live with yourself, to live in the middle is to live with God, but to live empty is to live in the creation, in the spirit. The point is to live empty, Ivy."

"Why?"

"There was emptiness before the premise came about."

"What will happen to me if I keep filling myself up?"

"You'll die."

"But I'll die if I'm empty, anyway."

"But you'll have lived in harmony with yourself and God. Because you lived in relation to those two ideas. Underneath them."

"How do you empty yourself?"

"I use this. The keys. Just not like you do. You use them to fill up."

"How should I use it? You won't tell me how to use it."

"I must liken the spiritual to the corporal. Iguanas and birds, my friend. Ants. The ancient, unspoken reactions. There are traditions that have been here longer than ours. And traditions infinitely more complex. They will show you how to use it."

I surprised myself by laughing. Didn't think I was in a laughing mood but there I went. "So why is it people," I asked, "that keep distracting me?"

"That's another simple answer," he said. "They've got shit to say."

And so this, dear reader, is where my strange fortune may inspire your forgiveness. You can call it convenient coincidence, I call it temptation. It was a most unlikely meeting. The devil meets you in the desert; Corbin Allen met me in the Rothko Chapel. That familiar tiredness had already crept over me. I had been sleeping deeper and longer, and what productivity and focus I had honed over the previous few weeks was losing to disorientation. Saturday afternoon I spent at Half-Price Books in Montrose, sleepily trying to scout out my inevitable subject until I fell asleep on the floor between shelves. The heat of my car's driver seat upon return induced such a broiling fatigue that I judged it better either to nap or load up on caffeine instead of driving home. I opted for refreshment, left my car on a neighborhood street, and walked south in search of a coffee shop. Passing Covenant House and a Kroger, I breathed consciously in defense against sleep, and focused on the movement of my muscles. I passed the Greek Orthodox cathedral in its gray glory, guarded by blasts of flush magnolias, and I turned west onto Alabama St. where in between a California-style bungalow and dog groomer's I found a busy little coffee spot with benches out front by a crowded bike rack. I ordered an iced Americano and drank half of it astride a bench, watching the waning day-moon rise. It occurred to me where I was and I tried to remember the last time I had visited the Menil collection or the Rothko Chapel. Wesley had seen the Flavin installation a few blocks away, and remembered its neon vacuum, but he didn't remember much of the main collection, and it had been years for me as well. Hoping to catch the peace before it closed, I walked toward the museum, but as I approached Menil park I became distracted by the grand oak trees lining the roads. I stood under one and finished my coffee, daydreaming. Germination, breath, and water— nothing else. If only the exhaustion I felt then could have been prelude to an earthen reading. I tried to imagine what time felt like to a tree. I was standing, but I wasn't rooted. I crossed the street, passed under the proscenium of two huge, nearly intertwined oaks, crossed the grass, threw my cup in a recycling bin, rounded the tan windowless fort of a chapel, and heaved open its obsidian door.

If you have never seen the Rothko Chapel, make a pilgrimage sometime. Dramatically, thematically, it is the overture of a suicide, and though some may say that's far too apparent, physically only the noise of your mind projecting onto the paintings could depress you. It is eight solemnly grayish stucco walls crooking neatly into the purgatorial glow of a baffled skylight, the souls of three walls shielded by triptychs, the other five by single views, benches and any open eyes always facing the chasmic canvases of black, bleeding thistle and plum, sunken purple, deepwater blue. Small, octagonal, quiet, its stone floor pimpled with black pillows. It looks like a civic installation or an armory from the outside, but inside it's hardly a building at all. Neither a mausoleum nor a shrine of paint. It's just you and the work in there. Racing thoughts, assumable reverence, the dark reflections of slathered hues off canvas and eye.

In the small, dim entry room, a librarian-like woman greeted me with a pamphlet, saying hello, then, "Just so you know, we close in twenty-five minutes."

"Thank you," I said, and I passed into one of two side halls where a lone bench displayed holy books of all stripes, books of moral concern, of philosophy. I opened the Tao Te Ching and read a passage at random. It is better to leave a vessel unfilled than to carry it when it is full. Go fucking figure. Is there no coincidence or only coincidence?

Leaving the book, I cursed irony, entered the chapel, and stopped short. There across the gray and purple, facing the furthest wall, in the lotus position sat Corbin Allen. I was almost certain of it, though I couldn't see his face. Surely I knew him from behind, I thought, and I quietly crossed the stone floor to the bench furthest from him, and I sat in line with his body and faced the same triptych. We were alone. I could hear only his slow breathing and the soft hum of the lights and AC. The God of Silence—so difficult to find whole, but still laced into every sound, yes, for sound arrives in waves and there is time between every two.

What was I still doing there? I had spent so many days trying not to think of this man, and now coincidence was rendering me curious. Or was my pre-read fog rendering me weak?

Wesley didn't know his father to frequent the Rothko Chapel, and it seemed odd that Corbin was here alone on the edge of a Saturday evening. Meditating, no less. Had it been me who pulled him there? Were we that gravitational wonder of two galaxies falling into orbit? When I ask myself this I also wonder to what degree I'm trying to justify my choice.

I waited, bargaining. What were the odds? What does chance have to do with it? What if I helped him out, afterwards? What if I helped someone for once?

Better to leave a vessel unfilled, I told myself, and I stared into the frozen royal void of the paintings before us. I slipped off my shoes, brought my legs onto the bench as it rocked gently, turned away from Corbin and assumed the same lotus position with my eyes locked on the midnight column of paint between the entrance and exit halls. If this was temptation, let it be his to acknowledge.

After a minute I closed my eyes and tried to meditate. I tried again to reach the total stillness which I imagined plant life knew. The premise. I breathed, counting ohm to thirty and back. I scanned for tension in my muscles and let it go, assessed my frame and settled it, repeated, repeated, and breathed. If you are tired enough, or relaxed enough, you can close your eyelids and slightly roll your eyeballs back, and this can trigger rapid flutters of your lids exactly like full sleep does, and you will feel your face go slack and the nerve endings in your brain cool off, and your combination of meditative focus and drifting-to-sleep just might keep you busy enough not to think of the preacher sitting behind you.

When the lady from the front desk came in a few minutes later and gave a small cough, I opened my eyes and blinked through the glare. "Hope you've had a nice time, ma'am," she said, shuffling across the chapel, "Unfortunately we've got to close up for the night." I watched her cross the room and realized that it was now just her and me in there. Corbin was gone.

The lady disappeared into an alcove and returned with a push broom.

"Is there ever music in this chapel?" I asked.

"Yes there is," she said. "We have a Summer Sounds series. Every other Thursday. Last week we had a mariachi band. But they played outside."

"I'll come by for one, thanks."

"Evenin." She began to sweep.

Out of the heavy front door, I saw the sky stealing into dusk, and looked to my right, where across the block a giggling little girl balanced on her mother's shoes and together the two took exaggerated steps toward the street.

"Howdy, Ivy," said a voice, and I turned to see Corbin standing by the flatter spread of grass. He was pocketing his phone and smiling, approaching. "Fancy seein you here," he said, and I said hello as we went for a hug. I'd almost forgotten how tall he was.

"I thought that was you in there," he said.

"I thought so, too. Didn't want to interrupt."

"Me neither. What a coincidence, really. If you needed proof I gave your form of prayer a whirl, there ya go."

"You don't come here often, though?" I said, turning my guess into a question.

"Not in a while, no. Felt right today. It's so funny, I was just thinkin of you."

"Is that right?"

"Thanks for comin to the cookout. I didn't notice you leave, wish I could've said goodbye. Sorry, I turn into a little pyromaniac around fireworks whenever I've got the chance. The excuse, rather. But thanks for comin, I hope you had a good time."

"Thanks, yeah. I didn't stay long, I wasn't feeling well. But it was lovely, you have a lovely home."

"Thank you. Care to chat for a sec? They won't kick us off those benches for a few minutes yet." He pointed to the other end of the plaza, beyond the reflecting pool and Newman's Broken Obelisk, where three walls of bamboo offered a bit of privacy.

I knew I should go. I was only getting myself closer to trouble.

"I wanted to apologize for Wesley," said Corbin. "He didn't tell me he was quittin, and I wish he hadn't dropped that on you at the party. He felt pretty bad about it."

"No need, it's alright." I said. "I wish he would continue, don't get me wrong. I'd encourage him to keep training. But he wants to get to it, and write songs. It's good. He's very creative. Very ambitious, you should be proud of that."

"I wish he would focus."

"How focused were you at thirteen?"

"Quite," he said, almost sternly. It was then I realized we had already walked the length of the reflecting pool and were sitting on a bench in a corner of the bamboo hedge. Time had cracked up and I still hadn't left. Couldn't I get out of this? Jordan reckoned Corbin a haunted mess. Didn't I have a choice?

A group of joggers passed on the sidewalk behind the hedge. The nocturnal insects around us gradually buzzed awake.

"Wesley is focusing," I said. "But there's a lot competing for his attention."

"I'm glad I was born when I was," he said.

"Why?"

"After Jesus, before the internet."

I nodded in agreement, but said, "The internet's not so bad. It's just a new medium."

Corbin shook his head while looking at the ground. "That's

too weak of a description. There are very few things that have affected what it means to be human, but the internet is one."

"What do you think is so different now? God is the same. People are the same."

He thought about it for a while. "People will never be the same. Like after the bomb or the camera or the printing press or fire. These were not just weapons or mediums or tools. They were not single moments of discovery. They were culminations. And what follows a culmination is revelation, then reformation. Usually. See, we're alive during a time of incessant advance, the past two hundred years, the past thirty years. We're cycling through these three states on a daily basis. The very essence of our literacy is being reshaped within us, by us, by our reaction to our power, at a rate beyond our control. It is... disorienting."

He stopped talking and his face became a blank. I watched for a twitch in his expression, a readable value judgement of his own words. Maybe there are myths a camera lens manifests on a face, maybe this is what's called fame. I watched the creases in Corbin Allen's face relax into neutrality, saw his eyes narrow and his gelled hair wilt in the summer wind, and I asked myself if he was just a beginningless continuum of his own self-reflection. Can you become a famous preacher and still humble yourself before God?

"You know what I don't understand about you?" I said, and I didn't wait for a response. There must have been venom in my voice but I don't know what Corbin heard. "You get to theorize for a living, but no one can tell how sincere you are."

His huge head snapped in a double-take. "Excuse me?"

I could feel my brow drooping, my posture caving with the need for sleep. "If we sat here all night I bet we'd have a beautiful conversation. We'd talk about God and the internet and the meaning of life. But I wouldn't walk away understanding how you reconcile your career with your religion. You have one of the loudest microphones in America, man. What you say goes far. If you can speak so beautifully about God and the literacy of our souls, why can't you talk about climate change, or systemic racism, or war profiteers?"

"So we're getting political," he said, and a wicked, angry smile appeared.

"It's not politics, it's people. You're the richest man of God alive."

"Probably not," he said.

"And you've changed. You're changing. Wesley knows it. Jordan knows it. I can see it. What are you the culmination of, pastor?"

He didn't answer. For a tense moment it seemed as if he would, but he didn't.

"If Sunday was your last sermon, what would you say?"

"I'd say... tune your head to the word of God and you will hear Him speak."

"And what should we do with our hearts?" I asked this full-cheese.

"Don't let them stop," he answered.

Our eyes met and I wondered why I ever distrusted them. They were mine, they were mine, a palindrome of vision. Corbin inched closer and the wind died. He nodded the faintest initiation of a kiss, and for a fraction of a breath she calculated the distance to her car, and then their lips met and they brought their bodies closer together, enveloping arm after arm, and they kissed as though some conclusion about their life could be determined by their chemistry. And now who wouldn't say that perhaps that day even their very atoms touched?

Corbin

A return, unknown as yet, which must exist. A product: this within, and all of that. Extremities now boundless, still there are barriers to movement. Improvement is: Now You Are This. Remember that? So what is next? What is next was always here, they say. Reach and crawl and say what you saw, say how they say it, yes, that's what you've seen. Cubbing, cobbling, Corbin, you. Momma knows and Daddy shows. You just listen now. You be quiet here. For every season and its claims all face fate just the same. Things return, like night. Sometimes, you'll get applesauce. And things return, like night, like sleep, and turns brush time away like dreams.

Your yard has no fence—property is different from land, you see. Your body is your sole property (these parts private), and the only ways into you are through your tear ducts, in your ears or nose or mouth, or down here. Some years the yard's grass loses to the dirt. This your fifth is one of them. Momma's and Daddy's house here fenceless on the hot dirt has thirty years to it. The land is much older. Everything but God has an age, even the world.

Night contains true mystery. Momma and Daddy sleep just like everyone else, and God can make them sleep okay even if they're mad because God can do anything. God already did everything first. He made the world, and made night time happen. He put beauty in everything, Momma says, and Daddy says He's in everything, too. And what's inside you? What's there with God? Blood, veins, guts. Pipes like a toilet. You're like a walking river, and you want to see a river, and you scream this to Momma and Daddy, "I wanna see a river!" "Stop bein a brat." "But I wanna see a *river!*" "Stop screamin!"

Time out. Sitting in the corner, facing the wall. But what are you supposed to *do*?

"Pray to God."

So pray for cool water. Never-ending rushes of water.

There is the Arkansas River. And God made Tulsa by making people build it. Someone built your house—planked, white and graying, peeling. Your home leaks into the city around it, and vice versa. Communal want and waste. "Does God love everybody, Momma?" "He loves them more when they do right." And people do a lot of things but not much of it is right. The Densons, the Millers, the Humphreys, strangers, four hundred thousand in the county, roundabout, and everyone's somewhere doing something. Tulsa isn't even close to being the biggest city in the world. "Packed with sinners nonetheless." Packed with God's doing. Money. Zippers. Handshakes and hugs. Bank lines. Colored people. The market. The supermarket. The gas station, so many gas stations. The price of candy. How some shops are open at night, but the post office isn't. Mail as uncountable as sand. And the candy comes from somewhere, and somebody makes it, and God made them. And Daddy says things like *protesters* with so much air. "Tulsa is a bust as always," he keeps saying. "They're missin God in all this." He builds a fence with Mr. Miller. Army men, these. Pilots. Daddy didn't fight in a war, like Mr. Miller, but they are tough, these men. And they talk about the new war like it's a lesser, uglier sally than Mr. Miller's. "Think if Normandy had been in your livin room three nights later." So like that a war across the globe etches the reaches of things, God's trials, the size of the planet. People talk about places, and some energy of His escapes raylike from them and burrows through the earth, the named place never quite antipodal to the namer, but receiving some of the light—what's that word Daddy likes?— nonetheless.

Prayer and Church and Scripture and Learning Every Bit of It. Above all else, God, raining Bibles down. Matthew Mark Luke John Acts Romans Corinthians Galatians Ephesians Philippians Colossians Thessa... Thess-lonians Timothy Titus Philemon Hebrews James Peter John Jude and Revelation, Revelation, Revelation! Mom and Dad agree—the only thing anyone's witnessed enlighten a soul is the revelation of Christ, the perceptible self-surrender to His comfort.

As a necessity, y'all go to a small Pentecostal Church outside town. They're just the only decent ones around, says Dad, though he never likes it there. He says he wouldn't like the Baptists either anymore for their currency of ideas, the spiritual payout. "God isn't who people think He is. He's who you know Him to be, somethin you gotta know from deep within. And you either get it or you don't." So God is within, but also above. Above home, above the car, the road, that dust-encrusted intersection up the road, where there's only stop signs and huge telephone wires and the passing population. Above Steak N Shake, between burger buns, in lines of cars, on little leather-seated stools, roaring over the clank of milkshake spinners, Himself the fattening size of communal want. Above communal waste, of course. Above the woozying smell of the mechanic's shop, floating on the papery air in the library, bursting from whatever communal want is chanted by the protesters downtown. Yes, everywhere, deep inside, but inevitably moving upward. Up and over the wide, columned dictum of the convention center's facade. Brown's department store. Light poles and petticoats and long-missed snow. Frayed mittens. That one brown pair of shorts you have always owned. Mr. Miller's Impala. Whatever's exchanging all the time between Dad and Momma. Marquees, high-heels, newspaper stands. The weather and fortune and knowledge and every line of questioning. Above any list you could make, there He is, and He is the list itself. And still you cannot picture Him, and Momma says that's okay.

Enter questions of community. Daddy doesn't proudly ally himself with any group. He curses at the radio. "A TV will rot your eyes," he says. "Tulsa is a bust as always." "I grew up watchin my pops gettin kicked out of churches and I hated it," he says to Momma. "I ain't gonna do that to Corbin no more. There are freethinkin Christians in this world, like us, y'know. People with the capacity, the real capacity for rejection of the world and acceptance of Christ's work. There are folks who can be slain in the spirit, Ada. God help us we'll find em." He plugs you and Momma into his ways, like he should, but his ways keep changing. He turns. "There's a good group meets at a farmhouse past Sand Springs. Been there just now," he says. "That's our new house of God, a'right."

At the home church, Daddy raises hell, of course. He raises hell at every turn. Maybe that's why Momma is so happy he's quit his job working on planes and now goes to school. "Your Daddy's gonna be a preacher," she says, elated. "God keep him from the war."

"I ain't goin anywhere," he snaps at Momma over a dinner of baked potatoes and bacon. "Men treat war like a game and they know not to consider men like me a piece."

"The drums have been beatin for some time," says

Momma.

She says he probably raises hell at school as well. You pronounce it—"Oral Roberts." Momma mutters it. "That's what he's probably doing, raising hell at Oral Roberts." And in echo of her profane catharsis you let the word slip. Turn turn turn—no "damn" no "hell" no "bastard"—Dad takes his fury at one word to the point of a belting. "Hell is a reality, son, not a curse you can throw around. God hears every single curse, and you best be able to defend em."

Toast and peanut butter. Bits of hot omelette. Daddy's favorite night is steak and potatoes, or leftover stew. Momma's favorite nights are all leftovers. Applesauce or chocolate if you're on good behavior. But more than not you're thanking God for baked beans and bread. Dinner at Jimmy Denson's is more of a pot roast and noodles affair, but his house smells like cigarettes because his momma lets his daddy smoke indoors. "Well, good for Mr. Denson," Momma says, but she doesn't mean it. And you can't fault her for the judgement, their dinners taste like smoke.

The Farmhouse is not named so to be literal, really, though they've got a big garden. It's a reminder—seeds, cycles, harvest. This you learn at the dawn of 1970, after Dad has left school ("...*these people think money is a measure of somethin, no matter the evidence, no matter the scripture. Let em think and grow rich and die, I say...*") and in the early moments of parental reversal. Dad now spends the day with you, while Mom works. An entire readjustment of spatiotemporal expectation becomes necessary, as though the moon and sun had swapped responsibilities. Where the chaos of a day with Mom might collapse into a central point like some lesson of starlight, days with Dad begin from a plane and diffuse like a stagelight focused on nothing. Such is the haze over reality by the time you reach the Farmhouse. By then you have heard from Dad all his views on God and life, views expressed with a rambling authority you suspect is particular to your father. He goes on and on about life with God—what it means to be *born again*, exactly how gradual sanctification can be. He has talked so much and will talk so much more. Isn't this verbal glow enough? Or does church never end?

"Why do we pray?" Pastor Eden asks. You have been seated beside his pulpit, an old music stand. He speaks to you but looks at his congregation, fifteen or twenty, most of them much older than Mom and Dad, except the Rolands, with their young twins. Everyone faces forward, stone-faced, layered against the winter, each with a copy of Pastor Eden's Bible, each, even Mom and Dad in the front row, with the impassable glint of reverence in their eyes, fixed on the pastor. Why do you pray? The food, nightmares. To whom do you pray but a big, hulking, faceless man with a staff, kneeled in some river? And these twenty people, do they imagine the same man?

"What do you think, Corbin?" says Pastor Eden. "Why do we pray?"

"To talk to God," you say.

"Very good. But why do we gotta pray? He can't hear us if we talk normally?" Chuckles dot the room. You shake your head. "No?" he asks with exaggerated shock, now looking to you. "Why not? Of course God can hear us if we talk. But then why are we go'n round prayin?"

"To be nice about it."

Pastor Eden slams his hand on the music stand, upending it, dumping paper to the floor, and he continues on like nothing fell. "To be nice about it, yup. Now that's *respect* you're talkin about, isn't it?"

"Uh-huh."

"Yes, sir," Dad corrects.

"Yes, sir."

"Respect for the Lord," says the pastor. "Good answer, son. Folks, he's right. Barely six years old and he's got his perception straight. John and Ada, my compliments." Daddy chuckles, Momma nods. She gives you a little wave from down at her hip.

"You can be a prophet or a priest or a king, but you ain't catchin God's ear unless you speak with respect. That's right. The Good Lord was good enough to give y'all a gift. All y'all. That's why we're out here in a comfy home, not some loft downtown. We've been given gifts. Not just life, not just food and prayer and the good book. Not just death, no. We've each got us a lens and a purpose. John Allen here's got a gift of power, ain't that right, John?"

Daddy nods.

"Here's our case family for the day, seein as little Corbin's birthday got him waitin for his own gift." More chuckles, Daddy puts an arm around Momma. "I tell ya, as annoyin as John's mouth gets, we're blessed to have him and Ada with us. John's got a gift alright. What they call it in a formal setting, John, how you can distinguish spirits and all that?"

"Somethin like that."

"Bet you didn't know your Daddy had that kind of grace, did ya, kid?" Pastor Eden lays a heavy hand on your shoulder and kneels beside you. His eyes sunken, his face deep with lines and blush and stubble. You gotta wonder again who Pastor Eden imagines when he prays, you just gotta.

"No."

"Don't worry," he says. "God's got big things in store for you, I can sense it." The group goes Hmm, Yuh. Oh, yes. "But can ya answer it, Corbin? God's given you somethin and you don't know what it is yet. But what else did he give us, what did he give us all as a gift? It's the reason we gotta show that respect, that's a clue."

You don't even know what He looks like, what He talks like.

"I don't know."

"He gave you," Pastor Eden starts quietly, then starts again. "He gave *us all* the gift of fearin Him. The gift of lovin Him. Yes, by heaven, He lets us sit in awe, He lets us know Him. He lets us be scared and happy. He lets us feel. Ain't that the mark of majesty?"

At home that night, Momma spreads peanut butter on a chocolate muffin, sticks a candle in it, and lights you a chance. "Wish," she says.

Puddles and wet socks. Paper cuts, Band-Aids. Balance on a bicycle, brace against a sinking gut when you feel Dad's hand letting go, praise kinetic energy. For every action, reaction. For every sin—no, for most sins—a chance at forgiveness. Sewer drain tops, gas caps, dumpster handles, tin lids. Mud puddles, mud cakes. Now brush way back there, on the insides of your teeth, lower, way back there, get all around, and count to sixty.

Mondays at the Farmhouse are for foundations, Bible study. Tuesdays for prayer and wisdom, Wednesdays Jesus, Thursdays prayer, and Fridays... Gifts. Y'all'll one day get your gifts, if you're good, if you believe enough. Tongues, teaching, exhortation, prophetic gifts. For an hour every Friday, you sit with Pastor Eden on the floor of his darkened office, staring into the licks of a burning candle, listening, accessing. God reminds—you get naptime, too. Some days, some Fridays, you can hardly tell the difference between prayers and lessons and hymns and dreams and the hypnosis of Eden's office sessions. The pastor holds his dry hand to your forehead, incanting, "Deliver This Boy From Illusion, Lord, Let Him Know His Purpose, Speak It Through Him,

Lord," and sometimes you just dream this until awoken by adrenaline.

Daddy says the education you need is moral, Biblical. "Do you know what 'practical' means?" He shows you how to clean yourself properly, how to sweep, how to rake leaves, pull weeds, wipe windows, roll lint off clothes. He teaches you special prayers and tells you to count your blessings. He tells you he's glad you're on the verge of figuring it out.

So tongues it becomes, trips of suggestion. They say they hear you channeling Him while you're asleep, so by autumn you're scared to fall asleep. God and the Devil only know what you'll say. Hell is a real place, and fraud can get you there. But to everything, turn, turn, and so on. At the domineering behest of the pastor, or Dad, you can recite yourself into paralysis, and you can feel all language bubble and burst in your head, and come drip-spat out of you, and even God can wince then, though He gives you that moment, locked straight on the floor, gobbledygook incarnate, enchanted, spewing perfect nonsense.

Deep in a second winter spent praying at the Farmhouse, Dad says it's time to leave Tulsa. "It's a different time, Ada, don't you see how much bigger it's gonna get? For heaven's sake, we already went to the moon. People don't believe anymore."

"It's uprooting. We would pull up all the roots we have."

"The car is in good shape. And you won't have to work anymore."

And so Dad answers God's call, and y'all have good gifts from the Lord, gifts too important to hide in Tulsa. So you pack it up. Sell the house, finally. You stay in a hotel—the first hotel room you've ever seen in person, which will imprint its dimensions and decor on you so permanently that it alone, instead of any of the hundreds it precedes, will serve as the template for every hotel- or motel-based dream you ever dream—then Valentine's Day 1971 turns you onto the road.

Life in the backseat. A vanilla 1965 Buick SportWagon, with a sunroof divided by a crosslike intersection of plastic, with its panorama of windows, the roving home a vantage point infinitely less definable than a plot of land in Tulsa. Dad used to say the car was too bulky, but now he and Mom do their best to reserve even their smallest complaints. This machine is precious. And it's now their only world, too—skeins of geese in the firmament, cows huddled in the sparse shade of anonymous pastures, litter accumulating in every crevice, a pillow folded into the fold of a neck, the fragrances of a gas station.

Upon arrival, pamphlet and advertise.

Throughout, sing and pray and demonstrate and preach.

After, solicit.

Repeat.

Move on.

Where y'all go is for Dad to suggest and Pastor Eden to approve or not. Those at the Farmhouse have to print and mail the material, they demand assurance of the purpose of Dad's direction and a proper use of their funds. Your contribution, Corbin, will be to solicit donations. Half of the money goes to the Farmhouse, the other half to gas, food, lodging, whatever else. You arrive somewhere—first Dallas, before a million other places—and you scout the Baptist and Methodist congregations, but mostly at Dad's itching insistence you scout the evangelical enclaves often discovered through word of mouth. Holy rollers, Pentecostals, the outcasts. If there's a permit office or sheriff to deal with, Mom deals with them, and fair warning seems to be the cost of admission to any town's spiritual foci. The first apparent cost to you? Epidermal. Paper cuts from the Lord.

"Do we have to keep doin this tonight?" you whine to Mom.

"We have to," she says. "Gotta get this batch done before the mornin."

"Can't we wake up early and do it?"

"That's puttin off the work."

"It's not. We'll work better in the mornin. And faster."

"You know darn well you're just tryna weasel out right now."

So you fold, place, fold, staple. "We're doin the same thing over and over."

"That's what work is, Corbin. It's all steps, like walkin up stairs. One at a time, eventually you'll get there."

"Get where?" Fold, staple, fold, place, pickup, fold...

In a way, that whole first year is contained in its early nights. They repeat, return whole. You may not know this as each day becomes the next, but all of a sudden Dallas is a bust and you move on, and Dallas is done. The road, a new motel, the same tasks, the moments, the healings, the gathering of donations, the accounting, the moving on. There's Dallas and Tyler and Nacogdoches, Natchitoches and Natchez and Vicksburg. Lessons every week, be they school or church. Dad says the reason people are friendlier after the healings is because they didn't believe him before. Mom says you'll have a quiet day of rest next Monday, how about that? Next Monday, rather. And it's spring, it's summer, fold, staple, place. You unpack your suitcase and pack it back up. You ask a thousand faceless faithful if they'll acknowledge the spirit they felt and donate to your cause. Only the people Daddy heals give very much, though there is, you must admit, some viral effect to generosity that Dad's talk of God induces no matter where you go. Looking back, from winter again, now spring, you think maybe you're learning not merely from the stuff Mom and Dad teach you but also from information they withhold, and what they don't know. Could that be possible? Maybe you learn a little bit from the people of each town just by seeing them. Maybe you can learn from land just by passing over it. Vicksburg tells you about the Civil War, but Dad's awkwardness around colored folks tells you that even he carries that war with him, somehow. He can only speak to some strangers if they're talking about God. The war was over a hundred years ago, but time flies by whether you're driving or not, so who knows, maybe you can still be caught up in something that happened before you were born.

Jackson, Meridian, Hattiesburg. Gulfport and Biloxi. Look at this self-serve gas station. Listen to this guy on the radio sing, "*Sunshine, go away today*," and hope you hear it again. Nap and throw a tantrum or two, admit so in retrospect, nap again across the back seat. Southern summer rain is a gray wash. Tires wear out. A deadbolt on the door does nothing to prevent a noisy neighbor. The folks with the nicest clothes are the least likely to donate. *Do you feel much like dancing?* Dad doesn't want to listen to news about the war or the election. Mom doesn't want to sit through all the other bad rock just to hear "the sunshine song" or "Turn, Turn, Turn."

For two months in New Orleans, you find a true friend in Davey, the son of the motel-keepers. He knows good jokes and is good at soccer and Mom and Dad don't mind you two going off on your own after dark. But Davey ruins everything one night down near the sewers when he asks if you want to practice kissing. An instinct prevents you from telling Mom and Dad about it. Oh and why did he have to try and kiss you? Perhaps it was a test from God. If so, you passed, but God had to go and ruin a friendship in the process. In Lafayette, you miss Davey so much it hurts. You liked him. He had to go and ruin that. Him, not God. The badness and weirdness of people ruin things, not God. In Opelousas, you hate Davey. By Port Arthur, he's just a memory.

In January 1973, in Houston, Dad goes ballistic. You may only be a fresh nine years old, but you can see the horror and rage in both Mom and Dad for what it really is, conviction wounded by societal scorn. Dad says the government made it legal to kill babies. And Mom and Dad don't know why, they just don't know, they say.

Until now, Dad's temperament has remained constant—a base of proud confidence overlaid with molten piety. Now that is noticeably, randomly, tossed about with anger. He invokes deities you've never heard of and just cannot fathom why every Christian isn't mad about this. Dad keeps saying, "They don't even realize what this means," and he's saying it about his congregations, his passing friends. His methods, though, and thus your and Mom's routines alike continue unchanged, despite his bamboozlement. Once a date and location are set, once the flyers and pamphlet materials with the correct info arrive from Pastor Eden, the demonstration is advertised at every library, post office, school, community center, and courthouse in the area. In bigger cities and many towns, only so many places can be tagged, while every *elsewhere* boasts at least one or two social centers. Out in the countryside it seems like you're spreading God's word, His healing, thinner than you're spreading all the paper. Still, Mom maintains that every place is ordained and approached with reason, and that's important no matter how tired or bored you get. With any luck, buzz will generate. "It cannot be hostile buzz," says Dad. That's why y'all never advertise right outside the local churches, you don't want people to feel their ways are being threatened. You catch them wherever they congregate for post-service Sunday brunch, at the very least. It's all about attraction, see. Intrigue. Invite, don't berate.

They come for Dad's revival. For deliverance. It happens in

public parks and town squares. Shopping districts, near the rows of panhandlers and buskers. The parking lots outside college or minor or major league baseball fields. Across from a dance hall, beside a farmer's market, at the edge of a popular, restaurant-packed downtown district. The intersection of a town's only two busy streets. As a crowd slowly takes shape, you and Mom court the people already in the area to come join. Sometimes Dad will give two dollars to a busker to sing whatever Christian songs he or she might know. More often he sings hymns on his own, a velvet baritone leading skeptical locals into confident song. Mom reads aloud from the Bible and makes a game of it. "There is believers' freedom!" she'll shout. When the crowd becomes a congregation, and ideally the earliest arrivals have been waiting no longer than twenty minutes, Dad begins, and the tension builds through music and prayer and scripture, but everyone is waiting for the healing.

"Who among us believes in Christ?"

All hands go up, including Dad's and yours. You and Mom look on from the side of Dad's makeshift stage. She breathes a calm, even rhythm. Dad picks someone near the front and confirms with a cheeky smile. "You know your Lord and savior is Jesus Christ?"

"Yes I do," they'll say.

"Good. I knew when we came into town that there were true believers here. This is a wholesome place. An oasis in this riled nation, ain't it?" Mmhm. People agree. If it's a bigger city, Dad'll make some concessions. But without fail he makes his point: "You folks here are the good ones, thanks for comin out. And there's one of you here who I'm very anxious to meet."

He'll quote scripture, he'll ramble. He'll say, "I know you may be wonderin what I and my family—my lovely wife and son over there—have to offer you that your local ministers cannot. What are we doin here anyhow? Well, folks, I must say up front that I respect your leaders here. We've seen some inspiring services in town, haven't we, Ada?"

Mom will nod.

"Haven't we, Corbin?"

You'll smile and nod.

"And the flyers you saw, the litrature we handed you on the street, is barkin, ain't it? We promised you a demonstration of God's grace like you never seen before. This is indeed a ceremony of healing. How many of you have seen a healing before?"

A few hands, maybe only one.

"Did you believe what you saw?"

There's a lot of answers to this.

"This ain't gonna be like that, I can promise you." At this point Dad goes toward Mom and hands her his Bible. He runs his hands through his hair. Sips a Coke if he's got one. "What was once a beautiful, God-fearin nation has been beaten down. We all feel it." Mmhm. "By non-believers, bless their souls." Amen. "By a military that don't know what to do with itself." That's right. "By a president who can't even seem to trust himself." People will laugh. If there are black folks in the crowd—and Dad almost likes it when there are, tells you this is because black folks got their own traveling healers (*competition*)—he'll say quietly toward them, "Some of us felt this long ago. Some of us started feelin it, this loss of unity, when President Kennedy was slain. Some when the war became a slaughter. Some feel it every night when we turn on the television. What happened to our world's good conscience?" Hmm. "Our good world's sense of decency. Our justified pride. Where'd that go?" What happened? "What happened to our common soul? Our collective brain is confused. The world is corrupt and only believers escape confusion." Lord above. "A lot of people like to place blame.

I'm not here to do that. You know who and what is to blame for the breakin-apart you feel in your life. Whether you feel it without you or within you, the breakin-up, you know what struck the blows." Yes we do. "I'm not here to tell you it's the fault of the hippies or the television or the Soviets. I'm not here to tell you to blame Gore Vidal or the thugs downtown." And Dad seems genuine with this part of his exhortation, until gradually he doesn't, and his larger forgiveness narrows throughout '73. "No, folks. You can blame who and what you want, but it won't put the pieces back together." Amen. "I'm here to help you heal. More accurately, I am here to help *one* of you heal." Silence swells. "Now, I know the good book helps you heal. Your pastors and family should help you heal. But healing is not always... relief. I'm here to give you relief, folks. The Lord knows healing hurts. He sent me here to show one of you why." Mm. "Are you feelin unwell? Maybe you can't even name it. Are you dizzier by the day? You cannot reckon why. Are you feelin the weight of God's spirit right now, within this crowd? Raise your hand. Be healed in the presence of God. Raise high your hand."

Dad knows the hand when he sees it. There's always someone God tells him is the one. He hears God's voice. He invites them up to his stage. There is no discernible pattern to the people who turn out to need these connections. They are men and women, teen boys and girls, big, thin, black, white, healthy, sick, whoever. They approach curious and perplexed, shining with good Christian hope. They move toward him like ghosts, stand still where he says to, and they don't look at the crowd. They look right at him. "Are you hurtin?" he'll ask. They'll say, Yes or I Am or Today or Always or I Think So. "Do you want relief? Are you ready to receive the grace of God?" Then he simply gets in close, smiles, and grabs their hands. He clutches them hard, maybe clamps a hand on a shoulder. He holds them in silence for a long beat, falters for a moment, gets in closer, and whispers something in their ear. Sometimes he'll say what must be just one word, other times he'll whisper at length, and every time, his volunteer undergoes a radical sharpening of demeanor. They will well up, or burst into tears, faint, stand frozen in shock, start questions they can't finish. They'll hug him harder than he hugged them. The demonstration ends shortly after that. Dad confers with the volunteer while Mom tells the crowd to pick up pamphlets and promises if they sign up for a magazine from the Farmhouse in Oklahoma they will understand as clearly as the volunteer just has. Irritated onlookers will demand participation, a second proof, they didn't catch what happened. Dad may briefly take the stage again, invoke Matthew or Proverbs, calm the crowd. But he wraps it up quick. Most healing afternoons end with a pack of confused locals glaring and lamenting a waste of time. You make your rounds with the donation basket, gaining little. Nevertheless, Mom and Dad count every healing day a success—failures only reveal themselves days later. So the days pass, and word spreads, and the townsperson lucky enough to have been chosen praises Dad to everyone they know. Once, in Brenham, an elderly man with an eyepatch stops you outside a corner store and says your Dad changed his daughter's life. "She's thrown herself completely at the Good Lord. It's really somethin else. She's not that kind of believer, you know. She wasn't. But your daddy got through to her. I'd call him a con-man cept it's my girl." You sometimes ask Dad how he does it, and what it is exactly that he does, and all he says is, "It's God's grace, Corbin. I've got my gifts and you got yours."

Oh, divers and sundry locales, in the belly of the U.S.A. Oh, God of Tongues and Night and Day! "History is written every day, son, by everybody. And all throughout history, a few thousand years which ain't all that long, that whole time, the only thing that lasts is God." "Just worry about what God needs from you." Oh, the marketplace of ideas, of religion. "The real market is a system. Money is an evil, Corbin, remember that. Remember that even when no one is sayin it. Even when we don't say it."

The road and radio. Oh, study time. On this unlabeled map, can you find all the states you've visited? Can you name all the oceans? How many seas? What does 'embargo' mean?

This is the holy road you've traveled in all these years. Cramped, communal navigation of space, strained negotiations of time, a pyre of the soul paternally fanned, a mother of burlap heart, endless contemplation of the Lord and Savior, the long flat parts of the earth and the stupefaction steepness provides. Swings up to Kansas, over to Florida, wherever the road and Dad's yearly unwinding takes you, even if it means to a place you've been several times, or to a place so generic that it feels the same. Garden City, Ponca City, Jefferson City. All these hours at gas stations, in gas lines until even Mom's breaking point. Sleeping in the car more often, seeking free accommodation in houses of worship with more gusto and creeping desperation. Dallas and Tampa and Atlanta and unshakeable Houston. *That's right, it was in Houston.* Of all the days—and there are, at the end, over two thousand on the road—which could ever stand out more than that one day in Houston? It was during the longest stretch of time y'all went without a room, one of those hundred mornings after another night in the car or tent. Mom wanted to sleep so y'all left her with the car and Dad led you on foot through a nascent subdivision of ranchlike homes the sight of which summoned memories of your old bed in Tulsa so vivid that you damn near cried. Dad conducted you miles through half-farmed suburbia to the park by Hunting Bayou. He laid out on the grass with no blanket and breathed deeply and you thought for a second he looked rather happy but the thought passed with the second. He trained an expression of apprehension at the sky and told you to lay with him on the grass, which you gladly did after the long walk.

There rang a heavy silence between you two while you thought about the short concrete porches and bench swings of the neighborhood close by. You swept bugs off your legs and arms and fiddled restlessly. A resentment flared, you found yourself thinking bitterly about never having siblings or friends, never having a home, and you realized being with Dad was little different from being alone. In terms of your natural regard, his eyes-over-shoulders, voice-in-the-head, cloud-casting-shadow, etc., his presence and absence were both so all-consuming as to render them indistinguishable. Sure, he and Mom could say your strength was in speech, recitation, until the cows came home, but what you've always been really truly best at is being lonely. Certainly so in your brief moments of physical aloneness, but also on the first and last adventures in friendships mined from motels and laundromats and diners and campsites, and you marveled there on the grass at how profoundly lonely it could get even with Mom or Dad sitting inches away.

"I gotta tell you somethin," Dad began. "I have to warn you about somethin, Corbin."

You turned your head on its side, at Dad, and the moistness of the lawn slowly permeated your hair. You said nothing and braced consciously for a vague but imminent... what? *Scare?*

"Listen, I know you think I'm cold sometimes. To you. But that's only because there's a kind of coldness, and seriousness, that a father needs, sometimes. Sometimes not so much, and I'm not always good at the not so much. Life is very beautiful but it's also serious."

He paused as though waiting for you to say something. So

you said, "I don't like sleepin in the car anymore."

"We'll get a room soon, I promise."

"I miss our house."

"We'll get a house," he said after a long beat. "We're not done yet. But I know. We can't be on the road forever. Your mother would kill me eventually."

"Mom doesn't like the car?"

"Hah," he snorted. "She doesn't really like the car, no. But she likes the road. And she likes bein able to spread the word like we're doin, as a family."

You turned back up at the sky, but the sun was nearing its zenith and the sky was hard to look at, so you turned back to Dad.

"Now the serious thing I wanted to say... Cor, I've gotten pretty good at sensin what's... at understandin people. I think you've got somethin inside you. You've got a lot of good things inside you, you're a good boy, but there's another thing. You have a gift, and you can speak in tongues. I used to think they were one in the same, but I don't think your tongues is a gift."

"I wasn't always doin that," you said.

"What do you mean?"

"Like when I'm asleep, I don't notice it. When I'm awake, like with Pastor Eden, or in Kansas at the fair... I wasn't fakin, but..."

"It's almost like it wasn't you?"

"You said that's because it was God."

Dad's face flushed. "I don't think it was God. You could be a very holy person, son, a holy man. But this... thing..."

"Inside me?"

He took a deep breath. "It might be a demon."

A quiet ruled for a long time. You turned the word over in your head, turned it outside, in. Eventually, Dad whispered, "I'm sorry."

"That's not real," you said.

Gravely, he shook his head. "It is."

"How do you know?"

"I know. It might be. I know it's possible. I've seen it before."

"The devil?"

"Not the devil. A demon. A presence. You can get rid of a presence, Corbin."

"How?" you asked, realizing tears were assembling somewhere behind your face.

"You have to pray. You have to pray a lot. You have to be good. If it gets bad, I'll call someone. I promised your mother I'll call someone if it gets bad."

"Mom knows?"

"We suspect. I suspect it more strongly than she does."

"What if you're wrong?" Tears rolled over your nose, to the grass.

"I hope I am. But I had to tell you, so you know. So you can listen for him, and fight it. You're brave enough."

"I just... pray? But why did God let a demon out? Dad, what would he want with me?"

"God has a lot in store for you."

"No, I mean the... thing."

"They only want mayhem. They want you to never believe."

A fool's theory. How wrong the righteous can be!

And the strangest thing about this memory is that it is woefully incomplete. Between this news and the long walk home—the length of which, with hot tears and snot flowing, you marched a hundred feet in front of Dad—there is a blank. Perhaps Dad sermonized a little, or maybe he guiltily bought you a burger before heading back. You never know. You just remember how stiff your neck got, staring at him as he pronounced the word. Demon. You always remember that.

He used that term. *With such unwarranted confidence.* You just remember that stiff neck and the soggy ground, Dad's diagnosis, his ghostly pursuit as you led the way back to the car. Could you ever remember it all? It was only one day out of two thousand. But significant. You knew it as it happened. *You knew it when you met me. I was real.*

And pray. For Mom to sleep soundly through the night. For the strength to endure the time with her and Dad. Pray for alone time. For friends.

Bland as it is with each month promised to be the last, the final year does not spoil so much as it insistently garnishes the previous six years with the finishing, overpowered tastes of itinerant life. And what a medley of a life God serves you —you serve Him, you pray in turn with humility or grizzled hope, you are blessed to have been homeschooled without a home, perfunctorily mailing test packets back to Oklahoma four times a year, your mother and the Word of God perfectly fine-enough instruction for grand swaths of your mind and time, and you see over half of the states, you taste a beer, hear your parents have sex on numerous occasions, wear three pairs of shoes down to their filthy ends, get cursed with a demon, gifted a voice, stretched thin and flat by puberty as by a rolling pin, and introduced, perhaps prematurely, to such fertilizing ills as claustrophobia, nyctophobia, insomnia, acute loneliness, obtuse loneliness, oppressive domestic attention, domestic negligence, fear of reprisal, boredom, anxiety, and the self-consumption which attends the feeling that God and Satan speak in a language you could one day understand.

So a friend of Dad's (believe it or not) from Houston offers Mom a job at the Macy's he manages. Houston it is. Enough with the draining movement, the nights with no dinner, the financial fruitlessness of Dad's prophetic pursuits, Mom's compulsive cleanings of the car. Enough with sweltering summers and the sheets of hurricane rain and those bitter winter frosts which have keys to every motel room. Enough with Athens, Durham, Bakersfield, Phoenix. See it really has been enough for Mom and Dad, and for Pastor Eden's church, the gradually receding organizational backdrop to your family's decisions, which has expanded in patronage and come as a whole to see Dad's peripatetic service as a less useful investment than stationary hubs of communal worship, local events, local radio. "I spread their word," Dad says, "and now they've got ten thousand ears listenin, and they've got a feedback loop but don't care how it all got set up." But despite his pride by early 1978 even Dad wants to stay in one place. Mid-summer y'all wind up with an apartment nestled atop a Vietnamese market and overlooking a mud alleyway that feeds onto a busy street. A two-bedroom roach's nest, but a home nonetheless. Mom gets to work, Dad gets to stewing, and you spend the summer studying up for ninth grade and ferrying paperwork between your parents and the district office as the system tries to ascertain exactly how much you know. Alas, you know enough, and can articulate as much.

Now behold—Northwest Houston. Kölner High School. More peers than you've ever seen at once. Hundreds and hundreds of students. The children of everything from farmers to accountants to firemen. Black kids and Mexicans. Six-buildings, campus-style. Six periods and a schedule. Principals, counselors, a militia of administration. Detention, you hear. Syllabi on the first day. Reading Reports due the first week. Circles of laughter in the morning. Baptists, Methodists, Episcopalians, Jews, Catholics, even Mormons, even kids whose parents are too lax to guide them to any God. Though obviously a minority of outcasts, there are kids who dress like the punk rockers you've seen in magazines, institutional eyesores amongst the jeans and cardigans and modest dresses. There are Texan twangs and twangless dweebs. An auditorium bigger than any church you've ever seen and which still cannot fit the student body all at once. There are hands and eyes and hair of every style and somewhere there must also be you.

Quickly you resolve to put aside your previous self. The past seven years, and Tulsa before that, for that matter, do not exist. All that exists is this class, now this one. This teenagedom you've read about, seen on motel TVs when you could. If your life were divided into chapters, well, this would be a completely separate volume. Part II: Public Life. Set in Advanced Math and English classes, remedial sections of Science and Social Studies (thanks, Mom and Dad) replete with characters vaguely aligned in cliques, absolutely overflowing with girls. Girls!

Socially, you're missing some understanding, and you're convinced everyone knows it. You never got those notes, the instructions about how to talk to boys or girls, so you rarely do. You join chess club, creative writing club, after-school Bible study, and you measure freshman year by how many days you can delay going home. Now hold your books like weights and lunge all the way home. Reward yourself at night with Ecclesiastes, Proverbs, Matthew, Mark. Bridge within yourself the knowledge of the ancients and the progress of modern America, Texas, Houston, you. Life can have a structure, a network of challenges and options that prove what you needed all this time was a body and mind and routine physically removed from Mom and Dad. Bear no guilt about this, bear only sympathy enough for the Sunday shopping to spare Mom yet another responsibility. Wear your pity like a shield as Dad sits rotting with a beer and the radio.

By November, have a true friend in Kevin Wallsten, his

shrill voice and snorting laugh. By March, try out for the school baseball team and get rejected, but appreciate how the attempt admits you into more and more conversations. Boys now use your first name. Jacob Gent compliments your consistently good Comm. class speeches in front of some girls. You and Kevin and a handful of guys on the chess team have inside jokes. Sure, you're still an enigma to them and to most people—what do you mean you never watch TV?—and you trip into moments of awkward pretense—huskying your voice around a girl, pretending to have heard Talking Heads amongst unfoolable fans—but these performances come not from a discomfort with your actual self, rather an eager desire to improve that self into someone you feel you deserve to be.

Bookworm, library rat. You volunteer at the branch library a mile north of school, where the books are stiff and unstained, and Mrs. Barry the head librarian after an extensive probing of your repertoire happily gives you Hemingway and Steinbeck and Agatha Christie and Twain and the Shelleys and Ayn Rand. *And I am there in Dante and Marlowe and* Macbeth, *cheering throughout* The Master and Margarita, *whistling through* Moby Dick. *Maybe I'm the devil or his minion, maybe I'm death or just Father Time, but whoever I am I can merely glimpse you in these years. I can only peek out from behind your eye, while the faucet's running and the bulb over the mirror flickers and you stare into a thinning, stubbled face, the only one we'll ever get.* And so high school is four pistol shots to the head. Chess, track, track, girls, with lonesome summers and never a car.

Pray for the strength to shrug off a demon. Pray this on your knees, pray always on your knees.

Life's static increases in volume, expands, intermingles with the electric future of the world around you. And it is electric, this new age. You hear it in the music, which was strummed or shrieked until its current punchiness, though you'll stick with your Cash and Denver and Nelson, thank you very much. You'll turn the outlaw rambles or honky tonk slam all the way up in Kevin's car, way late at night, delirious with beliefs about what it means to laugh in unison, to kiss Mary Rogers on the bleachers, and you'll believe that together and apart all y'all are hurtling out of childhood and into some great communal delusion. You and Mary go on five dates before you ask her to senior prom, and she accepts. She doesn't care that you don't have a car or that you want to save sex for marriage, but she in turn demands your ears and heart and an upright chin when you're holding hands on a walk across school grounds. Y'all pray together and y'all fumble in the dark together and at prom she takes you to the art supply room and unbuttons your shirt to kiss your chest and now your stomach and now she takes you in her mouth, she shamelessly guides your tongue onto her, and even if y'all barely know what to do you accomplish something and afterward you tell her you love her, completely aware that it's the wrong thing to say. She doesn't say anything back but she smiles and you both know it won't last the summer and that's alright. You slow dance with her, an erection tucked up in the band of your underwear, and you dwell on very sharp memories of discovering how to masturbate in the half-privacy of motel bathrooms, and when you smell her hair it smells like lavender and for the first time it really feels like you have reached out in the dark and found someone, if awkwardly.

You know what they say—vocation, vocation, vocation.

Mom spends the turn of the decade assuming managerial control over the Macy's shoe department, weekly then nightly withdrawn from *home* as she focuses on the house, a sadness blooming within her trimmed only with unwavering attention to the moment at hand. In motel rooms, or at odd hours in the car, she would philosophize with Dad, she would read. Now she watches him chomp carrots with something akin to disgust. She seeks ignored and dusty baseboards while you and Dad make polite conversation or tense debate. She finds reasons to polish the tableware and go to the hardware store and rearrange the closets. And she smiles somewhat rarely, mostly glaze-eyed staring at the floor, out the window, at nothing in particular. Dad, meantime, spent the first two years in the apartment drinking and scribbling into notebooks everything he could remember about his healings on the road. Were he to reach over and gently clasp your shoulder and begin a question in a soft voice, you knew in an instant he meant to clarify a name, or which town this memory of his was from, or what did that woman in Odessa say after he healed her son and he ran away from home? Dad attends his impulses to ponder, to reflect and revise, but this attention only lasts so long before Mom's iciness ensures he returns to thinking of the practical Now. "Get a job," she snaps more than once. He gets a gig overseeing the facilities and operations of a modestly attended Baptist church, so he works for someone else, for a worship unlike his. He is a man whose sin is pride and it tickles you to see it wounded. Your jobs have ranged from library assistant to burger chef and back, but your vocation, your ideal career, you know, will be so much more. You will be a preacher, perhaps a theologian, and you will become an Allen, Man of God, as a response to but not extension of your father's own career. So it's your duty then at one of your final summer dinners, while Mom works late, to interrogate Dad about his choices like you're looking for examples of failure.

"Your mother believed in what we were doin. You believed it, too, I'll have you know."

"Like I could understand. You carted us around for seven years. For seven years, Dad, you cared more about strangers than your own son and wife."

"How dare you say it like that."

"What kind of Christianity is that? What kind of preaching is that? I took everybody's money, and we left town."

"God needs voices in the world. He needed them then and He'll always need them."

"Yep, sure, a nice voice praising Christ and railin about communists. Judging strangers. Promising them... what? What did you ever do for those people, Dad, except bilk them?"

He gets very quiet for a moment and then resumes chewing his steak. "You saw it yourself. They needed me. Don't pretend what we did didn't help."

"What did we ever do? What was it, what did you ever tell anyone, how did you ever heal them in a way their pastor or their fuckin therapist couldn't?"

"Don't you swear, boy."

"I'm a boy, huh. I thought I was a demon or somethin."

He stares at his plate, takes another bite.

"I thought I was a demon, Dad?"

"I never said you were a demon."

"You said I was haunted. You said I had an evil presence inside me. You told this to your own son. You took us away from the only home we had so you could play prophet. I just want to ask you one thing, okay?"

"I'll eat in the bedroom," he says, rising with his plate.

"Just one thing, hey. If you thought I had a demon in me all this time, why didn't you bring it up more often? You told me to pray it away. You never checked on it. How am I supposed to think you ever cared, or believed your own story, if you never checked on it?"

He starts through the kitchen doorway but stops and aims

quiet words at his food. "I know you kept prayin, and I know it's still there."

"Well, I'm not tempting hell and there ain't demons roamin around so pardon me if I'd rather live a life with the awe and love of God instead of the fear of Him, like you."

He looks right at you—*right at me.* "I can't control how you feel. Some things can. Just make sure you know what's in control." And he shuts himself in his room and finishes dinner and avoids your eyes for the rest of the summer. *But it didn't end there, did it?* Later you asked Mom with tears in your eyes. You wanted her to have tears in hers but she didn't. You asked her why she never said anything to reassure you. "You knew he told me that shit, didn't you?" And she just said, "I knew." "So what? You wanted me to believe it?" "Maybe it's true." "How could you think that?" "Your dad is always right." And then you left the room. *You* abandoned. He may have left you, but you left her. Alone.

You enter the University of Houston undeclared and after flirting with Religious Studies soon pursue a dual degree in Communications and Broadcast Journalism. You work part-time in a coffee shop and subsist on burritos and espresso and freely waste your spare hours sleeping or chatting with the prayerful of your dorm. Skim a few hours off each week to debate God with some anti-religious Comm. classmates who will humor the topic over cafeteria food, who initiate the discourse entirely because you so enjoy it. "See Corbin, you believe in free will," says Bill Greene between drags of his Camel, "you've said so yourself. God gave man choices. Temptation and sin and all that. I think it's all chemistry and biology. Physics some."

"You don't believe in free will?"

"Nature and nurture. We are predisposed to ourselves."

"But nature's there."

"And you suppose that's God. I can say there's no free will because our biology and our experiences add up to our logic, faulty logic at that plenty of the time. But how can you say there *is* free will? If God gave us everything and knows we have choices to make. Some will get saved and go to heaven and others won't? Then where's the choice? God's picking favorites, isn't he?"

"God gives you the choice. He gives you the world, life. And He gives you the choice of how to act in it."

"So my granddaddy beats my daddy and my daddy beats me and I beat my son. Is that me choosing or is that God giving me a shitty lineage?"

"God gives you the willpower, but he's not interested in tests, I don't think. Satan likes to test people. Talk about temptation and sin, even just bad judgement."

"Don't get me started on Satan. I don't like a binary worldview, man. There's too much going on. I *think* I'm making my decisions, but I've got the nature and the nurture to deal with. That's always what I'm dealing with."

"There is always that nature."

"There is always nature, that's true."

So was I noticeably there in these years? Snaking up your leg while you read about the prophets? While you reconciled the social gospel with American freedom. While you thought about how to make money off God. Did you hear me in the rattle of Bill's smoker's cough, or the blare of the megaphones of campus extremists? I know where I've been, but, dear God, did you catch me in those weeks your prayer slipped? Did you feel my jaw clenching at the loose and liberal sin around us? I awoke with every ambulance siren and social faux pas. You must have noticed me—I was You the Righteous, You the Belligerent Student, You the Devil's Advocate.

Surely you noticed me on the top floor of a school parking garage, peering vertiginously over the concrete, or gleaming in the serration of a knife—you thought about it a lot, no?

Skating over your studies, *The Screwtape Letters* and such. Barth, Merton, Niebuhr's parsing. Good ol' Augustine and Milton and Cervantes. Burritos and pasta and broccoli, Arby's and McDonald's, where you fight memories of Dad. The occasional stirring glass of wine, where memories win. You get it now, why you focused academically on communication. You are to become a greater preacher than Dad had ever hoped to be, on a grander scale than he could have imagined. He was too concerned with the ideas on the ground, too local. He failed to heed the realities, outer and inner, changing rapidly against the century. For a preacher to be effective he must first bring his own soul (*note: his story*) to light before the masses, thus to open hearts the land over and mix up in everybody's minds the function of the self and the power of the group. You can both lead a congregation and speak to every individual. You can make a decent living doing it. You will, one day. But first you gotta whet that soul.

From Lao Tzu thirty spokes sharing a wheel's hub, the center being useful. Shape clay into a vessel and tell yourself you don't use it for the space within. Utility is the presence, usefulness the absence. From the Word, the taunting questions. Have you journeyed to the springs of the sea or walked in the recesses of the deep? Have the gates of death been shown to you? Ah maybe benefit's the gates, usefulness your passing through them. From weekly service at a buffet of churches (*you little sampler*) not much peace. From circumstance itself, a life Now, and a life before you met Cynthia. Before Cynthia came Duncan, and the house you shared on Opal and Washington. There you prayed on your knees for God's strength to chase stability in His name. You and Duncan split the rent and utilities and entertainment and hurricane supplies evenly, even though you hardly used the cable. You knew him to watch too much television and harbor small resentments until they coalesced. He probably knew you to go on far too asocial, to eat at once too cheaply and sweetly. You were compensating. Days turned and with rare exception you kept to yourself. You and Duncan were housemates for two years but you never really lived together. You operated in and out of the same home base. Your experiences and ambitions only crossed paths.

After graduation, you gave Dad a check, a return you'd been collecting for some time, and though you'd pretty much paid for college yourself it still helped to give a sense of the settling of debts. For a year you balanced continued service at The Coffee Spot with a gig organizing the tape archives at Houston's second-most-watched news station. You studied the anchors, shadowed producers, interrogated the crew. You made yourself known, though you weren't making friends. An opening in the control room allowed you a rise in authority and pay and so promoted you bade farewell to the graduate staff at the Spot and held fast to new work, Cue A, no, B, go B, cue C, go C.

With new money and time, you volunteered. Saturdays and Sundays, morning to night, Faithstone Church. It had lured you in with radio broadcasts of Dan Striker's sermons, compassionate and values-driven. Faithstone Church in West Houston in the late 1980s, then a 1,400-seat affair of Striker's charge, a comforting place full of good-humored and hardworking devotees. You'd finally found a prototype of what you'd dreamed to build: rooted but ambitious, inclusive yet distinguished, altogether a positive seduction. Though Striker was always stronger as a church administrator than a preacher, he kept the open Houstonians who came to his services *joyously* reverent. You but ushered and mingled at first, then you setup and cleared, inventoried supplies, remounted the audio system. On a rainy evening Leland Frank caught you leaving and you jumped his car and gave him a firm handshake and dominoes fell as his cowboy friendship brought you to Striker at poker and pool and into contact with all sorts of old moneybags. Striker came to like you anyway and asked you to write for him after you got the post of Outreach Director. With this some years passed and the great flora of your twenties bloomed and on a sunny day you met Cynthia. Circled just outside the metal door of the loading dock warming up with the other choir altos she stood swaying in time in the middle of a feral harmony. You watched her as you crossed the auxiliary lot and moved onward along the curve of the building. She sang with eyes closed until the last possible moment she could have opened them and still glimpsed you and then she did just that. It was a structured beginning—introduction, friendship, courtship, the quenching love—but then death appeared.

In the autumn of 1990, after a life of calcified faith and retail service and many years her missions grinding unremarked in the void with Sisyphean results, Mom left Dad in their yellow-brick house in Spring Branch and drove west on 290. The sun would've been setting. She crossed the muddy median into oncoming traffic and died. It was declared an accident. Asleep at the wheel. You exchanged more words with Dad in three weeks than you had in three years, and so few of them pleasant, not enough of them empty. He blamed you and you blamed him *and neither father nor son could acknowledge my role in the matter.*

Wept dry you went on living. You lived in mute bitterness with rapt attention. You listened to faint clinks in the church's air conditioner, loudest above the maintenance closet near the bathrooms. You looked at the cupboard door closest to your stove and saw it had only one hinge to the others' pairs. The plastic trash bin in your bedroom still had a price tag on its bottom. Your neighbor making a noise in the morning? That was not the sound of a blender, it was the buzz of a coffee bean grinder. You told yourself to always pay attention.

Enter Cynthia Nicolo, aged twenty-four and sharing a one-bedroom apartment on Westheimer with a childhood friend. In flats she stood just under six feet tall, her lips the slightest lean below yours, her earthen brown hair streaked with odd red, and curly, her green eyes huge and forever aswirl, her voice like checkered wool, her lips of peppermint and salt.

America stared down the oncoming millennium as the proud economic victor of the era, even as L.A. burned madly through its surface, even as AIDS continued a discriminate yet senseless slaughter. You and Cynthia fell in love and you made love and this sex at first engendered unconscionable guilt. But Cynthia never stooped to your guilt and you were going to marry her anyway. She made her living a voice for hire and had sung nearly everywhere in town and sotto voce in the night she told you stories of her childhood. How she and her sister Zelda ran away from home toward New Orleans not to escape their parents but to learn French and listen to jazz. They got as far as Tyler hitchhiking from Arlington but they turned themselves around before the road did. How she really only ever dreamed of comfort and a big yard and a man more confident in God than she and with these things provided she would spend her life singing not for fame but for the music, the glory of music.

This is the life you've fashioned and it suits you well. You were born in the dirt and raised on the road and God would've beat His words into you if Dad hadn't. You met thousands of people, handled their cash. Nixon resigned and the war ended and the economy tanked and then industry threw money at itself enough that—because of the past but more intensely than it—your nation came to worship the almighty dollar alongside the individual Christ. You understood this as it happened, the great beast of charismatic faith awakening again. The problem in American belief is that whenever Christianity reawakens, false Christians seize power—political *or cultural*—while worshipping money, not Christ. And if they understand this is a sin, they perpetuate it for their own gain. Dad gave up on others as he settled for himself, but you vowed never to settle. You ghostwrote Striker's book and with that money you and Cynthia bought a house and there came a day when you breathed deep and smiled at how you'd really made it and there came many days like this such that domestic peace became a basic fact of your existence. Do you remember sleeping in the backseat of the car, parked on some dirt shoot beside a windbreak, alone awake and doleful staring up through the moonroof at the trees and firmament? Do you remember the fruit of roadside vendors and the sanctity of free condiments?

Now here's a body (*deniably*) yours. Four fillings, four wisdom teeth removed, one root canal, once an arm broken and healed, twice bronchitis, failing vision, serious dandruff, a left rotator cuff forever hampered by a casual football game, creaky ankles, a height uncomfortable in many cars and showers, perhaps a demon, certainly lots of psychological baggage thanks to parents and travel, an onion-like faith, a need to confirm this faith's reality by sharing it with everyone, the frame and hair of your father, periodic sexual and racial thoughts too uncouth to attempt to phrase which manifest with surprise and disgust but which manifest nonetheless, at once a constant holier-than-thou type of internal filter and a complex of guilt designed to ignore that filter, self-indulgent prayers, self-effacing prayers, sessions of weeping few and far between and utterly unbearable, and no matter how many meals you serve to the homeless or proverbs you disperse to strangers there is still an ego-self with its lurching, well-fed, animalistic bias. Now get lost in Cynthia. Cynthia. The older-sister pressure of good behavior and fine example, the damnation of being artistically inclined, the tall-girl torment of pre-teen years, the thankless antics of her friends, the patchwork glory of a singer, her students and their parents, the dead end of a noble profession, the way older teachers talk to her, her allergy to wool, her dark leg hair, her mother whose sarcasm rivals some of the worst things your own parents said to you, a fear of falling so prevalent that she refuses to look over balconies but also a lust for outdoor adventurism that her husband lacks, and how she lacks so little in spirit. Tonight y'all bury your cat. Tonight y'all are lazy, wanna just get some pizza? Tomorrow you've gotta reboard the fence gate, got a dentist appointment. *And we just can't get enough of each other, can we?*

Once a season you drive to Lethland where Dad has bought a condo and you drink coffee and play chess with a set of green and black soapstone pieces you bought him years ago.

"Your mother's been gone a long time," he says, but he says it early in his grief so that he can say it from there on out. You fork his queen and dark bishop with a knight and he says, "I didn't see that," but then he sends his bishop across your forces and offers a trade of queens. Every conversation devolves to the news or politics or (*God forbid*) the past. Now here wax ridiculous about Pat Buchanan and Ross Perot and Bill Clinton, now O.J. Simpson, now Newt.

You never say them to each other anymore but still y'all know your differences. Scripture is his cudgel, your pillow. His sins are prideful and yours are greedy and your greed a child of his pride. (*The devil tempts you accordin to you, y'know.*) Dad says he built his part of the new foundation of Christian America when he could and he couldn't do it forever and he'll go to his grave satisfied so what if he spends a couple decades enjoying rest. Evangelism and deliverance were his prime objectives and though he still believes in the righteousness of seeking political power well only with Christians do the ends justify the means and he's sure as shit not gonna run for office but he'll grumble at the radio and say I did my part, I did my part. You'd like to think of yourself as more of a Christian universalist. You are a minority member among your peers, under the shifting spotlights of American ministry, because you showcase the church and the glory of a modern God without a hint of politics. Without many hints at least. Evangelism is your prime mission as well, sure, but you also want a healthy life and happy home and a merciful vision of humanity and the future. You believe in America and the freedom of capitalism and where Dad's dogma decrees anything less than an explicitly Christian state half-baked you understand the variety of the world's powers and religions to be yet more evidence of the glory and possibility of God. Nothing can be perfect, and the world hasn't ended, isn't that enough? Dad never had the strength for comparative religion. He could only believe in something if he knew he was mentally privileged enough to be correct about it. An ideological elitism. You hate that he traveled around the country seeking Christians and healing them and yet now he balks when you suggest confirmation bias. Every time as you're making to leave he hugs you with sudden compassion like he thinks he's gonna die soon, but he never does.

He says, "You don't write sermons, you make petitions for other people's money."

You say, "You preached. Don't people give the more they trust?" and he gets the insult.

In early 1998 you and Cynthia spend a week in Salt Lake City because she wants to be somewhere that isn't flat. You hike

Black Mountain and that night sleep like the dead. On a stroll through Liberty Park as you're rhapsodizing about your latest spiritual insight she turns to you and says, "I need you to write all this down."

"What do you mean?"

"Corbin, I don't want to hear it this year. All the time. I don't need to hear it. I'll hear it when you tell our kids. Until then, hon, I'm gonna need you to write it down like you did for Striker. Sell this. I can't listen to all of this."

"I thought you liked hearing me think out loud."

"It's not that. I do." She has a lilt in her voice as she speaks. A kind of regretful displeasure felt with great conviction, but obscured by a kind tone. A response of hers so rare you forgot she could react this way. She must mean it. "You torture yourself. You haunt yourself. And I understand why, it's how you get good work. But I don't need to hear you do that."

"I feel like this is the way I've always been."

"It is," she sighs.

"Isn't this a little unfair? Wouldn't this be like if I told you not to talk about what happened in your classes?"

"No, not at all." She's angry at some structural level. "When I teach, there's a dialogue. I influence the kids and they influence me back. When you write for Striker, he takes your words, your ideas, and spreads them. You don't really have a sounding board. You don't have a reflection of your words back to you, they go through him and get reflected back to him. So everything you give to him and all the ideas you keep for yourself you're just kind of stuck with. You throw them all at me but I cannot be that for you all the time. It's exhausting."

"But you said yourself it's the way I've always been. Have I always exhausted you?"

She shakes her head no, but it's a lie. A withholding.

So you sit down and write a book. But to what extent is it you writing? To what extent the sum of your history, your influence, and your reaction? How much of me is in there? Don't get me wrong, you struck up some real personal clarity in those months, in some of those moments of pure flow. There exist muses and sources of inspiration, there exists the immanent Godhead, and these things you can draw from so that what comes out of you is an admixture of self within the timeless. But you exist in the here and now, only in the here and now. So how could your creation be anything more than a reaction to everything that came before? Ideas are never truly new, but people always are. Still we come into being in reaction to traditions and conflict and this we cannot undo.

What was your addition to the world? Let Yourself Live. *No subtitle. Boy, did you really ignore me in that text. How could you do that, ignore the demon within? You felt me most in those moments of creative flow, did you not? You wrote about the hotels, the road, the times you saw Christ rise up within someone gettin healed. But barely. You didn't write about the time your own father diagnosed your affliction. You spent a hundred and ninety pages sellin dull and tired maxims about faith and self-acceptance but only two pages on what hell really is — not simply the lone mind but* your *mind.*

Your mind has been plagued by the devil since birth, and he tricked you into writing a book, sent you to chase the dollar. A'right he tricked you into whatever you ever wanted and after every favor you kept pretendin to work for God. But you work for me, not God. You know this because you can hear my command within, my command the only extra, in growin proportion to your own. And I am no God.

Dan Striker and Leland Frank sit you down to discuss taking over the KZZT hour, and later that night you ask Cynthia what she thinks. "It would mean life in the public eye," she says. "Public ear."

"The book was going to do that too."

"Doesn't it feel like too much at once? You'll be finishing the press tour and then jumping right onto the air."

"Everything's kind of linin up. Maybe it's linin up for a reason."

You two discuss this while laying in bed. She is silent for a long time and then says, "Radio is for the angry."

"I'm not angry."

"I know. I don't know if that means it needs you or it doesn't."

"What do you think?"

"You want to evangelize, Corbin. I won't stop you."

"You knew I would seek the public eye one day. Public ear." You smile through the dark but Cyn does not return one. "Don't have to drag you in, and I promise it won't drag ya down."

"It's gonna be your life, all your time."

"It would be a chance to build something."

"Then we should have a baby. We should try. If it's all lining up at once then we should have a baby sooner rather than later. I'll need you around."

"Are they necessarily connected?"

She seems hurt by your question, swallows a comment, then says, "You're gonna make some money, I imagine."

"I'm gonna try. But the book is no guarantee and you'll be makin more teachin than I will with the hour, unless it's a hit."

"It's gonna be a hit," she says, but she's not excited, she's worried.

"You want to try for a kid now?"

Something in your tone makes her say, "You don't?"

"It's not like we haven't been trying."

She gives you a look. It's a look you will be contemplating

for the rest of your life. "Hon, we haven't really been trying." In your memory this face of hers will take many shapes— grim surprise, pitiful embarrassment, amused disgust—for when you create a memory both intimate and unsettling you overwrite it immediately, and the vision of the original is forever elusive. "This hasn't been a marriage where we're trying to have a child," she says. Then, quietly, "But it should be. I'm thirty-one."

"It's time?"

She's crying now. "It's time." And here she bursts into a smile, and she wipes her eyes while teardrops dot the pillowcase, and she says it again, "It's time," and in her sudden relief you sense someone who feels heard for the first time in too long.

How many variations of yourself have you been? If life is a symphony, how many movements; if your soul is a product, which version is this?

Corbin Allen, a child, a fundraiser, a preacher's assistant, a teenager, a study bug, a professional. Corbin Allen here with KZZT and you're listening to *The Day's Light*.

Say Folks, money's not gonna give you peace. God's gonna give you peace. Say Folks, you're not gonna get a re-do, God's gonna tell you how your life went. You're not gonna magically quit drinking. If you wanna quit drinking you gotta take your hand off the bottle, and take God's hand. Say God's the boss that matters. Say God's the love that matters. God's the one in charge. Folks, you're not gonna die in His absence if you live with His presence.

Up at 4:30 to work out.

By puberty we move beyond the God figures of our life—our God, our parents.

Work out and see Cyn off, "Teach em up good."

We expand our frame of reference to peers, to groups.

Your pre-show ritual: bathroom, second coffee, crack knuckles, warm voice, ready table, sit and breathe and be present and watch the clock.

And when adulthood comes, we find we must narrow in on something.

Intro-music and welcome, the day's reading, the interpretation, the sermon. Ad break. Music break. Ad break. Anecdote. News. Callers. Ad break. Callers. Ad break. Reading. Signoff.

This is where we get lost. Zoomin back in. We zoom in on other people, spouses and family. Idols. Villains. We are tempted in the desert and get lost. We zoom around, zip around. We lose the frame of reference. We forget God is the frame.

Pray for the strength to ignore the dark and lonely voice within, pray it again.

Successful locally, then regionally. This is how it works. It happens but not overnight. You publish a book, you get a radio show, sell truckloads, find yourself with a manager and a publicist and two assistants, keep selling books, keep going on air. It's still a hassle to get the money for the church. It's a wonder to get recognized on the street, by face or voice, but you feel fame's scrutiny before receiving its payout and you curse yourself for wanting the latter first, for wanting either. And Cyn wants to stop teaching. She wants to have a child with you. *But you needn't worry, Corbin. You could let me take over at any time. Or just wait.*

Striker retires. He and Pam buy a home on Galveston and he says he wants to buy a sloop. He asks you what you think of old men retiring into privacy. You hadn't thought about it but tell him he's earned what he has. "Faithstone isn't for you anymore," he says. "You need to make your name."

Leland fronts most of the cost. He retains authority over real estate decisions but entrusts the business of things to you. "It's money I'm considerin already gone," he says with that oblivious poison of the ultra-rich.

Meanwhile the century has long since turned and Wall Street's still on edge from last spring and Cyn still hasn't gotten pregnant. She alternately hates or is humbled by her job while you're thrilled out starting your true career. Not apart you two bide God's fruitful time.

Then four planes explode upon impact and God will never be the same in this country.

You pray. But for what? Yet you pray it again.

Death at any moment. Did you notice how deep was the green of your wife's eye, how many glassy orbs shone to comprise the sclera? Did you notice that no matter how long you trained the parallax of your sight over Cynthia's eyes you could never perceive her whole self at once? Eyes are infinite and contain the soul. But that is to ask did you ever consider how your two eyes can only focus on one other?

And yet could no thought feel new? The country launched into war again but it seemed not a new war, rather the continuation of all the most ancient conflicts. Ancient misunderstanding. *Ancient foolishness*. Even the most hauntingly sweet moments with your wife over the years have felt cliché in some way. Is that the strain of a long-term partnership? Your pair's unique issues resurfacing a few too many times? You're indeed haunted by the idea that intense sentiments, joy and fear alike, can only be processed with an overwrought, prismatic dependence on archetypes and tropes. Your dead mom's birthday was September 11th, what does that mean? Why do you want it to mean something?

Pray for Mom's soul.

Remember Parkinson's law. Work expands to fill the time allotted for it. This is what it means to be a conscious mind, living, comprehending itself. Existence doesn't need to be this complicated but when we live beyond infancy our minds create work for themselves.

The infant century. By its toddle you knew time itself had changed. Everything sped up. War again—desert blood, across the globe. Everyone got connected but war reigned, terror reigned, and the machines of society and business only sped up their consumption, expulsion. What was the distance between the UT tower sniper and Palm Sunday? What about the time between the Killeen Luby's massacre and Oklahoma City, Virginia Tech and Fort Hood, the movie theater and the elementary school? The millennium felt inevitable, the dot com bust too. 9/11 felt inevitable, as did Fallujah and the iPhone and the Arab Spring and Occupy. That's what was unnerving right at the beginning, with the Blackberries and the flattening screens and the new gold rush in California— the 20th century had warned us what we'd do in the 21st and then we went and did it all anyway. Inevitable you would have a child with Cynthia—Wesley James Allen, born the fourth of March, the year of our Lord 2003. Inevitable an only son begot an only son. Inevitable the costs, diapers of course but think crib, rocker, clothes, babyproofing, maternity clothes, stroller, carrier, snacks snacks snacks forever. Inevitable the joy, inevitable the whiplash of two people looking away from each other and evermore toward a third. *Inevitable that your perversion of scripture and a huckster's Christianity would fill your pockets. Look at you, Mr. Grin, on TV, pennin drivel for The New York Times, bein translated into thirty different languages you never tried to learn.* Maybe it was inevitable that you would become famous. Famous like truly famous people are—recognized everywhere. At first, just in your hometown. Then maybe not everyone recognized you, but you were recognized in every place. Your face in shop windows and your voice in thousands of cars simmering under this Texas sun. Your century, the century you'll die during, see here, it's byte-sized yet stratified, with information infinite but results prescribed and limited.

Your life, to put it simply, gained inertia outside your control.

And I have inertia, too.

You never hated your father more than when you saw him with your son. It was as though he had been stockpiling a purer form of love out of your sight for all these years, only to deploy it in defense of some worthier progeny when the time was right and such love was beyond your use.

And always the firm hug at the end. Sometimes the whisper: "He's still in there, son."

You played chess with Dad and focused on your breathing and told yourself to just entertain a lonely old man and get back home to your boy.

You neglect your wife the same way you process your own neglect—gradually.

Your congregation and platform and bank account grew. Your prayers narrowed to the material—let Wes and Cyn thrive in health and happiness, aye, and let us reach syndication with our spinoff. Let us spread your word, Lord, to all the paying faithful of American satellite radio.

The money, the square footage, the temptation to make a career out of a callin.

You raised your son, when you could. *But let's face it* you were a man with a plan and that plan had little to do with raising a child in Godly earnest. You were on a mission to prove your worship more infectious than your father's. There was once a time and place for men of God like Dad, but no

more, not in this new century. You knew it by the time
Faithstone's attendance slipped and Striker retired. Crowds
of five thousand, eight, ten thousand Baptists or Methodists
or motley crews convened in huge buildings all over town.
The trends of the nation caught up every city, leaving only
fifty-follower hovels scattered about the shadows of the
giants. With Leland's money Riverbed sat five hundred until
it matured into one of the giants. And a giant you yourself
became, smiling everyfuckinwhere, saying *Let Yourself Live*,
have *One Life Under God*, and here's *100 Ways To Pray*.

Now here's hundreds and hundreds of checks.

Dad thought his preaching was more holy because it was
more personal, but you knew that in the 21st century
everything would be personal. The anonymous comment
screened across a planet, personal. The decentralized
thought. The most famous preacher alive can both be
speaking to everyone and talking directly to you. Need two
be face-to-face to get personal? Of course not. Not anymore.

Dad once said itinerant evangelical preachers built this
country. That's why he became one. But it's hardly true.
Slaves and workers built this country, while profiteers
collected on the work and rewarded the preachers. Or else
the preachers seduced themselves into greed and let the
meaning of justice pass them by. Men like Dad became
outcasts for a reason. A twenty-first century evangelical must
understand that we are all temporary guests in America just
as we are temporary guests on earth. We are no longer
building our nation, nor are we maintaining what we've
already built. We are merely occupying this land and these
ideals in the name of some design we have forgotten, or
never knew at all.

*So where's your sermon on guns, pastor? Where a homegrown
thought on gasoline? If you're so noble, grab that little leather
notebook you use and jot down: Blood for oil? Was Christ a fiscal*

conservative? Does God watch you in the voting booth? Didn't think so.

Riverbed Church—that was your legacy. Your prayer repeated by millions, for years:

Jesus is my God

~~I can be what He needs me to be~~

I can do what He needs me to do

I let Him into my heart

Forever

In Jesus name, amen

No politics, not too much Lucifer, little hell.

No guts, pitiful action, no shame.

All love, good business.

Phony sympathy.

There is footage of former president George H.W. Bush reciting your words with you.

And you reckoned with a demon in you every day, and you raised your son or didn't every day, and at times lost in the follow-boom of sixteen thousand people saying what you've written as mic'd-up you say it with them could you feel unlike your Corbin and then know a You was missing. *And I was with you every minute. Right above you, deep within.*

Jesus is my God *But fame is your God.*

I can be what He needs me to be *You'll be who I tell you to be.*

I can do what He needs me to do *But only if I want you to.*

Let me into your heart. Forever.

In Jesus name, amen.

And that's what keeps you up, my man. If opposition is definition, is lettin Jesus in a sin?

Did I screw up time itself? Did I single-mindedly disorder the chronology of your existence? No. I thought linearly and you thought radially, and as such we've thought up a mess. You lived your days as they passed, every moment. You raised your son and spoke to him. You loved your wife and told her. You worked and wrote and preached and ever the kid who grew up too soon you went through life cognizant of its patterns of disappointment and you earned much of your success in spite of this. Life happens and you lived in a manner you thought just and for all your money you always prayed on your knees. But I color much of our perceptions of the past and future, and in some ways only the worst or best of me can regard a thing. You're somewhat elusive to my influence in the moment but I come to inform your perceptions of moments like any old philosophy could, an idea studied deeply and subsequently unbelieved, a background radiation suspected yet undiscovered.

Cyn stopped reading and looked over from her Angela Carter to say, "You aren't admitting we're at an impasse."

"We're at an impasse?"

"Public school is the real world. Private school isn't, no matter how great a school."

You knew it was coming. "I have the resources to put him in front of great teachers, around other well-off kids who'll become friends for life. And they'll talk about Jesus, too, how is that not a win?"

"Just because you have the money doesn't mean you have to spend it."

"That's what rich people say. I earned this money. For this reason."

"Maybe it's not a good investment."

"How could it not be? It's like buying time."

She laid there, hips down on the floor of the bedroom, kicking her feet up in slow interchange behind her and curling her toes all cute like she would on the floor of that first apartment of hers, the one along the screech and sirens of Westheimer.

You asked how it was that you could raise a child. Didn't

some demon tell you long ago? You guessed you should become an example of something for Wes. Was your house example enough? The new enormous home. You counted the rooms. You counted those rooms like you counted all that spare change for your daddy. That difference enough? Your books enough? Was the fact of your creative process? *Those moments where I burst through?* Could run into old classmates all you wanted, but you knew it was your son who needed impressing. Could humor Dad all you wanted, but knew it was God who must forgive you.

Every night as your head hit the pillow your memory plunged up intimate embarrassments recent and ancient—turning from old Simon on the street, yes Simon was his name, from the Faithstone years, who served in Vietnam and twice divorced and lost a son to SIDS and never could afford medication for himself, who returned posted up on a corner near Riverbed to accost you at every sighting, proclaiming himself Jesus Christ come back to earth. That moment you first turned from him, replayed at random in your night-loosened mind. Or else the dozen flashes of anger at Cynthia over the years. Or Davey, from long ago, on whose childhood you often dwelled to wonder what role you played. You swam with him in the stagnant rainwater pooled between the hills of a golf course. At the sewer you almost kissed him before scolding him and fleeing. Did you let him kiss you? You can't remember.

To remember life's mistakes at night, or its obligations in the morning, indeed even just to think beyond the present moment and access past or future makes a mockery of experience. Our very cells change, in time. We are physically distinct from ourselves-not-long-ago, but we remain stuck in the same mold, the same patterns. Our cells either reproduce and die or were already dead at birth. Our senses, our memories, our wants and fears exist and cease in collage. There is no narrative to your life. How then can one plan anything? How truly recollect? One cannot exist in three states at once and yet we demand this of ourselves all day long. You busied yourself with sermons. *Helping Neighbors, Doing Favors; Living with God's Truth; today I wanna talk to you about Let The Light In*—that's what all this work and fame was for. You did not just greedily want to be a mover and shaker. You wanted validation. Accountants, assistants, interviewers. You wanted to abandon the responsibility of finding a narrative in the collage.

You made a church. You didn't show God to nobody, you just put people in a room together and told em all to imagine Him. You built a system instead of relationships. And like all the worst preachers you thought money was some kind of truth or Godly reward when in reality it is pure power. Worldly power. Sometimes evil, always effective. You said you didn't like to preach about hell or devils like me. You always said it was better to focus on the real enemy, one's own faults. I thought you meant to focus only on what we as men can know, ourselves. But then you turned around and implied that our circumstances—our money, our luck—measured something Godly. How could that be? One cannot measure things in heaven by things on earth, as the poet said. Money is a social metric. The ultimate system. And systems are the enemy, not minds.

You could've done it at any moment. You thought about it each time you visited New York, your camera-ready hair solid against the gusts of tunnel-wind, your heart slamming with imagination. Then you started taking taxis when you visited and figured there were plenty of other ways to die in New York.

You thought about it in Houston, on the balcony of the Gulf Light Theatre during their anniversary gala. In a boat off the Everglades. Descending a tower of la Sagrada Familia, with Cynthia right behind you. You realized 'jump' is a four-letter word.

Your son stretched before you—pencil marks on a doorframe, the widening frame of successive birthday photos.

Your wife wept on the eve of your son's ninth birthday. She grabbed your hand and held it tighter than you thought possible and she cried for fifteen minutes before she could pronounce the word 'cancer.'

At a certain point—probably the fatal chess match—I was able to gauge the degrees of my influence within you and so able to experiment in adjusting that influence. Seemingly shut off from the cognitive actuation of your present, I felt my own self actualized inside you only in the short deliberative moments of extreme emotion. I was much of the joy the night your son was born. I was the vacuum of the heavens of ecstasy, sex and music and preaching. I was the panic in you watchin your father's hands freeze mid-castle and his face pale and him stroke, shut down, disappear behind his eyelids forever. You were the consideration—to pull the plug, as they say—and I the rejection.

Jordan Barshius once said, "Your son will be an artist, sir, not a believer." For this insight you would always hate the guy, even as you sought his counsel. "I don't know what Wes is so angry about," you said. And Jordan answered, "He's angry that he's young."

I never touched your grief at Cynthia's death. She died a crueler death than your mother and even though it was many weeks slower than a suicide it felt just as quick. Cancer is an evil even I wouldn't claim a soul deserves, so I was there in the extreme of the shock but I was quiet.

A stroke, a coma. The death of your one true love and the clinging life of your oldest enemy. A new phone, never-ending email. The digital dominion, the new everything. All of it—changed around 2013 and still changing too fast but now with an air of finality like a rushed epilogue.

I suppose it's time for me to explain myself. First let me note that if I could have done things differently, I would've. If I'd realized the truth on my first visit, I never would've returned to you. But I returned again and again until I couldn't leave and the great irony of my work is that in tryin to purify you I caused half of your corruption. I wanted you to be a man of God, but what triumphed was some percentage of you that desired fame. In your status, you are not a channel for the Lord, you are a hypocrite laid bare. Don't let anyone tell you otherwise, Corbin. You are an emblem of all those lessons of mine which you failed to heed. God is private. He does not stay still. You can only bring Him to others if you chase after His wind. You must seek Him in places and in people. Your gift is speech, so you will not find Him, though you preach in His name. My gift from God, on our other hand, was an ability to fully feel His presence in people. Or His absence. We spent seven of our years on the road so that I could shine His light out of other people's eyes. But if this gift sounds appealin in any way, let me assure you it is not, not forever. One life is enough to bear. I lost millennia tryin not to bear my own. I did so in the valiant service of God, but, nonetheless, it stole my mind to an early grave. You don't know what it's like to peer into your son and see the devil.

Your mother understood what I had to do, aware of my ability and your potential. That's what you could never wrap your mind around. She knew it was real. Bless her heart her biggest fear was that you'd give up on life and end it. Look how that turned out.

You could raise children, but the world would raise much of them. You could love, but a lover would die. You could drop a toaster in your bath and be rid of your demons forever.

But then what?

You couldn't even write your petty little birthday letters anymore. *I began to write for you. I took your handwriting and then your voice. Or maybe you just gave yours up.*

I watched you loathe me and watched your mistakes unfold time and time again and again. Satan sleeps, Corbin, but not in you. It was me. It was me the whole time. Now, five years departed from my body, as miles away it breathes purchased breath, my consciousness gradually remembers itself within you, and so what's the difference? What's the difference now?

We still have the body and the doubt and our city. Houston, our beautiful swamp. The great swaths of cypress, their muddy channels and ponds. The ghosts of awesome pines lording over bright flatstone neighborhoods. Culs-de-sac like sparklin plates of grain, downtown routes potholed and littered as with clues leadin back to a more forgiving century, beltways and farm-to-market roads connecting any population, just name one, the ways ever alive with silent SUVs and growlin pick-ups. Houston's dome of perfect Texas sky. The remaining pockets of rurality, the gray-pink glint of the downtown skyline, the crammed hipness or strip-centered foreignness or dead-grassed poverty. Our famous annual rodeo. Hurricanes. McCain yard signs, now Romney bumper stickers. Lakes of blue and an openly gay mayor. The reaches that reek of sulfur or gasoline. The wretched brown port. A wary pride of the Bush family. The repurposed old Enron offices. The Astros and Rockets and Texans and what else. The city that gave us Beyoncé and Howard Hughes and Ted Cruz. The home of NASA Mission Control and the Rothko Chapel and Jones Hall. The enormous Riverbed Church and its revered preacher. God Almighty, bless this city, cast out its demons. God bless this city of taco trucks and crawfish boils and blonde realtors and oil money and fine art. This place is ours. We are its faith. We are the holy sweat of its every humid afternoon.

Praise the Lord's surprises. *And the greatest surprise of your life? How many people you've met. That's it. Greater than leavin Tulsa or gettin used to loneliness or my incremental embitterment or your mother's death or the fact that I'm in two places at once. The only surprise of life which expands with every acknowledgement is how many people you've known. An international celebrity preacher with bestsellin books who runs an organization so visited it needs a security operation like that of a baseball stadium, gee, that man's a far cry from the little boy knockin on the office door of a motel to see if the proprietor has any kids who can come play. This you remember every day, with every handshake, every stranger recognizing you in traffic or out at dinner, and you remember all those lonely hungry hours of the road with a criminal smile when you meet families and cops and power brokers and the homeless in line on Wednesday and Sunday morning.* Yes, you are rich and famous but think of the good you had to do to get here. No one's perfect nor ever was.

But let's not rehash the past again. Let us focus on the calculation at hand.

The fact of the matter is I will only get stronger. We both know it. You cannot pull the plug because you've got the church and everyone knows you've got the money and there's no excuse. You like your reputation. You cannot will or pray away my voice any more than you can resurrect Cynthia's. And why would I let you? I have been a messenger of God. He clearly isn't done with me. He has stuck me here for a reason.

You eye open medians and long knives and Leland's guns. You have rope in the garage. You have a doctor with a generous prescription pad. *This of course your only course away from me which also takes you far from Wesley and everything else.* And yet—(*oh, and I'm the ideologue?*)—there is the overriding fact that suicide is the dankest sin. To shuffle off your mortal coil, aye, there's nothing a demon would approve faster.

Pray for the strength to kill yourself. For the power not to.

Still you daydream about my demise. You imagine a murderous nurse doin you a favor. You think about a pillow over my face. Security cameras. Hitmen, like in the movies.

You vow to yourself that this will be your last year on earth. And how so? Do you expect me to believe you've got the courage now, after all this time, really, at your richest and most famous and most stable and forever a single father? You expect me to think you'll abandon the movement—the generations of believers, the values, the homeschooling, the politicking, the money? You have staked your career in reaction to my restlessness and so-called narrow-mindedness and my esteem of the individual. And now as American Evangelicals mature into one of history's most effective demographics, as everyone connects to one another conductin life across a screen, lonely together, the invisible and omnipresent new order alarmingly not omnipotent like the God it seemed to be, and as they say what's real is what's online and what's online is not reality, and with everyone confused or dreadfully confident and this the perfect moment for a true and honest Christian awakening, now, now of all times, you'd kill yourself? I seriously doubt that.

For I was never stronger than I am today, and my vision never clearer. And you're sitting here before a bamboo hedge with this rather odd young woman and she's spillin her thoughts like gossip and it all becomes clear, but for a split second like in a flash of lightning. You are seized with many ideas and feelings all at once and prominent among them is the notion that she is the answer to your problem. This you feel with extreme certainty, though you can't think far ahead and you've forgotten one important factor (see: my power in extremes.)

11

I Make My Bed In Hell

What am I supposed to write now? Would you bear more self-reflexivity? It is an all-dictating fact that Ivy Qualiana alone writes these words, and thus alone reflects to compose a history. How could I capture Corbin or Wesley? Or Xenu, for that matter. Might it demand a book that would take fifty-two years to read to fully capture a life of that length in words? Or could you capture it all with a pen just sketching on a deck of cards? With an album. A podcast. I don't know. But I must try to describe what it felt like in the moment. In the life. Maybe it's what stuck out? Jordan told me to write it all down and see what I missed, and all these years later I'm finally writing, though I've long known what I missed because Jordan told me when I asked. I needed a different reason to write, and if I'm being honest with myself I want to write this because I am now some years removed from it all and sufficiently afraid of death and deeply worried that I will forget it all in the final years of my life if I make it to them.

I must have finished the kiss. I probably opened my eyes and saw that face, the chisel and wax, wearing an expression of bemused inspiration. Sweat likely glistened at the gray roots of his hair and when I looked into Corbin Allen's eyes I probably saw in the turquoise my dusk-dimmed self and the bamboo behind me and the muted light through it as through latticework. I could have turned to look at the broken obelisk and its pyramid's throats of rust and in that summer evening fade the art and its water could have made a face and the art and the greenery behind it could have made a face and I could have stared at the trees and the chapel too and seen faces inanimate. Again I don't know. I don't remember what happened after I became Corbin Allen. I lost at least an hour after him.

When reason settled over me, when the immersive carnival of my uncoupled mind admitted in sensation, I found myself in my home, on the piano bench, staring as I often did at the clutter of my coffee table. The lives of Marie Curie, Frederick Douglass. I became aware of my body and dried tears on my cheeks. I rubbed my face, stretched. I became aware of a dread deep within me, but a dread shooting up like the capsule of a slingshot ride.

I checked the date and time. I tried to recall the last thing I did. Kissed Ivy. Or kissed Corbin. Yes. I checked the mirror, got sick of it. I stretched more, ran my palms together, ran my fingers over the slopes of their opposite knuckles. I watched the clock and felt the night coming on and felt very sure there would be consequences for what I'd learned. It is no exaggeration to write that the very moment Jordan knocked on my door was the moment I knew for a godforsaken fact that curiosities like mine terminate only at death. Someone's somewhere.

I opened the door and waved him in without speaking, then gestured to the futon. I sat myself on the piano bench. Jordan sat on the far side of the futon and took in his view of the place as though he hadn't already lived the life of its resident. Although the temperature outside had dropped with the dark, it was still sweltering inside no matter the boxfan behind the futon, the boxfan aimed out from my bedroom doorway, or the window unit's labored puffs. "Schrödinger's cat," he said. "Pandora's box. The forbidden fruit. What'd you find?"

"Why are you here?"

"Again?" He gave a tsk. "You called me, Ivy. Seriously, you need to—" he snapped his fingers "—get back to yourself quicker. I'm worried about what you'll choose to do in that state. Did you drive here?"

"When did I call you?"

"Like forty minutes ago."

"What did I say?"

"You told me to come over. You said you needed to tell me what happened."

I stared at the trusty old coffee table, counted the items scattered about the surface. Between or on top of the books, four weeks of TIME and some few loose pages of sheet music, three pens, a pencil, a washcloth orange where I'd wiped Dorito dust from my lips, two dirty mugs and my empty Nalgene bottle, hand lotion, a bobby pin, a bottle of 1000mg fish oil pills. I wasn't really one to clean up for guests then, was I?

"Ivy?" Jordan said. He was watching me space out.

"It's one of those moments, you know, where you're looking at nothing but you can't look away. Just a sec."

"Your eyes are moving, though."

I looked at him.

"You took Corbin for a spin?"

My mouth was dry and with its use I remembered what I wanted to say. "Yes."

"And?"

"It's not him in there."

"What do you mean?"

"I mean… he is there. But so is his dad. John Allen."

"John Allen?"

"Yes. He's like us. And he read Corbin. And he got… stuck in there."

"John Allen," Jordan repeated. "The man who's been in a coma for five years."

"He's awake. Inside Corbin. More now than ever."

In one slow moment, Jordan's deadpan expression evolved from disbelief to fear. "My God," he said. "He must've gone in so many times."

"You say 'take em for a spin' because you can control them."

His mouth ajar, Jordan nodded.

"Jordan."

He was still locked in that fear. "What?"

"What was it I missed? You said to write it all down and I'd see what I missed. Is this what you meant?"

After a while he said, "You want to know?"

I did. Of course I did.

"You never spun the same thing twice," he started quietly. "It's different the second time. It's different the third time. Is he controlling him? John, is he controlling Corbin—entirely—every day?"

"Not… I don't know. It got kind of… crowded… in there. He's more aware. Yes, he can control. It's gotten worse over the past couple years."

"Years," he marveled. "How many times did he do it?"

"I don't know. There's no way to know. Dozens. Hundreds."

"It does get stronger. Can I have one of those?" Jordan pointed to the coffee table. He leaned forward and moved one of the magazines to reveal the pack of Camels I had started outside of Whataburger almost four weeks earlier. I blushed at the thought that one of my students might have seen it. At my nod Jordan opened the pack. He overturned it and out fell a small lighter with which he lit one of the cigarettes. He scratched at his neck, where the ink of his tattoo peeked out from his collar.

"I've never seen your neck tattoo," I said.

He undid a button on his shirt and pulled aside the collar. On the left side of his neck was the simple, shadow-filled shape of a keyhole. A circle-topped trapezoid. The way into him. I reached out to touch it but he wasn't looking at me, didn't see my reach, and he let go of the fabric so that the shape disappeared again.

"Ash in the mug," I said.

Jordan smoked and after a few deep draws he said, "The most I've done is three. Thrice the same person. That third time, the last day... I was awake, inside. Fully me. I knew who I was and what I was doin. I could do things. As him. For a few hours, that man was me. I say it's havin someone's keys but that's a serious responsibility. I only did it with him."

"What did you make him do?"

Jordan reacted as though the question itself were an accusation. "Nothin. Nothin. I just had a day. A normal day. Of mine. Not his. I chose. That was trippy enough, I'll tell ya that."

"This is what you didn't want to tell me. This is what it's for."

"It's what it is. Mastery, not variety. The repetition is only part of it. You don't need more than a few spins. Why would you need more than a few hours? The worst I heard... you can take someone for a spin three times and on that last day you're basically you. I figured it out on my own because I was depressed. You know your little road trip around the country just reading and reading like a slob?"

"Hey," I said, but it was an accurate description. Jordan

shrugged and pulled from the cigarette. The room now reeked of tobacco.

"I had a time like that. Just dead. So many years. I was an addict like you, except I hit rock bottom. I was this close." He spaced his fingers in measure with the burning cigarette. "I was at this rooftop bar in Dallas. Tall enough to die jumpin off. I'm lookin down, I see these two dogs on the street. By now it's been a while since I've spun anything but a human. So I think okay I'll do a final dog and go out on that. Went to a different church at the time. There was this dog who came to all the events." He smiled. "With the owner, that is. I knew the family, knew Blitzen. Cute as anything Bernese. Dad was this camping type, they had an RV and everything. I knew that dog got outdoors a lot. Seemed like a good life. So I took him for a spin. To. This. Day. Best life I ever lived. I don't know what it was, the hiking, the food, family. Bernese don't live long, this guy was happily past his prime. I came out of there so... warm. It was like I felt somethin again. You know? Like a sex addict numb all this time finally getting off, if you'll pardon the imagery. It was so naturally serene and felt right, that life, so when I got back to me I just went right back to him, spun him again. And... I knew somethin was different. Those last few hours. Things looser. So I spun him again. I actually did take that dog for a spin five times, but he's the only over three." Jordan dropped the butt of his cigarette into the ash mug and leaned back. "So I knew I could do it to people. I tried the once. Just a guy who lived downstairs from me. Like I said I didn't do anything. But later. Later in life, after I had met a few people, and witnessed..." He trailed off. He had long since been staring through and beyond the mess on the coffee table.

"Tricked into an eternity," I said.

"After that I knew. That's how you exploit."

"Exploit the power?"

"The people. You can do a lot in a few hours."

"What was the worst you ever heard?"

He looked at me. The face of someone resigned to the cruelty of people, a soldier long abandoned behind enemy lines. "It's what you would expect. Money. Opportunity."

"And Corbin's father."

"Yeah."

"He's been in a coma for five years."

"Yes."

"They aren't on good terms."

"No?"

"Corbin knows... something. He knows his dad doesn't like me."

"So what are you saying?"

"What should I do?"

He seemed confused by the question. "What is there to do?"

"You've never come across anything like this?"

"Who in God's name would look into their son's mind hundreds of times? That's like double abuse. That's pointless. He deserves a coma."

"I don't think he understood. He thought there was a demon inside Corbin. He was trying to... find it, or exorcise it, or something. But it was him."

"He lost his fuckin mind is what he did."

"You're not wrong," I said.

"How is he so functional?"

"Corbin?"

"I mean I always knew he was a little off. But if what you're saying is right, then how... what was that mind like? How does he function? Split?"

"I don't know." I said, raising my voice. Jordan was the one who was supposed to have answers. "How is John Allen's consciousness not inside his comatose body? How the hell do we do what we do? You said you knew everything about this. You said you had a PhD."

"Look, it's the equivalent of... I don't know, in the PhD analogy, like a fellow professor spying on his son. I guess. Not part of the curriculum. It has nothing to do with the school, or the subject, it's just screwed up."

He scratched nervously at his neck again. He grabbed the pack but set it down again without taking another smoke. His leg was bouncing like mad. I'd never seen him so rattled. So unsure of himself. I reached over to him again and this time he saw my reach. I grabbed the hand resting on his knee. He froze. I squeezed his hand and we looked at each other. That must have been only the third or fourth time we'd ever touched.

"I'm tired of hints, Jordan. I'm tired of analogies and metaphors. Tell me who we are."

He looked away but kept holding my hand. He thought for a long time, swallowed, kept swallowing. Eventually he spoke.

"You're like I said. The collector type. You aren't anything much yet, you just have somethin. We're just people. With a power. And it's the power that becomes us. The power defines us. Control, mastery, that's our use of it. But the thing defines you, and it's bigger than you. You know where this is goin. You always knew, somewhere in you. It doesn't end with humans. Human beings are not the highest form of life, but neither is some other animal."

"What's the high?"

He took a deep breath. He spoke very slowly. "There are individuals. And systems. And the planet. Animals, groups, earth. You've thought about it. You wanted to become a cactus or a flower but you couldn't. You can only explore the plane of individual minds. But you got the keys, Ivy. So you can explore more. Sure, you could be horses or dogs or just people for the rest of your life. You could stay in the realm of the individual. It's not that bad. It's familiar."

"Or?"

"Or. If you work at it. You could become a school of fish. A flock of birds. I swear to my God. You could become an entire group of people. And transcend the individual."

"Groups."

"Groups," he said. "Systems. Networks. The shared sense of reality."

"And then? The earth? We can take the entire earth for a spin?"

He shrugged. "That's what they say."

"Is it true?"

He nodded. "Probably."

"Have you ever been earth, Jordan?"

"I don't know that anyone has. It might kill you to be."

"The entire planet."

"You can try. You might as well try. But you won't read the planet. Try for the desert. A mountain. Maybe you'll read a flock of something. It uses you, Ivy. The power uses you."

"How does it end? Earth is the goal but if I won't end there, where will I end? What am I working toward? What good is it for my real life, my real body?"

"We are suicides or sociopaths," he said with a strange dullness. "That's how we end. Is it how we would've ended anyway? Is it what the power does to us? I don't know. But I know how I've seen it end. And I've only seen it end like that. Numbness, a lack. Throwin everything away. The undiscovered country. Or else... emptiness."

His honesty was surprising. It felt like the first real answer from Jordan, even if it wasn't.

"Have you been a flock of birds, Jordan? Have you been a group?"

He closed his eyes. He squeezed my hand hard. "Ivy," he

said. "I've been an entire choir. I've been…" He opened his eyes and froze again. Terror suddenly across his face.

"What? What did you just think about?"

"Nothing," he said. "We got company. There's a Tesla parking on the street right now."

My stomach dropped. I let go of Jordan's hand and stood to look over the AC unit. Sure enough, Corbin's car was out front, blocking in mine and Jordan's.

"How does he know where you live?" Jordan asked.

"This is where I teach."

"I should go," he said, standing.

"No, please." I couldn't face Corbin alone. "He can't be thinking straight right now."

Jordan sighed his signature sigh, an implied God damn it. "Comatose," he said, glaring at the preacher's car.

I met Corbin as he climbed out of the driver seat. He was still wearing the suit he'd been wearing hours earlier at the chapel, and in that pale moonlight he was gray like a ghost.

"I don't remember planning this party," I said.

He looked past me and I followed his gaze. Jordan had opened the door and was raising his hand in salutation. He had lit a second cigarette. "I didn't know you two were friends," Corbin said.

"Did I ask you to come here?"

He shifted his weight, put his keys in his pocket. He came around the car but did not extend for a shake or hug. He looked very serious. "You told me to. I assumed we'd be alone."

I remembered the kiss. "Listen, whatever I said… I'm a little overwhelmed right now. Maybe we can do this another time?"

He looked me over, looked to Jordan again. "No," he said, and he walked past me. "You said you'd help. Tonight." He even moved like a ghost, like he floated past Jordan and into the house. I tried to remember what I'd said, what I might have whispered as our lips pulled apart.

Jordan and Corbin exchanged small talk while I put water in the kettle and the kettle on to boil. I looked at my three little boxes of tea bags and knew which Corbin would choose. A fly sat atop the box of jasmine white, rubbing its front legs together, antennae twitching. It stayed there. Patient.

"What's the sermon for tomorrow, pastor?"

Jordan stood smoking in the open doorway. I lingered on the threshold of the kitchen and watched Corbin as he sat on the futon, absentmindedly flipping through an issue of TIME.

"I'm not sure we'll have one," he said.

"Why do you say that?"

"I think you know." Corbin dropped the magazine back on the table. Text emblazoned on the cover offered 240 Reasons to Celebrate America Right Now.

"I don't know anything," Jordan said. "I don't even know who I'm talkin to." He leaned back and blew smoke out the door.

The kettle whistled and I returned to the stove and turned off the burner. I carried two mugs of steeping jasmine into the living room and placed one on the coffee table near Corbin and offered the other to Jordan. He took it and blew over its rim and set it on the floor. Outside the street was quiet and windless. I stepped toward my room and checked the digital clock by my bed and then shut the door as tight as it could go for the cord of the boxfan. I turned. Those men studied me in anticipation as if I were about to begin my own heathen sermon.

"I guess I asked both of you here," I started. "I wanted to help you?" I said, looking at Corbin. He didn't move a muscle. "I wanted to help you," I said again. Jordan puffed away.

Corbin was still. I looked over his suit and remembered its

smell, the wear of its seams.

"You've been there," I said to Jordan. "When you saw the dog from the roof. I've been there." I turned to Corbin. "I've been many kinds of people in my life and I have had a few days with this feeling. The absolute decision. Of course, no one I ever was went through with it. Successfully. But some tried. They got to that point. It has to happen now, it makes more sense to go through with it than not. This constant and kind of unbearable self-awareness. People who haven't been there think it's selfish but it's not. Self-centered, sure. But not selfish. It's logical."

"Are you talkin about suicide?" Corbin asked. He was holding back some expression, it could have been giddiness or it could have been terror.

"It's this weird freedom," I continued. "You get to that point and you make that decision and then everything just lifts off of you. Because you know. It's the last big decision you'll ever make. No more weighing the variables or agonizing or thinking. Trinity of the mind, you know. Memory, intellect, and will. Well, at that point the memory and the intellect don't matter at all. All that remains is the will. And that is freedom. The real sense of it for the first time. Since you were a kid, maybe."

Jordan tossed the end of his cigarette onto the front steps. He closed the door and the air inside immediately went stale. He leaned against the wall of the bedroom and then slid down into a squat beside his tea. I remained standing, presiding with some pretense over my humble abode. How strange, I thought, that this should culminate with two guests in my little shack.

"This isn't what I thought you would explain," Corbin said.

"Well I need you to explain something to me."

"What's that?"

"That feeling... that generous, open, loving, completely delusional point of no return. It doesn't last that long. If you get to that point, you try. Now, what I can't understand is how you're still there. You got to that point and you stayed there. You've had that weight off of you for a long time, haven't you, Mr. Allen?"

Corbin had sunk far back into the futon but now he uprighted and sat on the edge. "Do you know who you're talkin to?"

"Corbin?" I said. He spread that wicked smile. "John."

"Everyone," Jordan said, raising his hand like a student with a question. "Let me get this clear. Who wants to kill themselves?"

"He does," I pointed at Corbin. "Don't you?"

"If you're tryin to get him to answer," he said, "I'm afraid you're out of luck."

There was a moment of silence then so keen I shall never forget the stuttering breaths I took, wondering whether to respond.

"You got a gift," Corbin said, almost sneering at Jordan. He turned to me. "And you got a gift. And I got a gift. I am surrounded by threes. What a pattern. Memory, intellect, and will, is it? Two parents and a child. Id, ego, superego."

"Empty, half, and full," Jordan said, looking at me.

"Yes," Corbin said, faintly pleased.

"Zip, zap, zop," Jordan said, "Peter, Paul, and Mary, what the fuck are you on about?"

"Are you angry at somethin?" Corbin asked.

"I am concerned," Jordan said, and in his squat he rocked back and forth, "because you just referred to a 'him' and I think you mean you."

"Are you concerned?" Corbin asked me.

"Should I be?" I asked in return. "If you're Corbin, I don't know why you're here. If you're John, I don't know either."

"You can cut the crap," he said. He tapped his temple. "You've been in here. I felt you there."

"What did I say to you? When I asked you to come here."

"You said, 'Come by and I'll kill you.'"

Another memorable silence.

"What's that now?"

"I assume you were talkin to him," Corbin said, or John said, again referencing the mind unvoiced within the room, "but my curiosity's gettin the better of me. I know you were in here." He tapped his temple again. And whose temple?

My eyes fell to the floor and then I watched the floor as I folded my legs under me and sat on the wood. So we all sat there in my home and drank tea and discussed a murder-suicide.

I opened my mouth as if to talk and they waited for me to say something. I held the pause, peering or trying to peer deep into those eyes in that face on the body of the man known as Corbin Allen. "When I met you," I said to him, "in your office, was that you or Corbin?"

"It was me," he said. "But it's my son's office." A joke.

I looked at Jordan for a reaction, but he was watching Corbin intently and gave none.

"And when I talked to you about your sermons? Those were your sermons we talked about. Weren't they? Or do you even know who I'm talking to?"

"I could feel you in here, Ms. Qualiana, for Pete's sake, of course I can feel my son. He is in here, if that's what you're really after."

"I know," I said. "And he wants to die. So why did you come here?"

He laughed. Not like that breathy fake laugh Corbin Allen gave in every interview or at the end of each sermon's opening joke, but a full-belly laugh. "To see what the heck your plan was, quite frankly. What, you think I'm just gonna let you kill me?"

"I said to come here and I'd kill you?"

"See?" Jordan said. "I have reason to worry what you'll do in that state."

"How'd you know Jordan's got it?" I asked. "The gift."

"Context clues. I know my way around people."

"Why would you offer to murder a man, Ivy?" asked Jordan.

"He's trapped in there," I said. I fixed onto Corbin's eyes again. "You're trapped in there. You want to die but… it's not like you can question God's will. You're alive in there. And John isn't leaving."

"Why aren't ya leavin, Johnny?"

"What, you think I can just snap back into myself? I'm in a medically regulated coma. My mind is here now. That body will be useless."

"How many times did you spin him?" Jordan asked. He too sacrificed the final bit of space between him and the floor, folded his legs from their squat, sat down. "I've heard of people losing some days. Maybe you need to keep someone for a week, a month, some fraud shit, or just gettin your rocks off, and you spin em seven times, ten times. Come back with a desperate, hardly slakeable thirst and yeah you'll think, huh, how long was I just in two places at once? But a fuckin coma, man? What's wrong with you? How and why on God's green earth did you get to this point?"

Was there a glint in Corbin's eye that I could recognize as his father? Certainly in that moment I saw flashes of John Allen brooding in a gas line, smiling as he patronized some local authority figure, stifling some bitter comment meant for Mom. I saw John Allen then even though his eyes were on the other side of town. It is hard to overstate how bizarre this all felt. How bizarre for someone's body and soul to be so mismatched.

He sipped his tea and carefully placed the mug back on the table. "Suicide is a sin," he said. "Corbin knows this. He is a coward and he wants to take the coward's way out. If he can't enjoy his mind or his body, he can't enjoy his money. And it's only money he ever cared about." He stopped as if for a response. We waited for him to continue. "Life is temptation and it always has been. Jesus, full of the holy spirit, ventured into the desert to fast. To avoid temptation. And there He was tempted. Food? Man cannot live on bread alone, it is written. Power? God has the power, and only God. And Satan took Jesus to the top of the temple, quoted scripture, said throw yourself down and prove to me. Neither death nor life can tempt Him. The release of death could not tempt Him. The Godly survival could not tempt Him. Life is temptation and temptation takes the form of tests. This is another test for my son. You want to help him. He wants an excuse. To die. To be relieved of me. To be relieved of himself and the trap of a solitary life. It's almost pathetic."

"No one here is a god," said Jordan. "Man is susceptible to temptation. If my mind was not my own... when my mind has not been its own, when it wasn't just me in here, all the scripture in the world couldn't help. I wanted to die. The want is not the sin, is it?"

"He thinks only good can come from this," said the preacher. "Wesley would have money for the rest of his life. He would never have a father entirely... there. But he'd have money. There'd be a legacy he can look to. A church. Sermons. And he could be free of his father."

I saw Jordan roll his eyes. "Fathers and sons. This story is old news. You came here to test your son? If he wants to die, then you came here to torture him, no?"

The preacher looked at me. "You asked me here. I assume because you have no sense of sin. No sense of right and wrong. A man wants to die? It is a sin to give him what he wants."

"I don't know," I said. "But how else does this end? Are you going to waste away under medical supervision? Are you going to leave your son without a soul of his own?"

"Do you pity him?" he asked with contempt. "He has tricked an entire generation into thinkin money and God are the same thing. He gets up there every week, you see it. He says it. But even when he doesn't say it, he oozes it. Oh, just trust in God and you'll be fine. Count your money, that's God's will, you'll be fine. If you pray hard enough, if you believe enough, you'll be rewarded. Here and now. But you won't be. Not in cash, or any of the little carrots he can mention in a sermon that are all substitutes for cash. It's a lie. He lies to millions of people with every sermon. Just with his demeanor sometimes."

"Isn't it a sin," Jordan wondered, "to take what isn't yours? To take a body that isn't yours?"

"I created this man. I fed him as a baby. I raised him. I kept him alive. I showed him the world and I gave him everything."

"And then you took it all for yourself."

He was angry in that minute and he calmed himself by sipping his tea again.

"Wesley needs a father," I said.

"Wesley needs a man of principle. Wesley needs a father who will tell him what God really is. He has lost his God because he only knows my son's conception of God."

"And your vision is more accurate, is it?" Jordan scoffed. "You think because you've got the keys, you know God better than someone else?"

"Don't I?" It was a challenge of a question.

Jordan shook his head. "We don't know anything. Individuals can never know what God is. We can only hope. Sense. Look to the past."

"I know what God is," said the preacher. "God is the answer on the test. God is the rejection of temptation. Having millions of followers is nothin. A chasin after the wind. Having money, a big house, cameras on you all the time... these are the temptations that my son could never reject. My son is alienated from reality and so alienated from God. I won't let him pass that failure on to Wesley."

"So your solution is to erase him." I said.

"I'm just here now. You offered to erase us."

"He has no agency anymore?" Jordan asked. "Corbin can't go buy a gun and pull the trigger?"

"He has shame because he knows it's wrong. And he could never ask." He turned to me. "And you knew that he would never ask. So you offered."

"I gotta say," Jordan said to me, speaking with a tone like we were the only two in the room, "I almost pity the man now. With a dad like this."

"John, I think you can let this go. I am not going to kill you. I don't believe in suicide, either."

"What do you believe in, Ms. Qualiana? Ms. Constant Religious Crisis."

"It doesn't matter what I believe. Just how I react."

"How profound," said the preacher, sarcastic.

Jordan grabbed his tea and set the mug in his lap, gazing into the liquid. "I'll do it."

"You'll do it?"

"Yeah, sure, maybe I'll kill you." The men stared at one another.

"Jordan," I snapped. "What are you doing?"

"You'd have to be insane to spin someone so many times that you get trapped outside of your body. This man is fuckin sick, Ivy. It'd be an act of charity. For Corbin. No?"

Jordan found the pack and lit another Camel. He took a long drag and blew the smoke sideways from his mouth toward the boxfan by the bedroom. The cloud caught in the current and the combusted drug and the room's dust danced together and apart and everything ascended, expanding.

"God can forgive a lot," Jordan said, and he said this to himself.

I was getting heated. "Jordan, why the fuck are you entertaining this idea?"

"This is beyond our pay grade, Ivy," he said. Then with his mug he stood up and still smoking walked around the table and sat on the futon next to the man. He ashed his cigarette and took another drag, staring at this man, his boss. "Death is death, but life... Life can be lots of things. Life can be corrupted. This man is corrupted. What's the Godly thing to do?"

"God gives life," I said. "How could it be Godly to take it away?"

"God takes life away," Jordan countered. "That's not the devil, that's God."

"Okay, well how about the law? John doesn't want to die. You are talking about murder."

"Yes, you are," said the preacher.

"I am looking at the face," said Jordan, "of a man who thinks he's God. You probably never entertained the possibility that your power doesn't make you special. It's what you do with it, you know. And what did you do?"

The one did not respond, the other turned to me. "What did he do?"

"He healed people. He thought he did. It's how they lived. Traveling. Healing. Getting donations."

"Those people were healed. They were saved. Born again in Christ."

"But you never figured it out," Jordan said. "Did you?"

Again he did not respond.

"What the point of this was? The power. How it can

evolve."

The preacher blinked through the smoke. He coughed and coughed again. "I had my purpose," he said. "I opened people's hearts to the Gospel."

"But now you're stuck. Because you didn't know. You think living lives is just about people? You think the point in all of this was to rout people's demons? Anyone who thinks they can get somewhere on their own doesn't realize they'll go the wrong way. You thought you could heal a million people and get to heaven. But there's no heaven for people like us, John. We're on our last life, and it's an eternity."

The preacher shook his head. "What kind of Christian would believe that?"

"What kind of Christian," Jordan said. "What kind of Christian heals someone and then asks for donations? What kind of Christian keeps his son hostage?"

"You'll kill two souls?"

Jordan extinguished the cigarette in his half-drunk tea. "I'm not afraid of the afterlife," he said. "In fact I'm a little impatient myself. To get there. See if. It's there."

"You are a coward as well, then."

"Is it cowardly? To face the music. It takes guts."

"Hey," I said, inching forward on the floor.

"He's a coward," said Jordan, "who relies on a soul not his own."

"Hey," I said again, more sternly.

The preacher sat very still but I could see he was sweating profusely and gritting his whole body against some wrenching force within.

"If I mean it," Jordan said, raising one of his hands slowly. "If I totally intend to do it, what can you do?" His hand was opening, gliding toward the preacher, who with much stiffness turned entirely toward Jordan, a leg retracting up onto the couch as he pivoted, his head bulging out to expose his neck. A dare. Jordan's hand approached the throat and formed into a clasp-grip like he was simply reaching for a bottle. I thought: Jordan is smaller. With shame I'll admit I wished I was recording.

"I am sure of my God."

"If you're so sure," Jordan said.

In one instant he got both hands around the preacher's throat and drove his head back and kneeled over him on the futon. The men thrashed in quick fits.

I had already stood up and yelled for them to stop but they didn't stop and I hadn't moved again. The younger man pinned the older down, knees over legs, those longer legs crooked in their guard and splayed. Both men were silent and Corbin's arms came alive and stilled repeatedly but he never even balled a fist. I was stunned by the quiet of the violence. Then I realized I heard a buzzing sound and I came to my senses and started to rush forward, and at that moment Corbin flung Jordan off himself, sat upright with the force. He shoved Jordan's chest once. Jordan stood saying, "Jesus Christ, man, you wasted your life, why wouldn't your death be a waste, too?" He rubbed his hands and fingers and scowled. He stomped by me and around the table and stood in the corner. I watched Corbin, who noticeably did not rub his red throat, though he coughed. He did not look at Jordan again. He stared right at me. As if to say, "Your turn."

The buzzing continued.

Corbin stood and straightened his suit and pulled out his phone. He looked at the caller name for a long time until the vibration stopped. He called back.

He stepped outside to speak, and Jordan countered his approach to the door by storming into the kitchen. Corbin shut the front door. I followed Jordan and found him washing his hands.

"What the fuck are you doing?"

"I wasn't gonna do anything."

"That's attempted murder."

"He was asking for it."

"One of him was. Not the one you strangled."

Jordan turned off the tap. He faced me and scoff-sighed as he would.

The front door opened and he and I went back through to the living room. Corbin stood in the open doorway with the dewey shadows of night half on him, his outline in the rectangle the first marker charting a way through that flat image from him to cars to road to woods to business to homes and on directly around the globe as far as the back of my head. I couldn't believe it had come to bargaining on behalf of existence. That's what I was about.

"That was the nurse," Corbin said. "I opened an eye."

He stood there for a beat and then turned and left. That was it. He passed our cars and climbed into his own and pulled into the street, then pulled back for a three-point turn. He drove away gestureless.

I went to the front door and kept it open, turning to Jordan. "How did you know that would work?"

"I didn't. Did it?"

"I better not have to go to to court because of you."

"Come on," he said. "You were curious, right? Didn't you want to know?"

I didn't answer. I watched the empty street. It's possible I was thinking up resentful memories of Corbin's, of Jordan talking about my son, *defining* him like it was a favor. Or the memories of the new son, a warning about spying. After a while Jordan asked if I wanted him to leave. But I couldn't answer. I'm not even sure he asked that or that I heard him speak. Was I even in that room? Was I just somewhere in my skull?

The mind is its own place—so it's written. And it's written:

The brain is wider than the sky, the brain is deeper than the sea. *The Brain is just the weight of God — For — Heft them — Pound for Pound — And they will differ — if they do — As Syllable from Sound —*

Pastor's Father Wakes From Coma Hours Before Passing

HOUSTON—John Allen, father of televangelist Corbin Allen, passed away Sunday with his son at his side. The elder Allen was 75 years old, and had been comatose since 2011, following a stroke.

The family announced the news Monday morning in a statement released by Riverbed Church, the Houston church founded and overseen by Allen's son.

John Allen was also a preacher, a career touched upon in the younger Allen's bestselling book *Let Yourself Live*. According to the church's statement, Allen had shown no signs of consciousness in his coma since entering it in 2011. That is until Saturday when his caretaker noticed John Allen showing "rare physical responses and possible signs of awareness."

The statement called the elder Allen's last-minute signs of awareness a "Miracle in Christ."

Allen died in the early hours of Sunday morning, with his son at his side. The family will hold a memorial at a later date.

CONNECT / TWEET / LINKEDIN / COMMENT / EMAIL / more

Riverbed Church Names Pastor In Residence

HOUSTON—Riverbed Church senior pastor Corbin Allen, bestselling author and the host of syndicated evangelical broadcast *Riverbed,* has taken a leave of absence in the wake of his father's death.

Allen's father died in late July after several years in a stroke-induced coma. Allen has not conducted his weekly broadcast since July. Joyce Meyer, an author and the president of Joyce Meyer Ministries, has been leading Riverbed Church's Sunday service in Allen's place, but the church says Allen's absence will continue indefinitely.

In a statement this morning Riverbed announced the assignment of internet personality Maxine Adams as Pastor in Residence until October 1.

Adams is the author of several books and since 2012 she has been hosting an independent Christian talk show on YouTube. In a brief statement to press Adams said, "I'm praying for the Allen family, and sending them all the love and healing in the world at this difficult time, and I'm humbled to become part of their community." Adams's first service is this Sunday at Riverbed Church, available on TV broadcast and online.

CONNECT / TWEET / LINKEDIN / COMMENT / EMAIL / more

12

Finished Knowing

Corbin never reached out to me again, nor I to him. Never again with my own eyes would I behold the man. Barely saw him online either except for the occasional meme. In the months after his father's death, he hid far from the public eye.

Shortly after the ordeal, Jordan and I met up, ostensibly to talk things through, though neither of us knew what should be said. We reflected on the metaphysics involved. Corbin and John would have touched at some point during his overnight visit, and this contact would have brought about the actual final reading. Beyond that, who could know? John Allen died in his own body with at least one eye open and only God knows how his son's mind functioned after that.

For a long time, though able to suppress my impulse to contact him, I remained obsessive about Corbin. The fall of 2016 in these United States—the orange bluster and digital fog, the red caps, the seething ideological encampments like so many forces arranged on a forgotten battlefield—I spent overthinking, contemplating Corbin Allen. Imagine you've lost your mind in circumstance like a creature down a well, perceiving only shadow with survival out of range. Or imagine there was some core part of you—childhood interests, the ideas of early adulthood, some briefly known version of your ever-changing self—and this core, eroded by time anyway, compressed a little with every new influence, each new dressing or accessory, until at a certain point you realized what was once a core had been pulverized and become an ether-like filling, a thing pervasive but gaseous, sustaining but unsupportive. This is what may be termed a crisis of identity or purpose. I know these crises well, in others and in myself, but I could not imagine Corbin's. What it really felt like for him. I could not imagine what it must have been like to return from being entirely the thing lost, the self compressed. In me, in others, what was lost down the well was always an idea of our past selves, or an expectation of our future selves. But John took over his son's body and mind long before I entered the story. Corbin was denied the present. By the early 2010s, John was the active self and Corbin the core abraded into near-oblivion. How could either of them possibly be whole again? Or rather, what obstacle might sudden, unencumbered wholeness present each of them? With whatever effort this return demanded of him, John died. But the televangelist would have found himself true again in charge of a healthy body, a clear head. What would you find?

What did he find?

He never preached again. When it was clear he wouldn't, Riverbed officially installed a new pastor. There was quite a bit of speculation about Corbin Allen on Twitter and from some in the Christian press—Why did he disappear? Is he just hiding from the Trump era? Is he on a mountain somewhere writing the greatest self-help book of all time? Most people understood the context to be that a man of God had lost his wife and father, and had earned enough money and done enough good to retreat leisurely into private life. From the Riverbed rumor mill Jordan learned of the stresses on upper management and the general incommunicativeness of their former pastor. It was said that even his housekeeper and his lawyer had no idea what was up.

It's interesting to me how people can be lightning rods when they're at the top of an organization. During Hurricane Harvey, Riverbed delayed opening its doors to the needy public until there was a storm online. I have wondered about their public relations crisis, limited as it was like water damage to a 17,000-capacity arena, and how that crisis might have resolved or not had still the church its original figurehead. I do still often wonder what Corbin Allen might have preached during the Trump era, if he could have preached then, if he had really stuck around in Christ and spoke from the heart.

Once upon a time, I liked to say I had been Buddhist and Christian and Muslim and Jewish and agnostic to varying degrees. I really only ever worshipped my own perception, my expanding awareness. My little talent. This worship I thought a sin. Gluttonous. I understand now that I was right to revere the ability and also right to feel shame with its misuse. For the ability comes from without, the use from within. This I read in the Tao Te Ching long ago, translated some other way, and only by revisiting the idea and all its contrasting manifestations could I say that I've come close to understanding it. Only by rereading could I internalize, could I be internalized. It was good to measure my faults and excesses and foolish to do so alone.

So I let myself love someone, and I let him love me. He was not my Virgil or my Raphael, not a teacher or a counselor or a psychic. He was my Jordan. For several years we were happy together. He was, after all, the only person I'd ever met who understood me, and I apparently the only one he could stand to embrace. Our relationship developed as one continuous flow state, jams or dueling pianos in the Riverbed choir room and variegated sex and a succession of green meals and that ever-present negotiation of time and space that any two people must strike. We cooked at his place and watched movies at mine, then we moved in together. A thousand times I traced my fingers over the ink of his tattoos—the triangles on his legs, the keyhole of his neck, two musical staves and two lines of Marlowe and a crucifix made of skulls. In bed at night he had an odd aversion to my gaze like no lover I'd ever known. I would ask him questions about our kind and at first he answered in the slightest. He promised he'd one day introduce me to someone who could provide the guidance I needed, which person I think he imagined should come in the form of some monk or wanderer or underground lecturer. Maybe I did imagine someone like that. Maybe he knew someone who fit the descriptions. In any case, such a one was a fantasy. Instead, drip by drip, he told me a lot. He answered me. But upon every question I asked of the power, I heard in myself response enough to assume all possible intersections and diversions of the morals and ethics involved such that my understanding of the subject was less informed by Jordan's hints than by the casuistry within me. And let's face it—he loved withholding and I loved reaching.

Our time together is a story separate from this, one I will write someday. I'm not ready to phrase that time yet. The pieces are scattered. The words won't make sense—birds, worms, codependent. Still I realize Jordan's end matters to these pages because I should have seen the end in the beginning, but I didn't, and you should know that. You— nameless possible me, possible stranger. You should know or remember how Jordan Barshius died.

It happened eight years after I met him. He knew he would do it eventually and so did I. The climate in his mind.

Desensitization. He believed it was the inevitable conclusion of his life for an existence of such inhuman length to be self-ended in an instant. He believed in self-fulfilling prophecies and accepted his own, even as it clashed with the advice of his Bible. I think he liked the poetry of it. He had spent his life stealing the experience of others, and so needed to steal his own away. But I wish I had known ahead of time exactly when he would try. And of course I wish that, who wouldn't? It all happened so fast.

Despite what popular culture suggests, death by blade is an unreliable method of suicide with a low success rate. Especially a blade used anywhere but the throat, so it's better to go for the throat, and you better move decisively because you won't want to cut yourself a second time. Jordan doubled his effort by doubling the tool. The mess was not his message, but sensorily he preferred bleeding out to guns or rope or pills. In the end, he duct taped two kitchen knives to the sliding doors of our bedroom and leaned over the threshold. Slam, rip, fall. He annihilated his veins and arteries and he must have done so five minutes before I got home.

Taped to the front of our apartment door was a note:
READ ME

I found him on his back at the edge of the living room, his neck an absolute gore of skin and muscle and blood, and everything everywhere red, the blood still flowing and pooling beneath him like in insult to his oncoming stillness, his eyes closed. I found him like that and I wailed but I had started wailing when I saw the note and I only noticed the sound I made after having already knelt in his blood and emptied my lungs and breathed again. Tears ran into my mouth as my hands hovered over him. A voice from the front door said, "Oh my God," and I turned to see a neighbor holding some shopping bags, looking in from the hall.

"Call 9-1-1," I cried. The woman dropped her bags. I

looked down at Jordan and saw his eyes were open.

I swear he smiled at me.

People wouldn't believe me that he would regain consciousness like that but he did. Maybe he heard me. He lifted one of his blood-soaked hands from his side and offered it. Waited. He looked at me like he was giving me a gift. I stood up and backed away, blood all over my hands and pants. I ran to the kitchen and grabbed hand towels and when I came back it seemed he was using all possible strength to keep his hand up and out. He watched me with something like disdain as I pressed the towels over the gash. I was saying, "Don't go, don't go, don't go," and he kept looking at me and I think he started to resent the moment. Resent me. He had timed it just right. He didn't need to include me, but there I was, not taking his offer. An explanation of his life and decisions, perhaps. A vision of death. You can hold a bee in your fist until it stings and dies, but now isn't that too violent? Jordan's eyes closed and he went limp again and the blood kept flowing. He had offered me a kind of suicide note, but I couldn't read it. Yet what destruction, invitation. What a parting gift, temptation.

Later, in need of a hobby, I decided to farm my own ant colony, so I bought a sizable formicarium which at first sat lifeless on my coffee table while I searched for a queen. Then after many weeks trolling suburban fields with a little glass vial in my pocket, two letdowns later, I finally found a winged carpenter queen in my mom's backyard in May of 2025. Her wings never fell off but she had mated alright and she proved herself strong bringing forth a colony. So I loved them. Tended their world, provided them sustenance. Spent a lot of time and money. Got a lot back. Instead of television, I watched them. I saw those ants tunnel and by tunneling gradually engineer a world of their own. I saw them work away their lives in service to the others and saw them carry their dead to the midden. Every Friday afternoon I uncovered their world, let there be light, opened the top of the case, led one ant up onto a stick of incense and then onto my hand and read it. Returned, I just lay there watching them until I could understand my thoughts. Like that I read an ant every Friday for nearly two years and after a while it began to feel like I was reading the system itself. Dare I say it, I became something larger than a mind. But my God was I lonely.

Now I am writing this so that I don't forget. I was young in this story and exposed to a lot of valuable lessons about solitude and belief and the foundations of my own identity. I am writing this because there has got to be another lesson in here somewhere and if I couldn't recognize it when all this stuff happened, or if I can't recognize it now, maybe I will when I return to the text. At a later time, as a different me. I need to filter my memories through my present sense of self and thus allow for the discovery of some change in my constitution. There must always be a change, no? The context is the same but every day is new. Even if I've always been wrong, I'd've been different kinds of wrong. And Lord knows I'm less anxious than I once was. Even if I've yet to process my grief. Jordan. My father. Even if I haven't learned a single true thing about myself or others, still there must be a change at some point, recognizable in my history or my words, and in that change there might be a lesson. I want to keep believing this is possible. I believe so for now.

One night in 2027 I found myself at a show. I had gone to Austin for the weekend and started my Saturday evening alone at a bar south of the river. For a long time the only reading I had done was the ants. Much of my comfort with other people had died with Jordan. Life was tangibly better when escape meant community and flexible perspective. Of course, it was still escape. Someday a litter of kittens, for now an ant farm. For now a beer in a bar.

OK so there I am at a crowded bar and I hear live music start up out back. I go outside and five songs later I realize that Wesley Allen is the sound guy. He's like six-two and rail thin with long shaggy hair, and I haven't seen him offline in eleven years, but it's definitely him, I can see it right away. I freeze up.

The music plays while I tear my plastic cup and debate whether or not to say anything. I convince myself it's a bad idea for some reason, but I don't leave. I loiter in the back corner and watch the band, hardly paying attention to the show except to check Wesley's face and movement when there's a screech of feedback, which there is only once. At some point he spots me. After the set ends and a playlist comes on the speakers he walks directly over and plants himself at my side and says my name as a question.

"Well look at you, that's Wesley," I say.

"I thought it was you."

"You're running sound, huh?"

"Yeah, it's a good gig. They've got good equipment and I get free drinks."

"Can't believe you're old enough to be drinking."

He smiles. He's turned out a bit grungier than his dad, both in body and dress. He's got some acne scars on his cheeks and what's probably three days stubble. He notices me examining him and gets a little shifty and then points to a table. "Wanna catch up for a minute? Next group has to set up and I can get you a free one."

"That'd be great," I say. I claim the table and in a few minutes he returns with two beers.

"Jesus," he says, "I honestly can't believe I recognized you. I mean you look the same, it's just been so long."

"You look a little different, don't ya."

"Do you live in Austin?"

"I'm here for the weekend. Scenery change. Though mostly what I've done is sleep in the rental. You live here?"

"I've got an apartment not far, near Saint Ed's."

"Are you in school there?"

"For a year I was, then I dropped out. School was not for me."

"And you're in the music world."

"Yeah, and I play too. Workin in a restaurant, but music's the thing. I still sing. In my car I still do those siren drills. Y'know for the upper register? Every time I drive, I swear."

"Good. They work."

"They really do. You were a good teacher, sorry if I was a bad student."

"Oh, please. Why say that?"

"I don't know. I don't quite remember. I remember quitting. I was never good with teachers and lessons and things like that. My girlfriend says I'm stubborn about doing things on my own."

"Girlfriend, huh? What's she like?"

"She's sweet, she's in grad school. Urban Sustainability."

"Wow. Must be smart."

"She's a fuckin genius, yeah. Like twice a week she blows my mind."

"Twice a week, good."

"What about you? Are you married or anything?"

"Nope." For a beat I consider bringing up Jordan. I don't think Wes knows the extent of our relationship. Does he know Jordan is dead? "I dated someone for a very long time, but he passed away."

"I'm sorry to hear that."

"It's been a while, but you never really get over it."

"I know what you mean." He nods and sips his beer. "What about teaching, do you still teach?"

"I do. Not as many private lessons. Local community theatre stuff, sometimes hired out for high school productions. Musical directing."

"Cool. What are the kids like these days?"

"Kids. They're the same. It's everyone and everything else that changes."

"Ain't that the truth."

I take another sip and so does he. We're keeping pace with each other's cups as two polite semi-strangers should when drinking together.

And I just have to ask. "How's your dad?"

"Dad," he says with a sigh.

"He stopped preaching a long time ago."

"Yep. He retired. While ago. After his dad died he just… Really broke him down. For a while there he barely left home. It was pretty rough."

"Sorry about that."

Wes shrugs. Then after a pause he says, "When people realize who I am they ask why he stopped and never came back and I don't know what to say."

"It was grief?"

"A few years ago, after I dropped out of school, I moved back home for a while. It felt like *The Shining* in our fuckin house, I swear. I half expected to find a draft of some book with the same lines over and over and over. I don't know that it was only grief. He was always a bit of a narcissist so I was surprised when he stepped away from the cameras, y'know? But now he's… just alone. Watches TV. Reads a fair amount, but he sticks to what he likes to hear. Plays chess online. Doesn't mingle much, or go out at all. I think he retired too early. I'd go crazy, too."

"Would you want him to preach again?"

"I don't know," he says, then he thinks about it. "Probably not. I wish he'd write again. His books still sell. He should write another, but it doesn't seem like he's got the energy. He's not level. Not in a long time. My mom and grandpa dying had to do with it, but... It's not just grief, it's like his whole worldview confuses him because it hasn't gotten rid of the grief. He's unsure of everything and constantly surprised about it. What's on the tip of his tongue he doesn't trust. Lot different from the old days. He was like a Christian Robin Williams wind-up doll. If I told this to my younger self I wouldn't believe it. I used to fuckin pray he would shut up, and now he'll say he's gonna start on a new project, but he never really does. When I was there again, sometimes I saw him take notes. He'd be reading and he'd bolt up from his chair like he got some big idea. But he wouldn't find paper or a pen in time so he'd take notes on his phone. Get all focused, lasered-in on his phone, typing. I just watch. Like, shit, is this cranky old man inspired for the first time in a decade? Slowly the typing slows. He looks around like he forgot it. Like there's an end to this sentence he's just started and it's somewhere on the walls, or out the window. He wouldn't even notice I was watchin. So I'd be like, you all good? He'd mumble. Look at his phone again, look down like he's reading some suddenly foreign language. Every time. Says he forgot what he meant. Not forgot what he was going to say, forgot what he even meant. I could sit there and watch him get struck with some idea and then watch as he estranges himself from that idea. Like every idea has a foundation beneath it and he is skeptical of every material in the base. Doesn't trust his own inspiration. If that doesn't sum up how he's been, well... I'm sorry, we don't have to keep talkin about my dad. People get obsessed with him. I have to talk about him a lot. It's an easy habit to get into."

Wesley leans back, takes a big breath, and as he lets out the air he rolls his eyes I think at himself.

"No, like you said, he was famous. A lot of people felt like they knew him. I felt that. Those broadcasts aren't the same without his sermons."

"You watch the Riverbed shit?"

"Not anymore, no."

We sit silent for a moment, drink. Wesley watches over my shoulder as the next group sets up. He checks his phone for the time.

"I should get ready. Are you gonna stay around for the next band?"

The beer and the hour conspire against me. I am quite tired by this point and should probably get back to my rental to crash. But I start to wonder about this young man and who he might really be. God damn me if I start to wonder. "Are they any good?"

"Catchy at sound check. Sort of punkish. They're from San Antonio, I think."

"I'll give em a try."

He's got half a beer left and he says, "Sorry for this," and then he chugs it and burps. "Me and some friends'll probably go out after this, too, if you're lookin for a thing to do."

"I'm not sure I can keep up with your friends."

"Well, think about it. We'll talk about people besides my dad. Regular people," he says, bright, like these imaginary regulars signify something different and truer than his father. People with troubles worth discussion. "It was great to see you."

"It was nice to see you, kiddo," I say. I push my open palm across the table. He clasps my hand and I know. Oh, I know how I'll react. Not proud of it. But this is how it goes. You can always want to know another, so can others want of you. If unfulfilled, unchosen, the want's itself still true. So she gives out her hand, he takes it and she spins, and she spins again, again.